The CAMP DAVID
CONSPIRACY

The Original Geoffrey Wines Novel

By
Antim Straus

The CAMP DAVID

CONSPIRACY

Sometimes for the public good,
things occur that need to occur.

And whose means of occurrence
are better left vague.

Or not.

Prologue

"**M**r. Wines, have you ever experienced South Carolina in the springtime?"

"No, sir, I have not."

"Well then, Mr. Wines, I guess this story needs to start somewhere, and for me it started in 1930s South Carolina . . .

You see, certain events occur when you are young that completely change your life. This is one of them. It happened one day with my very best friend Clarence Robinson.

I met Clarence when his dad came over to our house to help my daddy fix a leaky pipe. I didn't know Clarence. We didn't go to the same school because the schools were segregated then. In 1930's South Carolina, a black kid would never be allowed in the same classroom as a white kid.

While our daddies wrestled with the plumbing, Clarence and I sat on the front porch talking about hunting, exploring the woods around the Greenville area, and fishing. Particularly fishing! We found we both loved the lakes and trails around Paris Mountain and just sitting on the bluff overlooking the little Greenville town.

From that evening grew a lifelong friendship.

Sure, we had other friends, but we found we spent more time with each other than anyone else. Our parents didn't mind, but they were careful to warn that our friendship could cause problems and that we needed to avoid situations that could lead to trouble.

We seldom went into town together, so we never had the problem facing the "white only" ordinances. Instead, we spent most of our time in the woods or at the lake fishing. There we were able to piss on the same tree, drink out of the same canteen, and tell stories about how we caught the largest fish or how we outran the biggest black bear.

But despite our caution, we did run into trouble.

I remember a spring afternoon when we were just lying on our backs under one of those broad shade trees, gazing at the sky and enjoying the most wonderful day God ever created. We weren't concerned about our fishing lines in the water or anything else. We were oblivious to everything around us.

Suddenly, our dreamlike state was interrupted.

"Hey, what's a nigger doing at our fishing hole?" came a voice from behind us.

We both looked up. Standing over us were two redneck seeds, each about age fifteen or sixteen. I didn't recognize either of them. Neither went to the same school as me. And in Greenville, if they were white and didn't go to the same school as me, then chances were good they didn't live in Greenville. These boys were from one of the smaller towns close by, maybe the Travelers Rest area.

"Don't niggers know they don't fish where white people fish?" the same boy asked.

The other boy joined in. "Let's teach the nigger a lesson."

He grabbed our two fishing poles and split them both in half. This wasn't really a big problem since our poles were just tree branches with a string attached. Still, the idea of someone breaking my property and telling my friend he could not fish in *our* fishing hole was too much to bear.

"Hey, cut it out," I shouted, jumping to my feet. Clarence was already on his.

The redneck boys stood their ground, with their fists clinched. One boy stood slightly taller than Clarence and me but appeared to be no more muscular.

Clarence was easing back from the situation, not because he was afraid or a coward, but because he knew fighting with white people could only lead to more trouble.

I, on the other hand, was pissed. I didn't like it when bigger kids at school picked on the smaller kids. And I certainly didn't like anyone telling my friend what he could and could not do. Especially in my presence.

I took a swing at the bigger of the two boys. I caught him in the jaw, but my power wasn't enough to do much more than knock him back a foot or so.

"Grab the other guy!" I yelled to Clarence.

Clarence moved in on the shorter boy, placing a grip on him in such a way that the boy's wild attempts to hit him were blocked.

The first boy came at me with all his force, ramming his head right into my stomach. We slid backward, with his head implanted in my stomach and my arms wrapped securely around his neck. Soon we found ourselves on the ground trading punches, head holds, neck holds, and twisted arms. Neither of us sought blood at this point. The fight seemed to be more on the principle of not backing away.

However, the shorter boy Clarence held came from another perspective. He hated black people and believed he had the right to tell any black boy what to do anytime, anywhere, and for any reason. And he did not like the idea of Clarence overpowering him.

He twisted himself out of Clarence's control, grabbed a stick off the ground, and swung it right above Clarence's eyes. A stream of blood started running down Clarence's cheek.

At this point, I knew we were in for something more than a schoolyard brawl. The intensity of my fight with the taller boy suddenly picked up. I grabbed him by one of his ears, trying to turn his head for a clearer punch at his eyes. He countered with a series of rapid punches to my stomach.

I glanced over and saw Clarence flat on his back, with the redneck sitting on his chest and pounding him in the face.

With a burst of strength, I released the boy's hold around me, jumped to my feet, launched into a flying tackle, and knocked the boy off Clarence, who was still trying to clear his head from the barrage of punches. He then staggered to his feet, and soon the four of us were mixing it up.

Then, like lightning, Clarence grabbed the boy who had hit him with the stick, centered his arms around the boy's head, and lifted him from the ground. In one fluid motion, Clarence thrust the boy's face down, meeting it with his sharply rising knee. Upon impact, the boy's nose exploded, splattering blood everywhere. The boy then released his grip and ran into the woods and away from his partner, who I still firmly held in my grasp.

Seeing this, I gave the taller boy a shove and sent him chasing after his friend.

I looked over. Clarence's eyes were severely swollen, one nearly shut with a deep gash above it and blood running down his nose and cheek. But his wound was nothing compared to the boy with the shattered nose.

Remarkably, I had only a few scratches. When I got home, I saw I had a pretty good shiner, too.

I took off my shirt, dipped it into the cool lake water and began to dab at Clarence's brow.

"You look bad, Clarence. Real bad." I patted the bleeding gash. "But where did you learn to fight like that?" We had known each other over a year and had spent days together, but I had no idea he could protect himself so well.

Clarence replied hesitantly that his father had taught him to defend himself.

"Why did you wait so long before punching the guy out?" I asked.

"My daddy taught me to stay away from fighting. You see, being colored, we can't fight every time someone threatens us. So, we have to be patient and hopefully avoid a problem in the first place."

He continued. "And, Bobby, you started this fight. And you didn't have to." He rubbed his swollen jaw and tenderly felt around the cut on the side of his face. "As redneck as those boys were, I don't think they were really looking for a fight. They were just looking to harass a white boy and a nigger."

We gathered up our things, cut the line off our broken fishing poles, rinsed our blood-soaked shirts in the cool lake water, and headed home for supper."

"You see, Mr. Wines, now, fifty-three years later, I am Robert S. Osbourne Jr, President of the United States. And I vividly remember that beautiful spring day in South Carolina when Clarence Robinson here, *my best friend in the world,* taught me the most important lesson of successfully thriving in the world of politics: *Never jump into a fight before you must, because often your opponent isn't looking for a fight in the first place. And if they do, enter it on your terms, not theirs.*

"And for reasons you may already know—and probably itching to report—my friend Clarence asked me for my help. Now, let us, and Chuck Harding here, tell you the whole story."

Chapter 1

Washington, D.C.

D EA Agent Chuck Harding stood on a ladder fixing a light in the courtyard of the Ashford Apartments Housing Project in the worst part of Washington, D.C.

Today, he portrayed a handyman. *A regular Schneider.* His disguise included olive-green coveralls with "D.C. Housing Maintenance" emblazoned in white letters across the back, a tool belt loaded with screwdrivers and pliers of various sizes, and other tools to make his role convincing. He had grayed his hair and eyebrows to make him look older and less imposing. And his purposeful slow and labored progress up and down the ladder completed the ruse.

Less visible in his baggy coveralls stood the six-foot-two, 210-pound, thirty-nine-year-old muscular frame of a defensive end with a 9 mm Glock that was as ready as the Phillips-head screwdrivers. Of course, all of this would have been a red flag to his prey.

Despite these efforts, Harding hated this part of his job. It seemed so meaningless—a waste of manpower and small return in fighting the *War on Drugs.*

Ashford Apartments represented prime retail space for the homeboy's selling cocaine and crack in the inner city. In D.C., the more familiar Bloods and Crips did not exist. In their place were crews of neighborhood kids who grew up together playing basketball and who found it a lot more fun to heavily arm themselves, sell drugs, and make huge amounts of money.

And that was why Harding was fixing a lamppost light rather than infiltrating a gang. There was no way to infiltrate a group who had known each other since childhood. So, instead of identifying the key members from the inside, he had to track them from the outside.

Harding stationed himself there for what he called the "Pusher's Parade." This somewhat odd, yet effective ritual the crews conducted to kick off the major selling season. They knew the residents would leave their apartments on the first warm days in March to enjoy the springtime weather. In key housing complexes like Ashford, the crews would march into the courtyards wearing their colors. It was a way of marking their turf and exposing potential buyers to the key crew dealers working the complexes. It served as both an enticement and a warning to anyone buying drugs: "You know who we are. Buy from others at your own risk."

Harding and other DEA agents had been monitoring Ashford and the drug selling crews for several years. Their objective had been to observe and then arrest the users. Their directive to "get enough users off the street, and soon the distributors would follow."

But recently, the Justice Department had changed the strategy to identifying and arresting the distributors and dealers and giving the users a pass. Harding wasn't sure this was going to be any more effective. It seemed like switching from a basketball man-on-man defense to a zone defense—that is, block out the dealer working in the zone rather than chase down the individual user. But to be effective, the agents still had to have an equal number of players on the court. *There were so many more bad guys than good guys.*

The Sons of Steuben controlled the drug trade at Ashford. Mostly cocaine, cut to a level that the folks in the complex could afford. Some crack, too. Harding knew this crew well. They were the largest and most established gang in the city, with a bungalow on Steuben Street that was both their headquarters and an active crack house. They moved considerable volume as well, several kilos a month, usually from the Mendez cartel. But Harding's sources reported they were playing a double game and buying from Cali—a dangerous move. The cartels did not give up business without someone getting hurt.

Harding needed to spot any new faces during the parade. He expected to see Blanford Childress, the crew's leader, and Goon, his number-one heavy. Maybe Spike, an incredibly scary fighter. But they wanted to trot out the new faces, as they would be the key dealers working the complex.

Having completed the maintenance job, Harding slowly descended the ladder, maintaining his ruse. If his wife Peg were still alive and saw him doing household maintenance, she'd laugh. He hated doing household chores.

The Ashford complex contained 240-units, housing mostly families. It had an open front entrance, and the six stories of apartments created a *U*. In each corner stood a large open tunnel where the outside stairs were located, as well as the two dumpsters designed to catch the refuse thrown down the garbage chutes from the above levels. The D.C. Housing Authority found a real upside in making trash disposal as easy as possible for the residents. The chutes were purposely large so they would not clog and back up. Even a man or woman could be successfully trashed, as the police discovered a couple of times a year. Ashford was not peaceful. There were plenty of murders, fires, muggings, and frequent gunshots—plus a robust drug trade.

★ ★ ★

Looking across the gathering courtyard, Harding sought an additional task to maintain his disguise. He knew the parade would begin soon.

The lamps in the dumpster tunnels always needed replacing. They were broken on a daily basis. The dark shadows in the unlit passageways were important for selling drugs. For this, Harding could leave his ladder in the courtyard and simply straddle the two side-by-side dumpsters to reach the fixtures. He placed the halogen replacement bulb on top of the left-hand unit and pulled himself up from the space in between. The higher elevation gave him a better view across the courtyard and into the driveway space behind the complex.

He checked his watch. Four o'clock. People milled around the complex as the kids were back from school. He saw mothers with babies, young boys bouncing basketballs, and a few older men enjoying beverages from paper bags. *A perfect afternoon for a parade.*

On cue, five members of the Steuben crew entered the open entrance at the front of the complex. They had on their black jackets with "Steuben" across the back in deep-maroon block letters. Harding guessed they would circle clockwise around the courtyard and exit through the southwest tunnel, where most of their transactions took place.

The members looked cocky. They waved to the residents sunning themselves and made a point of looking at the boys and men straight in the eye as if to say, "You're on my turf because we are letting you." Not exactly the Disney parade with Mickey, Donald, and Goofy that Harding had taken his kids to a few years earlier.

Something instantly caught his eye. The light entering the tunnel from the backside shifted ever so slightly. He quickly turned.

Lions and tigers and ghosts, oh my.

Approaching the tunnel from the outside were six members of the M+O crew. They were wearing their black ball caps with "M+O" stitched on the front. And they weren't there for a parade; they were there to bust one up. They had to know the Sons of Steuben were marking their turf. And they were there to let the residents know they had options.

Harding couldn't exit through the courtyard because the Sons' leader, Blanford Childress, would recognize him.

And he certainly couldn't leave through the back, even wearing his D.C. coveralls. These dudes took no prisoners. He sure as hell didn't want another broken beer bottle ripped through his cheek.

Harding made a quick calculation. His best move would be to stay in the dark tunnel and take cover between the two large dumpsters. While his line of sight would be severely limited, his exposure would be reduced, too. They could see him only if he saw them. And with his Glock in hand, he figured the ten rounds would cover the two groups. *If I am lucky enough to have one taken out by the other crew.*

He unbuckled the bulky tool belt and let it drop to the ground, scooted it behind one of the trash containers, and then hid himself in the shadowy space between the two dumpsters with his back against the steel access doors.

He waited. And listened. Slowly counting to maintain a sense of time. His Glock rested on his drawn-up knees. A bullet in the chamber, ready to fire. Although he couldn't see a thing to his left and right, he had a clear view and an unobstructed shot for his full ninety degrees of exposure. At this range, his 9 mm would blow back and kill any intruder. He would be safe. Tight, but safe. *Yeah, real safe.*

The sound of footsteps and voices filled the tunnel. There was an echo off the concrete ground and brick walls. He could not tell direction but would soon see as the crew members parade past his limited field of vision.

He then heard the footsteps and voices double. *Shit. Both crews were now in the tunnel.*

The pitch instantly rose as the two crews confronted each other.

Harding heard each leader ordering his men to stand their ground and not let the other pass. This signified the beginning of the season, and any show of weakness would spell the end of their control for the complex.

Harding could see the two crews pushing closer—thankfully, not looking at his position. Hands were poised on their weapons. Guns and blades. Each group knew a gunshot would ricochet or, worse, draw the attention of the police. In the tunnel, there would be no place to run.

Suddenly, Harding saw Blanford flash a switchblade out of his sleeve and slash the throat of the M+O in front of him. Instantly, blood started gushing from the major artery. The M+O grabbed his neck, eyes staring straight ahead. Blood covered his hand as he fell to the ground.

A short pause followed, disbelief and an eerie silence. Then all hell broke loose. Each member would be lucky to leave this tight tunnel alive. This fight represented more than gang honor or macho turf protection. This confrontation meant war, and each side would lose members.

Harding kept his eyes moving up and down his narrow latitudinal line of sight as bodies pushed each other back and forth. Fists, knives, shoves, kicks. The Sons were on the left, and the M+Os on the right.

Right in front of him stood Blanford, the only gang member in D.C. who could identify him. He was still holding the bloody switchblade and looking around.

Their eyes met. Harding could see Blanford squint to adjust his vision to the shadows where Harding sat. A flash of recognition changed his expression.

Ruh Roh.

Blanford reached into his belt, brought his gun in line, and prepared to fire.

Harding began to pull the trigger of his Glock when a light-colored M+O with reddish hair pushed Blanford out of Harding's line of sight. Harding could see the M+O pull a gun out of his belt and shoot Blanford point blank in the stomach. The deafening sound of the shot reverberated off the brick walls of the tunnel.

Relief.

If Harding had shot Blanford, the blast echoing between the dumpsters would have been deafening and would have alerted others of his position. He remained safe, for now. He could shoot anyone before they shot him. And with Blanford down, he now had more than enough rounds in his clip to cover the spread.

The shouts and shots in the tunnel increased. Harding remained alert as the action moved left and right across his line of sight.

Both sides attacked with guns and blades. A tall M+O caught the arm of a Son as it swung toward his face. The new Son's hand gripped a six-inch blade. Not yielding, the M+O pushed his tall body against the shorter man, forcing his back against the corner of the dumpster where Harding sat. With the young Son pinned, the M+O thrust his knee up into the Son's groin. The container rattled with each thrust, and Harding hoped neither gangbanger would end up on top of him.

The young Son had balls of steel; he did not yield or slacken. The seasoned M+O pounded the man's grip against the steel corner, causing the Son's knuckles to bleed. Still, there was no yield of the knife or of control.

As the M+O began to repeatedly knee the Son's groin and pound his forehead against the shorter man's face, he suddenly froze and fell against the trapped young Son. Behind him stood a stocky elder Son with a dripping knife. The rescued brother then pushed himself and the dead M+O away and reentered the fray.

At this point, Harding had seen five gang members—three M+Os and two Sons—killed and lying on the gray concrete in pools of blood.

Making a last stand, the two remaining M+Os pulled guns. One shot rang out, hitting the young, rescued Son in the shoulder. The other two Sons responded with gunfire, leveling another M+O. The last M+O shot the stocky Son square in the forehead and turned to run, knowing he was dead if he stayed. Having yielded the tunnel, the two remaining Sons stopped to see if their fallen leader and brothers were still alive. Before they could check them, they heard the sirens outside the complex. They ran out the back alley, turning right as the police cars started moving in from the left.

* * *

Harding stayed hidden between the trash containers. Exiting now would only draw attention to him. He felt sure everyone in the courtyard had scattered at the first shot. With the silence and the sirens, they would start to filter back down from their apartments to look at the carnage. Harding would wait for the police. Seeing the bodies and blood, the police would immediately erect a screen to keep the complex tenants from gawking at or entering the crime scene.

Harding wiggled out of his coveralls and got his DEA identification ready. In an abundance of caution, he placed his gun under his legs out of sight and placed his hands spread on top of his knees in case an anxious rookie discovered him before the more experienced officers.

Soon he heard a familiar voice.

Chapter 2

Washington D.C.

The police scanner squawked on the desk of *Washington Post* metro reporter Geoffrey Wines. He looked up from his monitor and listened to the call reporting major gang warfare with multiple casualties at Ashford Apartments.

'Tis that time of year, Wines reflected. How many years had he been reporting on gangs and drugs for the *Washington Post*? Many. Too many, even though he had recently won a Pulitzer for his series of stories on the mayor's office, its misuse of funds, and its use of cocaine. The tip had come from the street.

Wines grabbed his notepad and headed to his car, conveniently parked right behind the *Post* building. Metro reporters were given these primo parking spots so they could get to the news faster. The fancy dudes who covered the Capitol had to go through the hassle of the parking garage.

Within twenty minutes, Wines arrived at the Ashford complex. All the police cars and ambulances were gathered at the southwest corner of the complex. Yellow tape and patrol officers kept the public from the tunnel and a large black security screen blocked the view.

Officers McBee and Dugan were already on the scene walking carefully between the bodies that still lay where they died. Wines knew these guys well. Escorting them and pointing at several of the bodies walked a black man wearing black cotton slacks, black soft-sole shoes, and a black sweatshirt. He had the gray hair of an older man but looked far more robust. Most notable was a ragged scar on his right cheek.

After a few minutes, the man walked away, and Officer McBee waved him over. Wines figured McBee would give him a firsthand account of what happened.

Wines stepped carefully around the one-two-three-four-five-six-seven-eight bodies lying on the concrete. Blood pooled everywhere. Finally, he took a safe position on the landing of the stairwell leading up from the tunnel.

Wines noted the maroon lettering on the Sons of Steuben jackets, as well as the M+O cap on one of the dead gangbanger's head.

He waited for McBee to finish his discussions with the uniformed officers, EMS, and medical examiner. Wines knew McBee would share what he knew. In this case, he probably knew a lot, figuring the person they were talking with had witnessed the fight.

McBee stepped up to the landing where Geoffrey stood. "Yes sir, Mr. Wines," McBee said. "Seems the Sons of Steuben were doing their annual parade to secure the drug trade here at Ashford when they ran smack dab into the M+Os in this tunnel. *And the walls came down...All the way to hell....* Eleven entered the tunnel. Eight dead. One nearly dead. And two ran away. One Son of Steuben and one M+O survived. Going to be some major shit happening before this thing is all over."

Wines took notes as McBee relayed the graphic details of the encounter. Then McBee said something unexpected. "You can't report any of these details of what happened. Just the deaths, the names, the place, and some context about the turf battles between the crews. I'm telling you these details because I like and trust you and figure it will help us in later investigations. But today, they are off the record."

"You got it, McBee," Wines confirmed. "But why?"

"Do you know the dude I was talking to?"

"Nope. Never seen him before."

"The black dude I was talking to when you walked up is a DEA Agent. Chuck Harding. He was here doing surveillance on the crews, collecting faces, and we can't blow his cover. Too much detail would alert the crews. A lot of questions would be asked. Besides that, who really cares besides us in the drug-wars business?"

★ ★ ★

Washington Post: Section B: Page 2
Eight Gang Members Die in Turf Battle
By Geoffrey Wines
Metro Staff Reporter

Washington, D.C. — In the first major exchange for turf, rival District of Columbia crews, the Sons of Steuben (SOS) and the M+Os, went head-to-head in armed combat for the Ashford Apartments Housing Project. During the fight, eight gang members were killed, including the SOS leader, Blanford Childress.

The meeting appeared to be an accident. "From the looks of the scene and the closeness of the combat, we surmise the entire altercation was totally unplanned," reported Officer Frank Dugan of the D.C. Drug and Gang Unit. "It appears each group ended up in the service tunnel completely unaware the other group was in the vicinity."

According to Officer Stacey McBee, "The Ashford Apartments are prime turf for the gangs. There are a considerable number of young families in the complex, therefore a ready market for crack and cocaine. The gangs are now trying to increase their turf prior to the peak summer selling season."

Historically, the warfare between the gangs and crews heightens during the spring as each set their boundaries and demonstrate to rival gangs they will not give up any territory without a fight. The sale of cocaine and crack in Washington, D.C., continues to thrive both inside and outside the metro area.

The death of Blanford Childress will cause greater violence

between the gangs. It is common for the gangs to seek revenge for any murder, but typically the death of a gang leader will result in a high level of intergang bloodshed as one gang seeks revenge. Further, according to the Washington, D.C., Police Department, there will also be competition within the SOS for the leadership position.

Last year, D.C. police reported seventeen gang-related murders between March 1 and October 1. According to police, this year's number could be more than double last year's, based on this one incident alone.

Chapter 3

Chicago, Illinois

Dwight Jones awoke with a start—sprawled across his king-size bed, fully clothed, and feeling like shit.

His tall, slightly emaciated body ached all over. He itched and could do nothing to relieve it. He rubbed his hand through his blond hair and across the three-day growth of his beard. The stench of body odor permeated the room. The sheets on his bed were damp with perspiration, and his mouth so dry he could hardly lick his lips.

His stylish Chicago Lincoln Park efficiency was a mess. The shades on the floor-to-ceiling windows were completely drawn, letting light in only around the edges. Clothes were thrown everywhere, dishes piled in the sink, newspapers strewn on the leather sofa, and a scorched pot sat on the stove.

And Christ he was hungry.

Two years ago, Dwight Jones had it made. Today, he wasn't sure whether he even wanted to live.

As he struggled to sit up, he surveyed the surrounding mess and wondered what day it was, what time it was, and how long he had been out of it.

"I really fucked up this time," he muttered as he stumbled across the floor into the kitchen. Thank God in his stupor he had turned off the stove.

There on the counter laid a clear cellophane bag containing about a gram of cocaine, assorted teaspoons, a glass pipe, and spice bottle containing the wonderful white free-base cocaine he had been mixing. Through the fog, he barely remembered preparing it.

He opened the refrigerator door and stared at the half carton of milk, two eggs, empty orange juice container, and open loaf of bread.

God, I wish this fucking itching would stop. Shit. He slammed the refrigerator door and turned to his large screen Sony television in his living room. On the oak entertainment stand next to the television sat his compact disc player and a Harman Kardon receiver. A pair of Infinity speaker towers guarded his audio lair—all his pride and joy.

He turned on the television and switched to the Weather Channel.

The local Chicago weather forecast crawled along the bottom of the screen. The time and date were displayed in the top-right corner. The printout reported a perfect fifty-one degrees on this Tuesday, March 5.

"Tuesday!" he yelled, staring at the screen. "Oh fuck! What time is it? Shit! It's ten twenty-seven. Where the fuck did Monday go? Where the fuck did the morning go? God damn, God damn, I'm fucked."

Dwight ran into the bathroom, threw his clothes in a pile in the corner behind the toilet, turned on the cold-water shower, and jumped in.

Unfortunately, this was not an unusual occurrence; it happened more and more often. He hated it. He despised it. Each time, as he crawled into the freezing shower, he swore he would stop using the blow and clean up his act.

It hadn't always been like this.

Dwight Jones exemplified the classic young, urban, upscale professional. His breeding, education, profession, good looks, and outgoing personality screamed of the socio-type of individual who could succeed in almost any endeavor.

A few years earlier, he had graduated a semester early from the University of Michigan School of Business with his MBA. Throughout school, he knew exactly what he wanted to do. He wanted to become a money broker working on the Chicago Exchange. He loved the idea of making huge amounts of money in the financial markets, driving the latest German sports car, living the successful urban life on the Gold Coast facing Lake Michigan, and doing the young urban bar scene of drinking beer with friends and bedding the pretty ladies he met.

He accomplished all of this.

He adored Chicago! The only place he wanted to live as an adult. He loved the Bears football team and hoped they could reclaim a winning attitude. He treasured the heart-wrenching Cubs and their impossible chances of ever winning a World Series. And he prized the vibrancy and heartbeat of the "city that really works."

Upon graduation from Michigan, he headed straight for a job with the Seaton and Earnst firm as a commodity broker and salesman.

His friends and parents thought he was crazy entering the financial markets for a living and lifelong profession. After all, it had been only three months after the latest stock market crash. With the massive decline of the Dow Jones Industrial Average, brokers were falling by the wayside, totally busted, and disillusioned with the earning potential of the financial markets.

But to Dwight, it was just a game. He had been playing the markets for years. Ever since he first began to earn money as a paperboy for the *Muskegon Chronicle* in Muskegon, Michigan, he had invested in the stock market.

He started buying the typical blue-chip stocks. For a young high school kid to be able to brag to his friends that he owned IBM, General Motors, and AT&T stock thrilled him. His parents encouraged the investments and, of course, saving his news route money.

However, by the time he reached his senior year in high school, he tired of the conservative movement of the blue-chippers and sought other types of stocks that would be more exciting to watch. So, he cashed in much of his portfolio and tried his hand in the speculative oil-drilling stocks.

He loved their volatility. He looked forward to seeing actual point changes when he opened each day's paper; and watching his skill at picking stocks pay off with constant increases in the size of his portfolio. With pride, he beat all the stock, bond, and money market averages with his selections.

By the time he headed off to the University of Michigan, he had amassed about $5,000. This gave him a nice base to continue investing during his college years—and to provide a little play money to make college even more enjoyable—though he didn't have to worry about paying any of his college expenses. His parents had planned for his education and had socked away more than enough money to cover the UM tuition, books, room, and board.

Dwight enjoyed college and earned decent grades, though not one obsessed with making A's.

During his second semester, he pledged the Alpha Tau Omega fraternity. Dwight's fraternity roommate was Bruce Zimmer, a street-smart, rich Jewish kid from Philadelphia. Bruce, also a good student and business major, prided himself as quite a lady's man who spent little time cracking the books. The two hit it off almost immediately.

Dwight and Bruce, like most other college boys, were completely into the coeds. They couldn't wait for their weekend "trawling," as they called it, to begin on Friday afternoons. Typically, their last class adjourned at 3:00 p.m. and that's when the action began with beers at Duffy's and then whatever.

One Friday afternoon late in the school year, as Dwight and Bruce sat in their usual booth setting up their plan for the weekend, they noticed a couple of girls neither had seen at Duffy's before. The babes sat a couple of booths over in the rough-hewed pine-paneled bar, with a pitcher of beer between them. They were talking emphatically with each other; gulping their beers; laughing; and animating their conversation with their hands, eyes, and facial expressions.

Unlike most of the coeds on an early day in May, they were dressed in shorts and loosely fitting sleeveless blouses. Their tans were darker than one would typically have this time of year in Michigan.

Dwight and Bruce eyed them, then eyed each other, and without saying a word picked up their beers and walked over to the girls' table, knowing they had their "catch" for the weekend.

"You guys doing all right?" Dwight asked in his smooth midwestern style as he eyed the dark brunette with the piercing-brown eyes sitting on the right side of the table. Her red-and-white-striped blouse set off her black hair, dark complexion, and full red lips. Dwight wasn't sure whether she was Spanish, Jewish, Greek, Italian, or a combination of all. *She's beautiful!*

"Yeah, you girls new or what?" Bruce asked in his sharp Philadelphia accent. "We haven't seen you around here before." He then sat right next to the redhead on the other side of the booth, moving her deeper into the booth until their hips touched. "Yeah, I don't remember seein' you girls around here. You know, it's late in the school year and all. But I'm sure glad I do now."

He turned his head, leaned forward, and looked straight into the redhead's green eyes. Her naturally light complexion highlighted the red blush of her tan, freckles around her pointed nose, and exceptionally white teeth.

Dwight continued standing next to the table, showing more manners than Bruce.

The redhead broke eye contact with Bruce and slowly looked up at Dwight. "Well, honey, don't just stand there with that beer in your hand lookin' down on us. Sit yourself down there next to Anita," she coached with a slight southern lilt in her voice.

Dwight nodded to her and anxiously looked over at the brunette, who scooted herself deeper into the booth. She patted her hand on the seat next to her as an invitation for Dwight to sit. Then she glanced at her friend across the table and let out a quiet giggle as Dwight sat.

"My name's Holly," the redhead said moving even closer to Bruce. "And this is Anita."

"My name's Bruce, and the goon there's Dwight," Bruce said with a broadening smile. "So, are you students here at Michigan or what?"

"Naw, we're not—not yet, anyway," Holly answered. "We start at the summer session. We've been livin' in Gainesville, Florida. We thought we'd come up and see the campus and have a little fun before summer classes start, maybe meet a few people," she continued, tilting her head, and looking directly at Bruce.

Anita broke her silence. "Yes, we are taking some special classes at your school of chemistry this summer." She spoke with a slight British accent, the type usually acquired from English schooling in a foreign country.

"University of Florida?" Dwight asked. "Classes out already?"

Holly nodded. "Yessir, our classes ended the last week in April, so we said, 'What the hell? Let's get on up there and see the school before we hit the books.'"

"Chemistry. What kind of special classes are you taking?" Dwight asked Anita, trying to pull her more into the conversation. He sensed she was the more studious of the two and probably would be more apt to talk about school.

"We are in a special honors chemistry program at Florida," Anita said quietly. "Florida and Michigan have a summer trade-out cooperative where students may elect to take their summer classes at the other school. The schools believe it provides a change of scenery and the opportunity for students to get a better education by seeing other campuses and how different academic departments work. Besides that, we're ready for a little cooler weather."

Beautiful. And smart, too, Dwight thought. *This should be an interesting evening, and maybe an interesting summer*. He would also stay on campus, taking a few extra electives to graduate a semester early.

The four grabbed a bite at Wally's Pizza and Subs around 8:00 and decided some dancing at The Hangar would be fun.

Holly turned out to be a wild woman, just as Dwight had figured. She and Bruce were meant for each other. The moment they entered The Hanger, Bruce ordered shots of tequila and the two of them picked up on a conversation from dinner about how plastered they got the last time they did shooters.

Anita—last name Mendez—lived in South America. Her father was a well-to-do Colombian businessman, and she had been educated in special English prep schools before coming to the States for her college education.

THE CAMP DAVID CONSPIRACY

The reserve and shyness she displayed when talking or meeting new people transformed into open passion when she hit the dance floor. *The woman could dance!* She was graceful, passionate, suggestive, and absolutely eye stopping once she walked on the dance floor. She moved fluidly as her hips thrust to the music and her arms waved about her head, grabbing her long dark hair about her face and eyes, then letting it drop suggestively across her shoulders.

At one point in the evening, even the band noticed her and played a special Latin medley they thought would be especially provocative for the tall blond kid and his beautiful lady.

As it turned out, the girls were living in one of the women's dorms.

For Holly and Bruce, the dorm wasn't conducive to the way they wanted to spend the remainder of their evening. The two seemed to be hitting it off extremely well, spending a lot of time talking; dancing aggressively on the floor; and drinking, drinking, drinking. The shooters were followed by a pitcher of beer to cool them down, then another pitcher for the rest of the table. When that pitcher was gone, they departed for the ATO house.

About an hour or two later, Dwight and Anita left The Hangar and stepped into the cool Michigan night. For Dwight, the evening had been something special. He had met *an absolutely beautiful smart woman* and had a splendid time as the center of attention, and he was now walking hand in hand with her to *his* fraternity house.

As they approached the steps to the house, he asked Anita to wait in the parlor while he ran upstairs to–determine whether Bruce and Holly had commandeered the bedroom.

As Dwight entered the living area of their suite, he could smell the sweet, pungent odor of marijuana smoke and hear Bruce and Holly laughing in the bedroom.

"Hey, Dwight, is that you rousting around?" Bruce shouted.

"Dwight, honey, is Anita still with you? Y'all having a good time?" Holly purred from behind the bedroom curtain. Then Dwight heard a giggle and the rustle of bedsheets.

"I guess we're going to settle with a little nightcap downstairs," Dwight said, knowing the "first in" rule he and Bruce had set years ago.

"Come in here, honey, I want to talk to you," Holly whispered. "Oh, it's all right Brucey, honey. We're both under the sheets. I want to tell your friend something about Anita, and I don't want everyone in this damn house to hear me."

Dwight slowly passed through the curtain into the bedroom area. On Bruce's twin bed, Holly was sitting up with the sheet pulled around her chest and legs. Bruce was lying on his back smiling broadly and rolling his eyes around while looking at Dwight and stroking Holly's bare back.

"Dwight, honey, you should know that you and Anita aren't going to end up in the sack like Brucey and me. Anita comes from a strict Catholic family. I think she's still a virgin and probably will be one until she marries the man her family agrees she can marry. Please don't push her or try to do anything that will embarrass her. OK, honey?"

Bruce grinned at Dwight. He winked, as if to say, "Bruce one, Dwight zero."

* * *

The next morning, Bruce walked Holly to the women's dorm where Dwight had taken Anita the night before.

For Dwight and Anita, their relationship remained casual. Something told him the last thing he wanted was to get in trouble with a strict South American businessman from Colombia. But Bruce continued to see Holly until she and Anita left at the end of the summer session. Bruce and Holly were truly peas out of the same pod.

One night during one of their dates, Holly suggested she and Bruce use a little blow to liven up their sex life.

Even though Bruce was a street-smart kid from Philadelphia and had smoked pot for years, he had never once used or considered using cocaine. But, with Holly, he said, "Let's go for it!"

He told her he had no idea where to get the stuff. She said she had a small amount in her room and knew someone in Gainesville where she could get more if needed. She taught Bruce how to cut the lines and snort just the right amount to set the perfect high. He found the experience to be about the best thing he ever imagined.

Before the end of July, Holly and Bruce did a little "blow dicking" a couple of times. Holly's Florida friend was glad to keep her cocaine stash well supplied with double-wrapped shipments through the mail. And before Holly left Michigan, she gave Bruce the name of her contact.

★ ★ ★

Bruce continued to use cocaine in addition to marijuana. Dwight refused to use either. He knew some of the financial firms fingerprinted and drug tested their entry-level applicants, and he did not want to take the chance of losing his opportunity to enter the business.

While Bruce kept his consumption of cocaine in check, he found out his Florida contact could get him better weed than he was able to get in Michigan. So, to offset some of his expenses of obtaining the "Florida stuff" and the bit of coke he was using, he started selling pot on the side. His customers were mostly fraternity brothers who were looking for something better than the local crop.

Upon graduation, Bruce moved to New York City, where he took a job as a sales representative with a major food company. He stayed in contact with his Florida connection and continued the recreational use of cocaine.

Dwight continued to play the stock market during his last year at Michigan. He was doing quite well heading into his last semester. His portfolio had grown to $8,000, riding the wave of the bull market. This was an exceptionally fine performance, especially given the fact Dwight had pulled $3,000 to $4,000 out during the past few years to liven up his college experience.

However, on the day the market crashed, Dwight's portfolio, composed primarily of high-yield junk bonds and speculative stocks, took a sweeping dive. His portfolio consisted of exactly those instruments the market revolted against in the days leading up to the crash.

But to Dwight, it really wasn't any big deal. *So, how many students leave college with a $2,000 nest egg?* he thought. Besides, he knew if he had been watching the market more closely, instead of being so immersed in his MBA studies, he probably would have been able to avert the destruction of his portfolio.

★ ★ ★

Now, here he was in Chicago, fulfilling his dream. He liked being a "Captain of Industry."

He loved having a Lincoln Park apartment that faced the lake. He loved the feeling of stepping out of his building in the morning, waving to the doorman, and catching a cab that would take him to his office in the Chicago Exchange Building while he read the *Wall Street Journal*. And he always purchased the *Washington Post*, too. They reported the scandals earlier than the *Tribune*.

The excitement, speed, and huge amount of money he dealt with every day was invigorating. During the past three years, he had successfully built a good client base, was learning his way around the various worldwide markets, and was considered one of the rising stars at Seaton and Earnst.

Well, he had been considered a star until the past few months.

Even though he was making $95,000 in commissions per year, that figure was dropping fast. His lack of concentration, his frequent absences, and his failing enthusiasm for the job he had so dearly loved was costing him his lifestyle. He had no savings left—living from paycheck to paycheck. He had used all his money to buy cars, cameras, stereo equipment, furniture, and cocaine. Ever since he first started using cocaine eighteen months ago, his habit had increased to $500 per week.

As the beating cold water hit the back of his head, Dwight began to think rationally for the first time in three days. He realized this was the end. His supervisor at S&E had warned him about his rising absenteeism and had put him on notice. Missing work wasn't a problem unto itself. However, making sales was. And Dwight's frequent unexplainable absences had caused him to miss appointments, important meetings on new issues, calls from his growing clientele, and the opportunity to make money for himself and the company.

Chapter 4

Washington, D.C.

Attorney General Patrick Miller threw the briefing paper across his desk. "For Christ's sake, how in the hell do they expect us to ever stop this?"

For the second time in a month, the Justice Department's case against a well-entrenched drug dealer fell through. The judge had ruled there was no way to prove the defendant, Ben Marks, ever distributed the drugs found in his apartment. There was no money, no records, or anything traceable to prove the drugs were unsold goods. No one came forward to claim they purchased from or dealt for Marks. And big-time dealers would never be caught in the middle of a transaction.

Therefore, only possession charges could be brought up—not exactly the *kill* the department had in mind when they started the investigation eighteen months earlier.

Miller knew the legal ramifications of *Marks v. United States of America*. As the attorney general of the United States, he knew the brilliant defense strategy used by Mark's lawyer would be copied by every two-bit drug lawyer in the country. It would be an easy maneuver to have the charges reduced to possession from distributing and selling. The fines were much less, and the prison sentences virtually nonexistent.

Miller recognized this turn of events reflected the shift in priorities he had personally established during his first year as AG. As part of the president's second-term pledge to make significant inroads in reducing the nation's drug problem, he pressed to concentrate law enforcement efforts on the dealer, distributor, and trafficker—not the individual user. His simple logic—*if maximum pressure targeted the supply side, then it would be hard to conduct business, and sales would dry up.*

Therefore, during the past two years, most of the government's cases focused on sellers and distributors, not the users. In fact, to get to the dealer, charges were typically dropped against users with cocaine or other narcotics in their possession.

And this, of course, set a precedent that would be the ticket to freedom for many of the dealers they were now investigating. Without money or something else to tie the possession of illegal drugs to their *selling commerce*, more acquittals like *Marks* would occur. This made it more difficult to utilize the 404(b) statutes to convict someone by tying other acts to the case. The dealers were getting too smart, and their workers more closemouthed.

Miller felt besieged. He knew he had to do something and do it quick. President Osbourne had set the war on drugs as a priority. With the status quo, current investigations would blow up in the government's face.

A new way to audit the trail of drugs needed to be found.

Chapter 5

The White House

President Robert S. Osbourne Jr. sat in his inner office reading the day's briefing papers. On his desk sat a heavy crystal tumbler of Maker's Mark and cracked ice.

As each day drew to a close, he instructed the few remaining aides and his chief of staff to not disturb him. He reserved this as his hour of reflection on the events affecting his country. His think time to make any real sense of the day. And short of a national emergency, he should be left alone.

Osbourne had served as the US president for the past six years. He had won his last election by a comfortable margin—though not by the landslide everyone had predicted. His presidency continued to be considered a success by a large majority of citizens, the press, and a very reluctant opposing Democratic party.

As he sat reading the papers, he reflected on the real meaning of his presidency and the effect his life in politics had on the American people. Like many before him, he started out as a state representative in his native Greenville County in South Carolina. He was one of the few Republicans to hold a state seat in the South Carolina legislature. From there, he was elected to the US Congress and then on to the Senate, where he became the Republican minority whip, vice president, and then the party's ticket for president.

Osbourne was considered a moderate. He had southern conservatism but wasn't so conservative as to turn off the northern supporters who favored a more progressive direction for government.

His arrival in D.C. in 1964 as the congressman representing the Piedmont region of South Carolina seemed unusual for the time. It reflected the changing attitudes in the South, the civil rights agenda of the Democrats, and Osbourne's open style.

This openness was due to his wife, Emily Rose, a Democrat who had always made sure Bobby understood the other points of view. Emily had often been asked how she could be married to a Republican congressman.

"I just loved JFK, and when he was killed, I couldn't see any reason to switch. Besides, I always believed black people should have the right to vote."

From the first day when Emily arrived in Washington in her shiny red Cadillac convertible with a potted palmetto tree in the back seat, she and Bobby had made quite an impression on the D.C. social scene.

Emily Rose had been a southern belle with a smoky voice, deep Carolina accent, and a gift for storytelling. With a cigarette in one hand and a snifter of Old Grand-Dad bourbon in the other, she would captivate the other congressmen at the various cocktail receptions with her tales, humor, and observations. She had become friends with the wives from both parties and, in the southern tradition, had encouraged rounds of social invitations for lunch, brunch, bridge, pinochle, dinner parties, and cookouts.

Bobby and Emily Rose had no children. Rumor back home was her "lady parts" had been damaged during a back-alley abortion.

As part of a political couple, Emily Rose had always been Bobby's link to the thoughts, ideas, and concerns of the other party. Women would talk politics, and Emily Rose shared their comments with Bobby.

During the period her husband served as the minority whip, Emily Rose had been unexpectedly diagnosed with stage-four lung cancer and died after a very short illness. Her funeral attracted hundreds, and given her ability to turn a tale, attendees were encouraged to tell their own *Emily Rose Story*.

Notably, many politicians from both parties told their tales, but a beat police officer on the D.C. force stood up and told a story that most agreed captured the spirit of Emily Rose.

The officer told how she made a U-turn on Pennsylvania Avenue right in front of him and asked where the Cannon Office Building was located.

He replied she was not allowed to make a U-turn on Pennsylvania.

She retorted with a simple, "Listen, young man, that is not what I asked you. I asked you where the Cannon Office Building is located."

The officer had been so taken aback that he told her she *had* been going the right direction. Whereupon, she then made another U-turn, and proceeded to the right location to meet her newly elected husband.

Her sudden illness had left Osbourne stunned. He loved her, and her humor had brightened each day. Her death left a huge hole in his soul that he filled by delving deeper into his work.

Nothing could replace Emily Rose's contact with the congressional wives. But to fill the void, he would channel his *inner Emily Rose* and ask these men what their wives thought about something. The answers were always telling because they often distilled the thoughts of the office holder while still hinting at nagging concerns or overwhelming support.

The widower president, Robert S. Osbourne, also made it a practice to invite couples over every week to join him for dinner at the White House. His guests were from both parties and included freshmen and seasoned legislators. For him, it filled a social void. For the invited couples, it was an incredible honor. And for the good of the country, he always engaged the spouse as both a courtesy and a window into the thinking of his guest.

★ ★ ★

At this time, the country comfortably sat about nine months away from the political fray that would begin as the two parties stalked their next presidential candidate. Although Osbourne certainly enjoyed his years as president, he relished the fact that he did not have to go through the political race a fifth time. The upcoming election would be one he could enjoy from the sideline.

These were typically the most comfortable days for the presidency. The wolf was off the door, and the president had time to rescue the party from any political blunders. He had learned through the years that a political crisis could arise from almost anywhere; and that it usually took the solid handling from the president to quell any lasting effect on the party. Even after the number of years he had spent in political office, it never ceased to amaze him how the president would be held accountable for the misdeeds or appearance of misdeed by anyone associated within the White House, executive branch, or often any branch of the government.

Most citizens and politicians who were complimentary of his political success cited his nonaggressive approach to politics and solving the nation's problems. Throughout his years in the Congress, Osbourne was noted as having a clear head when it came to seeing through a problem and marshaling the resources necessary to create a well-thought-out solution.

He knew what it took to get things done in government. As the minority whip, he had been able to wield an incredible amount of power simply by drawing his opponents in with support and then checking them when they disagreed. He avoided fights.

Osbourne usually discovered the perfect timing to get things done. He instinctively understood if he could find himself on common ground—even with his political adversaries—he could always be more effective with his own agenda. And it was always easier to have a group who wanted to get something done than to have folks fighting the idea.

He demonstrated this successful strategy with his handling of the government's budget deadlock.

The budget was a continuation of the problems that had hampered every president since Lyndon Johnson. The nation's budget had ballooned to such an astronomical figure, and so little of it could be manipulated because of long-term commitments contained within the budget. The national social programs needed to be maintained and placed on a sustainable path. National security was of vital importance via a strong military with cutting-edge weapon systems. The latest conflict with Iraq, not to mention the "new world order" with Russia, had proven the wisdom of pursuing some of these systems.

When the Democrats and Republicans, the administration and the Congress, the liberals and the conservatives could not reach any agreement on the budget, Osbourne simply borrowed a page from the strategy used by the founding fathers during the Constitutional Convention of 1787.

He used an approach where all parties could claim victory. All could take credit for bringing about a successful solution to the budget. And, most importantly, the unpopular decisions would be equally shared.

As president, he asked the Democrats and the Republicans to send to the White House the two senators and two congressmen who most understood the budget and the goals of their party. No staff would be allowed.

The Democrats sent their majority leader and the chairman of the Senate Budget Committee. From the House, they sent their leading moderate voice and leading liberal.

The Republicans brought their Senate minority leader and the House whip; plus, the ranking Republicans on the Budget and Ways and Means Committees.

The White House commissioned their budget director and chief of staff. A cloistered staff of aides were kept close to answer any technical questions.

The process was amazingly simple. The Democrats and the Republicans each had an equal number of votes. The White House representatives did not vote. They were there for informational detail only. The president did not have a vote except in the case of a tie. The discussions and the votes would be highly confidential. Only the final recommendation of this bipartisan committee would be reported to the House, Senate, and the public.

There would not be any reporting to the press or to anyone outside the committee. Both parties understood leaks would put an end to the proceedings and mean a return to the ineffective process they were seeking to avoid. Further, given the extremely tight group working on this committee, leaks could be easily tracked down, resulting in an embarrassing situation for both the individual and the individual's party.

The rank and file of the House and Senate would be asked to confirm their leadership's plan. If either party failed to uphold their recommendation, it would be an indictment on their abilities. This would not be the position either party would encourage.

In the end, through this unique political process, the elected leaders from each party hammered out the solution to the country's budget mess. Each party considered the process a success. The internal votes were never known. Passage of the final bill flew through both the House and the Senate on a bipartisan basis. And Osbourne signed it into law with over four hundred lawmakers standing behind him on the Capitol steps.

President Robert S. Osbourne took great pride in the results. He succeeded by putting different minded people in the same room with a common goal; and who were motivated in getting the job done.

With the budget situation now behind him, there remained one other urgent problem that needed addressing. There were still the burgeoning court dockets, overflowing prisons, and the growing evidence that illegal drugs were having an irreversible impact on the nation's kids and parts of society.

For months, he had bragged to the press about the success of his drug-enforcement programs. The street prices of cocaine and crack cocaine were up indicating the interdiction programs were effectively cutting supply. Yet the jails were still filling up, the number of gang- and drug-related street deaths continued to rise, and the urban government housing projects were becoming unlivable.

The cherry blossoms were now in bloom; and Osbourne knew spring and summer represented the peak seasons for drug-related crimes throughout the country. The streets would become alive with the "commerce" of drugs. With this season, the turf battles in the inner city would echo with a death knell that would continue until the first freezes of winter. The gangs would become more active as the sale of crack, heroin, and cocaine increased threefold during the hot summer.

Inner-city sections of New York, Los Angeles, and just around the corner in Washington would become totally out of control. The police were basically ineffective to this wildest form of commerce. The playgrounds and school grounds became the storefronts for the pushers, the couriers, and the dealers.

Unlike organized crime that centered itself on adult participation in alcohol, prostitution, and gambling, this form of organized crime was much more violent. Street-spraying gangs paid little heed to who else may be in the path of their gunfire. A victim's age or actual participation ignored.

Osbourne thought about the constant stream of headlines he would see during the next several months. D.C. alone ranked the highest in the United States in violent crime and murder. Little could be done to stop it. The demand for illegal drugs was too high, and the astronomical earning potential of those engaged in meeting the demand overcame any feeling of common decency.

And it just wasn't the poor and impoverished who were "bettering" themselves by selling drugs. The industry enticed professional men and women who risked everything they had going for them to obtain the windfall profits that an illegal-drug deal offered. Recent headlines exposed major selling organizations operating from the most respected law, accounting, brokerage, advertising, and medical practices in the country. Even fraternity houses at the country's most prestigious universities were being investigated for housing some of this nation's most successful dealers and selling organizations.

The formula for success was simple enough—basically a multilevel selling scheme where each entrepreneur built his or her own business by attracting and servicing a specific clientele. The product mix included various quality levels of cocaine and marijuana.

The opportunities created by the likes of Amway and other companies were surpassed many times over with this growing market. Where Amway could promise an ambitious person only a few thousand dollars per week and potentially Diamond status, the illegal-drug version of this free enterprise system promised something much more lucrative.

In the drug business the reward for outstanding performance created all the money and power in the world. A few hundred thousand dollars per year was just the beginning. The successful people in this industry could turn $100,000 per month or $1 million or more per year.

Jewelry and heavy gold chains replaced the diamond lapel status pins. An entrepreneur's success was visible to all by the weight of gold chains around his neck, the type of car he drove, or the additions made to his home or investment account. And money was only half of the rewards. Status and women made the lure of entering this business twice as attractive.

The dealer's status in the inner city was above that of almost any other person. Dealers were the people who were going to beat the odds and make it out of their impoverished neighborhood. They were the people the young kids admired and emulated. They were the people who could afford to be good citizens and pay medical bills for a sick friend or the attorney fee for colleagues in trouble. The successful dealers were at the top of the food chain.

Beyond the status, the rewards of the flesh were unbelievable. Women. Beautiful women. Women of every size, shape, and color were ready for the exploits of a successful drug entrepreneur. All they asked in return was a little free coke, maybe a favor from the law, or a break for a friend entering the business.

The lure for people to enter and protect their place in this business was simply too much. If Amway could promise only a one-week conference vacation at some Marriott resort, the drug business could provide private jets; yachts sailing the tropics; and beautiful, scantily clad women to replace the aging wife in furs and a support bra. If one's professional career took several years to build into a lucrative business and a cushy lifestyle, the drug-dealing business could place someone into that lifestyle in a fraction of the time.

The basic problem with illegal drugs was that it served both the ambitions of the rich, as well as the despair of the poor.

★ ★ ★

It was now 7:00 p.m. No guests tonight. Osbourne shook himself back into reality and took one last sip of his Maker's Mark. These thoughts about how to bring a solution to the nation's drug problem were never far from his mind. He constantly asked himself: How could he convince people to stop selling? How could he get people to stop using? How could he stop the insane madness illegal drugs wreaked on the American people?

Chapter 6

Mendez Cartel Headquarters

Colombia, South America

The business of illegal drugs taking place in the South American country of Colombia garners so much press that it is literally a joke to the kingpins of the Mendez cartel. Most everything the American people read about the "war on drugs" is either a misnomer or purely false.

The federal justice and enforcement powers in Washington, D.C., believe the only way they will eventually bring an end to the nation's drug problem is to convince everyday citizens the full force of the US government *will win the war* against the drug cartels. But the reality is the cartels are firmly in control of their business.

No aspect is left to chance. The quality of the product, its distribution, pricing, and marketing are all carefully planned components of this highly lucrative business. The practices the cartels apply to maintain sales and profitability are the same as those taught at the finest business schools in the United States and used by the likes of Procter & Gamble, Kraft, General Mills, and other sophisticated packaged goods giants.

Four key individuals run The Mendez Cartel. Like any corporate structure, there are executives responsible for production and procurement; financials; distribution and sales; and security. Juan Pablo Mendez is the ex-facto president—chief executive officer and founder.

The skills and leadership abilities of each of his lieutenants would enable them to succeed in any business in America. Their educations are from the finest schools; their computer equipment and management information systems unsurpassed by any Fortune 500 company; and their financial controls and network of banks and capitalization surpass anything found in the United Kingdom, Germany, Switzerland, or the United States.

Their success is solely predicated on their ability to get cocaine into the United States. Like the legal ethical drug business, the US market is also the bread and butter for the Mendez cartel. America's appetite for Colombian cocaine grows every day with steady demand and no end in sight.

Their daily strategic concerns center on: maintaining a steady stream of cocaine into the US; having couriers to transport product to the proper distributors; maintaining a network of dealers, optimizing price and profit. Too much cocaine on the market lowers the price and margins—too little escalates the street price to prohibitive levels and reduces overall tonnage.

Today's drug cartels expertly practice the lessons the oil cartels learned in the 1970s: Supply dictates price and profits. And the drug cartels work with each other in maintaining price levels—versus the Arab practice of working against each other by constantly lowering the price to maintain volume. This pricing discipline is possible because the drug cartels keep their expenses in line, thus minimizing the need to maintain a high level of volume just to assure a certain income.

The man responsible for the Mendez cartel's marketing and distribution network is Feliz Herendez. Outside the cartel brass, he is simply known as Zorro—a moniker given because of the z's in his name, sophisticated Latin manner, elusive background, and a legendary quickness with a sword if he is ever crossed.

Feliz is a complex man—known to all within the cartel as extremely brutal in business yet very loving to his friends and family. His credo—*loyalty, livelihood, and life.* He demands complete loyalty to the cartel, to Juan Pablo Mendez and to him personally. In Zorro's world, there is no room for anyone not loyal. Period. Persons trying to take the upper hand over the business, steal from the business, or hurt the business in any way are eliminated. No HR involvement. No exit packages. No second chance. No questions, no trial, no leniency, no excuses.

As an added precaution, if any person is arrested or questioned by the police, they are deemed suspect, and their loyalty immediately questioned. Any man arrested best not return to the cartel for they will be marked for "extermination by Zorro."

Feliz' number-one lieutenant is an American-born Hispanic from south Texas named Luther Gomez. Unlike the tall, handsome features of Feliz, Luther is a bulldog of a man—squat and brawny—with dark pocked skin and slicked back hair. His presence brings fear, but his smile disarms in a frightening kind of way.

In their world, Feliz sets strategy, and Luther implements it. Feliz regulates the flow of cocaine out of the cartel and sets the price. Luther establishes new avenues of distribution and protects existing avenues to ensure the product reaches the American streets.

To accomplish this, Mendez operates a multi-tiered distribution network. First, there are boats and planes to transport uncut cocaine to the American coastal cities or up the Central American corridor. The key is to maintain multiple pipelines and not overwork any one avenue—no matter how ingenious or lucrative. Repetition usually ends in a bust—though some busts are planned to draw the American authorities away from the more fertile paths.

Container ships carrying imported goods are often used to provide large-capacity shipments. In these cases, the cocaine is slipped into porcelain figurines, machinery parts, clothing, bananas, or any number of seemingly innocent shipments. The secret is to package the product in such a way that drug sniffing dogs cannot pick up on the slight ammonia scent of cocaine.

Small planes flying low over the seas are also used to fill the distribution gaps. Though the payload can be only 1,500 to 2,000 pounds, a successful delivery places several million dollars of coke into the US domestic pipeline.

The delivery points are the who's who listing of American cities. Containers holding cartel cocaine arrive daily on ships unloading in

New Orleans, Houston, Los Angeles, Seattle, Baltimore, Philadelphia, Boston, and Miami harbors. To reach the interior cities, a complex array of surface vehicles transports the product to Chicago, Saint Louis, Detroit, Cleveland, Denver, Oklahoma City, Las Vegas, Atlanta, Dallas, Minneapolis, Indianapolis, Salt Lake City, and Phoenix.

Luther oversees the shipments to these interior areas and the major distributors receiving the cocaine. After that, the middlemen and smaller operators take the cocaine, cut it, repackage it, and distribute it to the thousands of independent dealers throughout the cities and rural areas of the United States.

Feliz and Luther maintain a constant watch over their responsibility. Feliz seldom leaves Colombia. Luther is on the road most of the time. The two of them had worked as partners for the past ten years. Before the cartel, Feliz had been a small-time importer and smuggler in Colombia. Before the current immense popularity of cocaine, he made money bringing the white substance to New York on frequent business trips. His "day job" at the time had been importing South American pottery and ceramic art. Luther was one of the "local gentlemen" whom Feliz sold twenty kilos of cocaine a month which he liquidated through a wide group of pushers, pimps, and fringe Mafia types. Each made a good living.

When Juan Pablo Mendez started to form his cartel, he asked Feliz to head distribution because of his knowledge of exporting goods to the United States. Feliz selected Luther because of his established contacts, knowledge of the street, and toughness.

Both had anticipated the new cartel would make them individually rich, but neither guessed their wealth would accumulate at the rate and immensity of the past five years.

★ ★ ★

Each spring, Feliz and Luther see the immediate increase in the demand for cocaine. Like the way retailers preorder and stock frozen turkeys around Thanksgiving, the cocaine dealers increase their inventory in anticipation of the seasonal rise in sales. The key distributors place their orders for greater amounts of cocaine to get an early jump and establish themselves with their dealer base.

"Luther, come here and look at this," Feliz called out, spinning in his chair back to the computer screen on his desk. "Look at these orders!"

Luther examined the rows of numbers on the screen. The first column showed point of entry (POE) where the cartel ships to the US mainland. The second column showed the number of kilos shipped in the current month. The third, the kilos shipped the preceding month. The fourth, orders still unshipped for the current month. And the last column reviews the amount shipped last year during the same month. For every city—the current month's shipments shown in column two were significantly higher than the year-ago shipments displayed in the last column.

Luther whistled. "Jesus! The natives are thirsty. We're up almost twenty-five percent from last year, and last year was a great year. And our initiative to build the white-collar trade seems to be taking hold."

Feliz looked up and grinned. "Something, isn't it? Our dealers must be moving it because there are still plenty of unshipped orders." He ran his finger down the fourth column on the screen.

Luther returned his grin. "Where the fuck you think those D.C. dudes are coming from with last week's announcement that 'usage is down, shipments of cocaine into the US are down, and street prices are up?'" he asked sarcastically.

"Heh, it's just part of the game they're playing. And we help them with it." Feliz smiled. "Remember in January when we cut back shipments when the street prices were beginning to dip? We were just setting ourselves up for the key season—getting the prices up for when the big volume hits. Heh, higher sales with higher prices. What else could a good businessman hope for?"

"Yeah, it's pretty amazing their DEA isn't doing a better job than they are. If you open a newspaper, you'd swear we were going out of business. It doesn't look like we're going under, does it, Feliz, my friend?"

"Nope. And it looks like we need to start setting up the new routes for moving product into the US. This added demand is going to stretch our current channels." Feliz stared at the screen. "Man, this would be a lot easier if we were based in Mexico."

This was a problem every time demand for cocaine stepped up in the States. The network of imports through the container ships stayed constant month in and month out. That was part of the disguise. The custom agents at the various seaports paid little attention to ongoing familiar shipments arriving on a steady basis. So, Feliz assured they remained constant.

The large cargo container shipments were extremely important to the cartel. Various means were used to protect their integrity. It was not unusual to ship coke-free containers, called "empties," through the system just to maintain the disguise. Even more extreme, the cartel would plant a container on an alternative ship, with every intention of having the container discovered by US Customs or the DEA.

These decoy containers would hold as much cocaine as regular containers. The only difference being the "imported" materials surrounding the coke would be different, and the recipient fictional. The strategy was to allow the US government to intercept sizable shipments.

When these decoy containers were "discovered" through this kind of deception, the benefit was great. The US feds typically felt they had accomplished a major hit, and the street prices usually rose for a short period. But it was just the cartel's way of maintaining a balance of supply and optimizing pricing and logistics. *Simple business practices.*

To the cartel, the three thousand kilos of coke wasted for this illusion was merely a cost of doing business. In all, Feliz's numbers showed less than 2 percent of their total tonnage was sacrificed to protect the hundreds of thousands of kilos moving through these important distribution channels.

"Luther, we also need to begin setting additional cross-country routes. Our business in the central part of the US is picking up. The gangs are beginning to make inroads into some of the smaller towns across the Midwest." Feliz looked out the window of the office and at the garden below. "The Bloods and the Crips are expanding their influence into the towns of one hundred to two hundred thousand people. It's easier for them than fighting for a greater share of the business in the major urban areas."

Luther nodded. "We'll start on it. Perhaps Saint Louis will be our best central point for supplying these Midwest markets. We have a good facility in East Saint Louis, and the DEA isn't as strong there as in Chicago. We can move the additional product via the I-40 connection from California to Amarillo. Our drivers are also having exceptional luck in moving along I-44 through Oklahoma and on to Saint Louis. Less than five percent of our runs are being intercepted."

Conducting business was that simple for the cartel. Feliz devised the strategy regarding distribution and supply, and then Luther made it work. It was streamlined management in a very flat organization.

And they were making boatloads of money doing it.

Chapter 7

Chicago, Illinois

It had been three weeks since Dwight Jones was fired from Seaton and Earnst. His search for a new position completely stalled. In fact, it had never started since Dwight had two problems. One he admitted. The other he would not acknowledge.

Dwight knew his ability to return to the financial markets was virtually nil. He knew it was a tight industry, particularly in Chicago. He knew any check of his experience would reveal that Dwight Jones had been a rising star at Seaton and Earnst, but for the past six months had been totally unreliable in his position—missed days of work, missed calls from key clients, and failure to keep up with the newest issues. In confidence, the references would say drug use was suspected.

Dwight wasn't the first person in the financial business to use illegal drugs and lose their job. It was more common than the captains of the commodity markets would like to admit. The nature of the business attracted type A personalities, who were motivated by change, the pressures of the market, and the ability to play hard when times were good.

Typically, a young, highly motivated MBA would enter the field. During the first couple of years, they would work their ass off building a client base and learning the business. They would slowly succeed and soon begin to attract more and more money.

The first stage in their metamorphosis would be buying a BMW, Mercedes, or Porsche. These were their first badges of success.

Soon, the novelty of the dream car would wear off, particularly in Chicago, where it was virtually impossible to simply park the car while trawling the Rush Street bars or to take the car out during the icy days of the long Chicago winters.

This led to the second stage, with the new "master of the financial universe" furnishing their pad to use for entertainment and, of course, "to nail a little pussy." The prerequisite for the apartment: it must overlook the lake and be either on the Gold Coast or Lincoln Park; the furniture had to be exquisite, modern, and expensive with real leather, solid wood, no veneers; and they had to have the latest in electronics, usually a full-size Sony television set, a VCR, a compact disc player, and the finest audio amplifier and speaker system available.

★ ★ ★

Unfortunately, Dwight's second problem was his addiction to cocaine—and it altered the way he thought about himself and others. He had become highly paranoid, had no sense of well-being, and simply needed to be under the influence. He used more and more coke—plus freebasing—to maintain a level of equilibrium, but even that became harder. His money went up his nose, and he pawned some of his possessions to score.

★ ★ ★

For Dwight, his entrée into the world of drug abuse started innocently enough. Even though Bruce Zimmer, his best friend and college roommate at the University of Michigan used cocaine, Dwight never did. He dedicated himself to pursuing his profession and wanted to make sure nothing would impede it. No marijuana and no cocaine. Period.

After he had been at Seaton and Earnst for about a year, he began to have tremendous success in spotting issues and market turns that would generate faster-than-normal returns for his clients. He successfully made the few 'sure-kid-I'll-give-you-a-try investors' a handsome return on their paltry first-time investments. Soon, they began to give him larger sums of money and tell their friends about the new whiz kid at S&E who was exceptionally good at spotting new opportunities.

After he had been at Seaton and Earnst for about fourteen months, Dwight began to work on a deal that showed tremendous potential for both him and his clients. It was a new European bond issue for a high-tech German company seeking to expand its share of the European market. The company had been having trouble getting European investors to buy-in to their issue and looked for Americans to help. By using the devaluation of the dollar versus the Deutschmark, the company was able to offer a higher-than-normal yield.

Dwight examined the financials and determined it would be a fairly good investment by itself. But by studying the money markets, he determined if the dollar fluctuated positively against the German mark, the return for the US investors would be tremendous. And Dwight's charting showed there would be a positive correction in the US dollar and German mark exchange rate during that spring.

Most of Dwight's clients took his advice and bought in. He himself shifted about $10,000 from his own portfolio.

A few months later, his instincts proved right. The German mark dropped versus the dollar. The computed selling value of the issues took a large jump, providing a short-term window for his investors to sell off their positions for a fifty-two percent gain.

His clients were ecstatic. Other people in the firm were also impressed, particularly the senior partners who had been watching the kid. They commented to themselves how Dwight reminded them of the old breed of broker, who could sniff out a good investment for himself, rather than following the herd or only the advice of the research pundits.

Dwight made about $15,000 in added commissions on the deal, plus a capital gain of about $5,200 on his private investment. He certainly didn't mind being $20,200 richer.

This put him "on the map." He was no longer just another smart kid in the financial markets business. He was now a *professional* who people trusted to make them money.

With this new status came other responsibilities and trappings. Now, more and more people clamored around Dwight and continued to applaud his success. He no longer felt as if he were in training. Everyone expected more from him. His clients expected a repeat of the German success. The partners asked his thoughts on many more issues than before. His colleagues looked to him for advice and a cut into *his programs*.

This had a dual effect on Dwight. On the one hand, he had to act the part of a very successful commodities broker. He liked the attention and respect. On the other hand, he now had the constant pressure to succeed.

He had already settled into a new apartment overlooking Lake Michigan. He had bought the furniture and accent pieces to make it seem like home. His CD collection teemed with rock, as well as romantic mood music. His apartment and lifestyle were right where he wanted them to be. He was fulfilling the dream he had imagined throughout college.

During this period, Dwight met Marsha Tidman, a secretary in one of the thousands of offices in Chicago. Marsha was an extremely gregarious woman with an infectious laugh; a full chest; and tight, slender hips.

And almost from the start, they began to see a lot of each other. They both thoroughly enjoyed the other's company and never ran out of things to talk about—politics, music, travel, and building a good life. He loved going out with her, meeting her friends, and introducing her to his business associates and clients. She was marrying material, and he even liked her parents, who lived in Rockford.

Their sex life was pretty good, too. During some weekends, Marsha stayed at Dwight's apartment. Off and on, they discussed moving in with each other, but neither could make that sort of commitment. They both really liked each other, but they both knew they weren't ready to settle down quite yet.

One Wednesday evening as Dwight sat at Mother's bar, having a beer, Johnny Malloy, a Seaton and Earnst colleague, pulled up the stool next to him. Johnny was a year older than Dwight, and also viewed as one of the up-and-comers at the firm.

"Hey, Dwight, how's it shaking? Still riding the big wave?" Johnny's California analogies often punctuated his speech when he wasn't on the phone with one of his clients.

"Yeah, things are going pretty well. Market's good. People are confident. Still making money."

"Hey, Dwight, see that guy over there in the green coat?" Johnny pointed to a tall man across the bar who appeared a bit older than Dwight with dark hair and even darker deep-set eyes. "If you need any stuff, he's a good one to talk to. His name is Vinny. Good quality. Prices in line. He's always around here, so you don't have to look far. Don't have to travel to Cabrini or some gang-infested neighborhood to make a score."

"Oh, I don't smoke. Stinks up the apartment."

"Hey, baby, we're not talking about grass; we're talking coke," whispered Johnny. "Cocaine. Blow. We're talking the *big wave*. The *big breaker*. We're talking twelve-foot waves! The real thing!" He waved his hand like a surfer gliding down the face of a big California wave.

"Oh, yeah," Dwight said, covering his tracks as not to appear uncool.

"Never used the stuff before, huh?" Johnny looked Dwight right in the eye. "How can any successful financial wizard make it without a little blow once in a while? Here, let's go get you some."

For Dwight, the bulb suddenly went off. He was doing well. Things were on track. His hard work over the past year and a half was paying off. He had the apartment, the car, and the perfect girlfriend. He deserved a special reward for his hard work and success. He had heard coke afforded a fantastic high, a wonderful release, and according to his old college roommate Bruce Zimmer, it provided the best sex around.

"Hey, Johnny, if I buy, will you show me the ropes?"

"Well, hell yeah! Let's go surfing!"

★ ★ ★

It had been nine months since Johnny first introduced Dwight to cocaine. During this nine-month period, Dwight's life and values totally changed. He was no longer the ambitious commodities broker living the good life of a young professional in Chicago.

Within the first three months of using the stuff, he turned from a social user to a recluse. He found he enjoyed using the stuff as much alone as with someone else. Marsha refused to partake.

As the frequency of Dwight's usage increased, Marsha and Dwight would get into terrible arguments about his growing dependence on the drug. After a particularly heated exchange, she gathered her personal belongings from Dwight's apartment and left. Permanently.

"Fuck her," he said when the front door slammed closed. "I don't need her or any other bitch to get my jollies."

Wanting higher highs, Dwight had Vinny teach him how to freebase. Soon Dwight found the high from freebasing better than screwing Marilyn Monroe herself—he supposed.

As he used more cocaine and freebased more often, particularly on weekends, his life began to unravel. His habit began to cut into his savings. His income began to drop because he wasn't being as aggressive with his clients. He was becoming more and more isolated from everyone around him. By the time the snows of winter thawed, Dwight was helplessly hooked. Cocaine now completely consumed his life.

Vinny, sensing Dwight's dwindling finances, offered Dwight a means of reducing his outlay of money. One night at Mother's, as Dwight was buying a couple of grams, Vinny made an offer.

"Hey, Dwight, you're such a good customer and all, why don't you start a little franchise yourself. Sell a little blow to your friends. Make your personal outlay less, or perhaps nothing."

"How's that?

"Simple, Dwight. You just bought a couple of grams from me for two fifty. That's one hundred twenty-five dollars per gram. If you bought an O, about twenty-eight grams, I'd sell it to you for twenty-five hundred instead of thirty-five hundred. You'd get your personal amount for free—and a nice profit, too. 'Course, you stay away from my clients here at Mother's."

Dwight paused for a bit. He figured the margins in his mind. About 40 percent per transaction, $1,000 per ounce. Not bad. He thought about whom he could sell to: a few guys at work; maybe Bruce, his old college roommate; perhaps a couple of neighbors he thought were using the stuff.

"It's tempting, Vinny, but I'm in the commodities trading business, not the drug business. Thanks. In the meantime, I'll stay one of your better, smaller, customers."

★ ★ ★

Now, three weeks after being fired from Seaton and Earnst, Dwight was no longer in the commodities business. He had become one of the untouchables at the Chicago Mercantile Exchange.

He had bills that must be paid. He owed the March rent, the monthly payment on the BMW, and a few personal loans for the furniture and the jewelry he had bought Marsha. And the expenses of his habit were not moderating. In the past two months, he had driven his credit cards to their limit.

Dwight was almost out of cash and made up his mind to enter a different commodities business. He wanted a steady income and decided to take Vinny up on his offer.

He now needed to buy the start-up inventory for his new venture.

Chapter 8

Chicago, Illinois

"Hey, take it easy and relax a bit, it's nearly six o' clock," David Klein said as he was getting ready to leave the office. He and Eric Robinson had been putting in several long days preparing for a major client presentation.

"I need to finish this one section before I leave," Eric said. "Go ahead, I'll meet you at the Brasserie around seven thirty."

"Sounds great. See you there. I'll keep a place warm for you."

Eric busily finished the section of the project he was working on. This was his first solo assignment at the Leo Burnett Company, and he wanted to be sure the job was being done right. Not that anything anyone did at Burnett was a solo. Still, he felt the responsibility for putting together the initial agency position on this project. And he felt good his account supervisor was entrusting him with this important assignment.

The Leo Burnett Company stood out as one of the world's premier advertising agencies. Within its walls were some of the most talented people in the field. Its advertising campaigns included many familiar long-running campaigns: McDonald's, the Marlboro Man, Tony the Tiger, the Keebler Elves, the Jolly Green Giant, Morris the Cat, and Charlie the Tuna.

Despite all of this, Eric still had a rough time coping with the layers of management and the lack of independence.

Within a few days, he would review this work with his account supervisor. From there, they together would present it to the management supervisor. And lastly, the three of them would take it to the Plans Board for the final blessing before the client presentation.

Sure, he understood the importance of keeping top management involved, and he appreciated their input and experience on the major marketing problems that needed solving. But the constant oversight by so many levels on every project smothered him. It seemed to water down every original thought and recommendation they made to their client.

Although Eric would never admit it, it also grated on his ego when the 'superiors that be' changed his brilliant thinking. Eric had never been at the bottom of the totem pole in any place or in any organization.

Throughout high school and college, he had always been at the top of the heap. He stood six foot one, extremely handsome, black with a strong yet manageable physic. His face had a smooth complexion, and because the corners of his mouth turned up slightly, he always appeared to have a warm smile.

Eric's real strength was his mind, with an exceptionally quick wit most found to be charming, and he exuded a warm, self-assured manner. In high school and later in college, Eric's teachers noted his leadership qualities. His peers respected him, and his professors at Northwestern University found him to be the ideal student. He possessed a genuine desire to learn, to stretch his mind, and to find better ways of doing things.

★ ★ ★

Eric grew up in a strong family environment in Greenville, South Carolina, the last of Clarence and Ellen Robinson's three children. When the Robinsons had been in their late thirties, they had thought their childbearing years were over, but Ellen had suddenly come up pregnant. They had two children, Elsa and Eli, before they had Eric. Elsa had been just about to graduate from high school when Eric was born. Eli had been in the ninth grade.

Eric's dad, Clarence Robinson, worked as a security officer in one of the J. P. Stevens textile mills in the Greenville area. He started working with the firm in 1955 when he left the military after twelve years of service. His own daddy had worked there years before.

Clarence had joined the army during the concluding years of World War II. Like every other red-blooded American boy, he joined on his eighteenth birthday. After a few short months of training, he was sent to Europe just after the D-Day invasion. He, like all colored troops, served in a black regiment.

At the conclusion of the war, Clarence Robinson stayed in Germany as a military policeman. His job assured order in the defeated country and not allow either the Americans nor other Germans to exploit the ravaged German people.

Because so many of the American servicemen were so eager to return home, the army was delighted to have men volunteer to stay. Of course, because Clarence had joined so late in the war, he didn't have enough points to return home before many of the well-seasoned GIs, anyway. But he was very interested in learning about police work and felt the military would provide the skills required by police forces around the country.

So, when the war ended, Clarence signed up for another four years of active duty. He spent two of those four years in Germany and later trained at Fort Leonard Wood in 1948. At the conclusion of this four-year stint, he signed on for another six years. He served as an MP at Fort Leonard Wood until he retired from the service in 1955 to return to Greenville.

During those years in Missouri, he met Ellen Thorpe and married in 1950. The following year, they had Elsa; two years later, they had their first son, Eli.

Then in 1965, Eric was born. Despite the surprise of it all, both Clarence and Ellen were delighted to have a new son.

By this time, Clarence had built himself quite a track record at work. Though his black skin would not allow him a management position in their security force, he had job security, the respect of his fellow man, and the eye of the more senior management of the company.

Clarence's time in the service and his growth in his current position allowed him to provide Eric with many of the advantages often reserved for white children. Clarence's salary level allowed them to live in the fringe areas around the better neighborhoods, so Eric was able to attend the better schools in the vast Greenville school system. And because Clarence had seen so much of the world during his years in the service, he had a better insight into life than men who had been quarantined in their own communities all their lives.

When Eric turned six, both Eli and Elsa were no longer living at home. Elsa had married a nice young man who worked in the Stevens plant, and Eli was a student at South Carolina State.

Eric's years of growing up in the Greenville community were wonderfully constructive. Clarence delighted in having a young son to relive the years he had enjoyed as a boy in the woods, streams, mountains, and lakes. He shared with his young son the stories about how he and his good buddy Bobby Osbourne would spend countless hours on the banks of the streams, with fishing poles in hand, hoping to catch the next big one. He shared with Eric about the day he and Bobby were attacked by a couple of rednecks and about how he had to bust one boy's nose to make them leave.

He also taught his son how to wrestle, how to break a man's grip, and the importance of avoiding a fight, if possible, rather than running headlong into one.

When Eric was fifteen, he realized *the* Bobby Osbourne whom his dad had been referring to all these years was the same Robert S. Osbourne who was now vice president of the United States.

This realization had a profound effect on Eric's life. It demystified the notion that famous people were somehow different from the start and that truly successful people were a result of some peculiar circumstance that didn't touch the everyday man. Even famous people came from the same roots as the common man.

Eric realized that if his father had grown up hunting and fishing in these very same streams with Vice President Osbourne, then he could grow up to be anything he wanted, and all his hard work would pay off. He realized a man with ambition could achieve anything he wanted. After all, if the vice president had drunk from the same cup

placing the money into his shirt pocket, he headed down the steps to Lower Wacker to get his car.

Chapter 9

Chicago, Illinois

Dwight Jones nervously prepared for his first big score. He would meet Vinny outside of Mother's on Rush Street around 8:30 p.m. to complete the transaction.

He had managed to scrape together enough money to make his first twenty-eight-gram purchase—*a Big O*—with $2,500 in his pocket, the proceeds from reaching his final limit on his Gold Master Card. Any additional cash would have to come from selling his merchandise, or selling his car, or hocking his furniture or stereo equipment.

Vinny had been selling to Dwight for the past nine months and had always treated Dwight with a great deal of respect. Of course, Dwight knew nothing about Vinny, his last name, where he lived, or how long he had been in the business. Other than Vinny's line of work, Dwight had no reason to believe Vinny would do anything to harm him. Despite this, Dwight thought it might be smart to carry some protection in case something out of the ordinary were to happen. To help quell this fear, he tucked a hunting knife into his pants before leaving the apartment.

Dwight decided a nice long walk would help calm his nerves before the meeting. After all, it was a beautiful March evening—cool, not cold, clear, and with only a soft breeze instead of the harsh winds of Chicago winters.

As he turned south on Michigan Avenue at Huron Street, he took a short snort from his snifter. The snifter was a small sterling silver inhaler that held a pinch of cocaine. It fit easily into the palm of Dwight's hand. Unless someone watched Dwight closely, the smooth ease in which he took a snort would have looked as if he were just rubbing his nose.

Instantly, the effects of the shot began to take effect. Dwight's apprehension began to disappear, and his gait picked up as he strolled past the various bookstores, hosiery shops, jewelry stores, and office entrances on Chicago's Magnificent Mile. On Wednesday nights, the streets were fuller than normal, not because the stores stayed open later, but because Wednesday night was "bar night" for the young professionals working downtown.

As Dwight approached the drawbridge crossing the Chicago River, he noted a tall black man standing at the automatic teller machine near the entrance of the Wrigley Building. The man appeared to be taking a sizable sum of money and placing it into his shirt breast pocket. Then the man placed his credit card into his wallet and headed down the stairs to Lower Wacker Avenue.

Dwight decided to follow him. The amount of cash enticed him. He figured he might have the opportunity to isolate himself against a slow start in sales with the extra cash.

The idea of robbing a man had never entered Dwight's mind before. But he knew he was on the brink of complete financial disaster if he couldn't generate some cash fast. Every dime he had in his pocket right now was for Vinny and his first Big O purchase. He wouldn't even have enough cash to buy a beer afterward.

Well, Dwight, let's go for it, he thought. *The opportunity seems to be availing itself to you, so why not take it?* The snort of coke running through his system made him feel particularly sure of success.

Dwight followed the man down the stairs into the dark, shadowy Lower Wacker sidewalk. The man walked briskly toward a group of automobiles parked against one of the brick walls on the west side of the street. The amber halogen streetlamps cast an eerie shadow across the cars, partially bathing their hoods but leaving the doors and rear ends in the dark. There wasn't much traffic.

★ ★ ★

Eric Robinson headed toward his car when he sensed another person walking in precisely the same direction. He glanced around. Out of the corner of his eye, he noted a man with blond hair wearing nice casual clothes. The man appeared innocent enough. *Must be someone lucky enough to get a parking spot down here too.*

Usually, Lower Wacker flowed free of traffic, as it was right now, or moved more briskly during the rush hours because of the limited access. In contrast, the surface streets were always congested with cars, cabs, buses, and pedestrians.

As Eric approached his sleek two-door Toyota Celica, he noticed the man stood appreciably closer to him than he thought he would be, according to their earlier pace. Eric paused for a second as he shuffled his briefcase to his left hand to take the keys out of his right pocket.

★ ★ ★

Dwight was now within ten yards of the man, who had paused in front of his car to retrieve the keys from his pocket.

How in the fuck should I do this? Dwight needed to do something that would catch the man off guard. Given his age, size, *and build*, this guy could handle Dwight without too much trouble. Dwight's mind raced for a solution. He was now closer than five yards away.

Suddenly, he had it. He coughed loudly into his hand, bringing up as much mucus and spit as he could. He rubbed it across his face, leaving a smear of snot dripping from his nose. Then he started twitching his body and face in a manner that replicated the actions of the junkies who were frequently seen on the streets of Chicago. Dwight figured if he were somewhat irrational in his approach, then odds were the man would hand over the money more easily for fear the assailant would do something totally rash.

★ ★ ★

Eric looked over at the blond man. *What the hell is this son of a bitch up to?* The guy just spread snot and spit across his face. Must be some asshole on drugs. I better get out of here.

He quickly thrust his key into the door lock, twisting it until he heard the unlocking click. Then with the hand holding the briefcase, he lifted on the handle and swung the door open.

Just as he swung himself into the car, lifting his arm to throw his briefcase on the passenger seat, there stood the junkie between him and the door, making it impossible to close.

"Give me your money," the junkie hissed.

Eric thrust his briefcase into the man's chest, shouting some obscenity at the top of his lungs. However, the junkie only bounced against the door, not yielding any space for Eric to close it. Eric dropped his briefcase and struggled to grab the top of the door to try to force it to close.

★ ★ ★

The force of black man's push was strong, causing the small of Dwight's back to impale itself on the sharp corner of the door.

Without thinking, Dwight reached with his right hand and grabbed the knife out of his pants. The man had dropped his briefcase and had his hand on the top of his car door to close it.

With his left hand, Dwight grabbed the man's wrist, pushing it straight up off the door. Dwight noticed the man had no leverage with which to fight. His right hand was completely neutralized by the steering wheel and the fact that Dwight was standing behind his body. Further, the low seats in the Celica made it practically impossible for his target to quickly lift himself out of the seat and onto the pavement, particularly since Dwight was holding his left arm straight into the air.

"What do you want, motherfucker?" the man shouted.

Dwight hissed, "Give me your money!"

"Fuck you, you fucking junkie."

This last phrase hit a nerve with Dwight. Anger and rage came over him. He was not a junkie! He still had his faculties, his dignity, if not his job. He was not the dredge of the earth. He was not one of those lowlifes roaming the streets of the ghetto and housing projects, doing anything it took to scrape up enough cash to make a score.

"I'm not a junkie, I'm not a junkie, I'm not a fucking junkie!" Dwight screamed.

Then in a fit of anger, he thrust the knife up into his accuser's armpit, piercing his suit jacket and entering the soft tissue between the shoulder socket and rib cage. Instantly, the gray pinstripe coat turned a muted red as the man's arm relaxed and fell limp in Dwight's grip while his face turned from anger and outrage to disbelief. His eyes looked straight up at Dwight and then widened as his mouth started to form one last word.

Dwight backed up from his position within the swing of the car door. He dropped the man's arm. It immediately fell forward, with the man's chest hitting the steering wheel and his head hanging over the top of it.

In complete panic, Dwight slammed the door shut, dropped the knife, and ran back the way he had come.

What the hell have I done? His head throbbed like it would explode at any minute. *What the hell have I done?*

Dwight kept running until he got to the top of the steps and once again on Michigan Avenue. The fresh, cool breeze on the surface street seemed to clear his head. He then realized he had to meet with Vinny. He also realized he did not get the money. But in a strange sort of way, that relieved him from the last charge the young man spoke. "I am not a junkie," Dwight kept saying over and over again to himself. "I am a businessman. I am not a junkie."

He reached into his pocket, grabbed the silver coke snifter, and instead of taking a sniff, cast it into one of the litter baskets along Michigan Avenue.

Chapter 10

The White House and

Greenville, South Carolina

President Robert S. Osbourne sat at his desk in the Oval Office looking over his appointment calendar. The day appeared to be the normal type of day in the life of the president of the United States. There was a meeting with his cabinet, a few meetings with select members of the Republican Party, scheduled phone calls with key members of the House and Senate, and a few scheduled photo ops. In between these scheduled appointments, Osbourne found time to write a few personal notes to old friends and acquaintances.

Pat Hayes, his personal secretary, buzzed his line.

"Mr. President, there is a Clarence Robinson on the line. He claims you and he are personal friends and that he was invited to the inauguration. I checked, and he was. Would you like to speak with him? He claims it is of the greatest importance."

Osbourne paused before answering. Of course, he knew Clarence Robinson. He was his old fishing buddy from his days of growing up in South Carolina. The last time he saw him was during one of the quick flybys on the night of his second inauguration. What was that? Two years ago? Ever since Osbourne had become vice president fourteen years ago, he spent very little time in South Carolina and no longer scheduled his annual visits with the Robinson family.

"Please put him through," Osbourne told Pat. "Clarence is one of my oldest friends. We grew up together in South Carolina. I owe a lot of my personal success to a few lessons he taught me when we were young boys together."

A click sounded on the line as Pat transferred the call from the main White House switchboard to one of the president's private lines. "Hello, Clarence, this is Bobby. What a surprise!" Osbourne's voice showed the genuine delight in having a chance to talk with his old friend.

"Bobby...err...Mr. President," a deep southern voice said on the other end of the line.

"Clarence, you can call me Bobby, just like you always have." Osbourne had this same experience with many of his old friends and acquaintances. He allowed most of them to call him Mr. President. But for Clarence Robinson, it was Bobby—now and ever after. Osbourne continued. "How's your family?"

There was a pause and a deep sigh from Clarence. Osbourne knew something wasn't right.

"Clarence, what's the matter? Is there something wrong with Ellen, someone in your family?" Osbourne knew something must have been terribly wrong for Clarence to sound the way he did.

"Bobby, my son Eric is dead." Clarence's words came out slow and sad. His voice completely hollow. "He was murdered by a junkie, a drug addict."

"Oh my God." Osbourne whispered into the phone. "Eric?"

Osbourne knew Eric was the apple of Clarence's eye, the child he spent so much time sharing the same fishing, roaming, and hiking spots they had explored so many years before. Eric, the boy who did so well in school and now employed in a prestigious Chicago advertising agency.

"I'm so sorry. I don't know what to say." Osbourne felt a large lump forming in his throat. "When did it happen?"

Clarence spoke just above a hoarse whisper. "Two weeks ago. We...we...we buried him last week. He suffered badly from the wound. He held on for...for a couple of days." Osbourne could hear the tears of his best friend.

"Bobby, I must see you," Clarence said much louder and clearer. "We cannot let Eric's death be in vain. We must do something about this drug problem. You have got to help me. Only *you* can do something about it."

Osbourne heard the pleading in Clarence's voice, the hate for what had happened to his son. "Clarence why don't you and Ellen come to Camp David this weekend. We can talk about it there."

"Bobby, I'll come alone. We need to get rid of those druggies. We need to put a stop to this killing of innocent men. I need you, Bobby. I need you, Mr. President."

"I'll have your trip arranged. Pat Hayes will handle everything. But you can always call me direct on my personal cell line. No need to fight the White House channels. See you this weekend, my friend."

Osbourne placed the phone in the cradle, his eyes welling up with tears from the thought of his friend's suffering and anguish.

Clarence's words kept reverberating through his head. I need you, Bobby. I need you, Mr. President. We need to get rid of those druggies. We need to stop this killing of innocent men.

For Robert S. Osbourne, the nation's drug problem just hit home. His best friend's son was dead because someone had needed a few bucks to buy drugs.

★ ★ ★

Clarence knew he could trust his friend Bobby to do something. They would talk about it when he visited Camp David the following week. No sooner had he finished his call to President Osbourne, the phone rang again.

It was ringing a lot these days. When someone loses a son, folks call. The past two weeks had included flying Eric's body back to South Carolina and fielding probably fifty calls. There were friends, folks from church, the Greenville media, and acquaintances from work.

Clarence Robinson understood death. He also knew how hard it was for all these folks to pick up a phone and reach out. It was always awkward. Everyone wanted to know what they could do to help, but there really wasn't anything. Just knowing others cared was enough.

"Clarence, this is Dan Murphy," said a big voice on the other end of the line.

THE CAMP DAVID CONSPIRACY

Dan was an old army buddy who had served in Germany after the war. And like Clarence, Dan, too, had stayed in law enforcement. He was on the Chicago Police Force and had worked his way up to detective. They had stayed in touch over the years, mostly via reunions of the old platoon of MP officers. And, of course, they had traded Christmas cards every year since then. These relationships were strong. Dan had also helped Clarence ship Eric's body back to South Carolina from the police morgue.

Dan and Clarence had already shared the tragic loss of Eric, so Clarence assumed this was an official call.

"Clarence, as you know, I've been on the Chicago force for over twenty years. But the circumstances surrounding Eric's murder are driving us crazy. I've asked for extra effort on this. But…but nothing is breaking. We have no suspects. No other witnesses. No leads. Nothing but a couple of fingerprints from Eric's car and the knife. And a big goose egg hit on those."

"Nothing?"

"Zilch."

"Nothing, huh? Uh, Danny, I appreciate your pulling strings to put extra manpower on this. I'm confident you're doing everything you can."

"Clarence, as you know, the best time to find the perp is within a few days of the event. It's now been two weeks, and still we're no further ahead than we were the night, err, the night your son was killed. His murderer just vanished."

Clarence started to say something, something nonchalant to help reduce his friend Dan's guilt, but then he had a thought.

"Hey, Danny. There is something you can do for me. Can you send me a set of those fingerprints?"

"Sure. But what are you going to do with them?"

"Not completely sure yet. I'll let you know."

"Clarence, what are you thinking?" Dan asked. Clarence knew Danny suspected something. He had to know his desire to work every angle and would put those prints to good use.

"Don't know yet," Clarence answered, "I'll let you know if I find anything."

Dan Murphy finished the conversation with complete understanding in his voice, "Please tell Ellen we're thinking about her. And you, too, Clarence. You, too."

Chapter 11

Camp David

President Osbourne looked forward to this weekend with bittersweet anticipation. He always loved going to Camp David. The woods reminded him so much of his boyhood home in South Carolina. The lakes, woods, fishing, and even the occasional hunting always brought back fond childhood memories.

During the years he had spent in the House and Senate, he wanted these things while he lived in the congested Washington area. He missed having the vast outdoors during his time off. And, whenever he visited his South Carolina home, his schedule required official business—some constituents who needed attending or a self-appointed power broker demanding to be stroked. *God, those years had been tough.*

Occasionally, he would be invited to Camp David on business with the president. But those trips had usually been packed with meetings, leaving little time to walk the beautiful woods, or to simply enjoy everything the premier retreat had to offer.

As vice president, he had been afforded the opportunity to spend more of his free time there—certainly not as often as now—but enough to remind him of the things he missed about the rural South and his roots. And as vice president, when he did visit the camp, he had been able to take advantage of the nature.

One of the things he most looked forward to when he became president was having complete access to all the Camp David facilities. He made it to the camp at least two or three times per month. And while there, he usually fished in the lakes and small streams or just sat on a rock and thought. Somehow, the peace and serenity of the hills made things clearer to him. The pace more natural. The environment more real. And the quiet—a welcome change from the total lack of privacy he endured in the White House. At Camp David, he controlled his own schedule. This made the camp even more attractive.

And now, this weekend, he would be spending it with his old friend Clarence Robinson. It would have been such a wonderful reunion under different circumstances. Osbourne hated himself for not inviting Clarence to the retreat sooner. He knew Clarence would absolutely love the hilly countryside, the amazing fishing lakes, and the woods covered with a mix of hardwood and pines. He knew the two of them would have had a marvelous time recounting the lovely days they spent growing up doing what they were now doing in the most prestigious retreat in the world.

Considering the number of times he thought about Clarence while he walked the Camp David woods, Osbourne felt aggravated and disappointed he had never extended an invitation before now. He guessed the power of the presidency had more of an impact on him than he would like to admit.

But the reason for the visit was not to recount those good ol' days; not to spend their hours mindlessly fishing and hiking; and not to relive the innocence they felt as kids. It would be serious and deeply emotional.

Osbourne wanted to help his oldest friend find some sort of comfort in his son's death. He needed to find a way to bring his tremendous power to bear in finding a real solution to the drug situation in America—that inflicted pain and suffering on almost every family in the country. It hurt not only those involved in selling or using drugs—but also everyone else—as its effects rippled throughout society. Drugs impacted everything: from the murder and burglary rate to medical costs; the spread of the deadly AIDS virus; the rape of potentially agile minds; and the diversion of welfare and educational funds to fight drug-related violence and building prisons.

And now, on a much more personal note, drugs were responsible for the death of his longest and oldest friend's son.

★ ★ ★

THE CAMP DAVID CONSPIRACY

Pat Hayes had arranged a driver to meet Clarence's plane at Washington National Airport and transport him directly to the hills of Camp David.

The moment Clarence stepped from the secret service van, Osbourne felt his stomach tighten. The man hadn't changed much over the years, still tall, a bit lanky, his hair graying, but he did not look his full sixty-plus years. The biggest difference Osbourne noted was the missing spark in Clarence's eyes.

"Clarence." President Osbourne hugged his old friend.

Without saying a word, Clarence hugged Osbourne around the chest, buried his head on his shoulder, and started crying. He held Osbourne there for at least five minutes without saying a word, just a strong embrace and a quiet sob on his old friend's shoulder.

Then, Clarence moved his hands up to Osbourne's shoulders, straightened his arms, and held his old friend in front of him. Large tears were swelling out of the corners of his sad bloodshot eyes.

As if he were about to explode, Clarence let go of the president and turned around, with his back facing him. And there he stood, with one hand down at his side and the other barely touching his forehead.

Osbourne placed a gentle hand on his friend's shoulder and nudged him ahead. Quietly, they walked down the driveway a few hundred feet and then turned left on a narrow dirt path that could hardly be seen behind a large holly bush. As they walked by the bush, Osbourne pushed the branches aside with his bare hand so the needles would not scratch Clarence's arm.

As they stepped along the narrow path, Clarence turned and began, without prompting, telling Osbourne about Eric's murder.

"Eric was working late at his new job in Chicago. He's with a large advertising agency there—the one that does the Marlboro advertising, the Green Giant, all the little Kellogg's animals.

"He told his friends he would meet them at their favorite bar when he finished working on this important assignment." Clarence recounted with a certain amount of pride that his son's profession had progressed so well.

"Anyway, he had to get his car. He parked it in an area they call Lower Wacker. It's a street under the surface street. It's kind of dark and dingy with a lot of newspapers swirling around and not many people. The basements of the buildings empty out on this Lower Wacker. And there are all these large concrete supports that hold up the top street.

"The police report said Eric was entering his car when a large man, about age nineteen, grabbed the door and slammed it on Eric's arm. The report said the man was on drugs and was probably trying to gather enough money for his next hit. Typically, there had not been any problems in the underground area before."

Osbourne looked directly into Clarence's eyes and listened intently to his friend.

"Eric evidently shoved the door back against the man and was managing to get out of the car when the man grabbed a knife and thrust it under Eric's arm. Eric lost a tremendous amount of blood. The druggie didn't stay around because several people passing in cars started honking their horns. These people identified the man as having wild, erratic movements and a totally unkempt look." Clarence again buried his head on Osbourne's shoulder.

Then lifting it, "Bobby, they still haven't been able to identify and capture Eric's murderer. The police have added resources, but that's not helping my son." He brushed the tears from the corner of his eyes.

They walked without saying a word for several hundred feet.

Finally, Clarence turned to his friend. "Mr. President, you have to help me. You must help me avenge my son's death. You need to ensure that other innocent boys don't die because of illegal drugs."

"I will, so help me God, I will," Osbourne whispered, patting his friend's arm. "Clarence, I promise you, I will."

Chapter 12

Justice Department—Washington, D.C.

For Attorney General Patrick Miller, the war on drugs became more frustrating every day. He was blocked at every turn. The latest *Marks v. United States of America* make it even harder for him to prosecute the everyday dealer. And the efforts against the cartels were not working, either. He simply could not outmaneuver the incredible speed and agility with which the cartels did their business. And unlike them, he was required to stay within the confines of the law.

Every lead he wanted to follow, every hunch he wanted to sniff out, and every person he wanted to prosecute demanded warrants, writs, court orders, and incredible bureaucracy. The use of informants and reduced sentences for valuable information yielded mediocre results.

The highly publicized murders of two drug informants while awaiting trial seemed to be working for the cartels. People were not talking. They were more afraid of the cartels' security forces than of spending a lifetime in prison.

And to make matters worse, publicity about a few informants who were thrown out of the Witness Protection Program made that lure that much tougher for the Justice Department to promise.

True, they were still getting their share of the little guy—the everyday pusher and dealer. But they were not getting anywhere with the cartels and their major distributors.

Miller's war on drugs was a mess. He owned it because he had changed to the "dealer first" strategy. There was no way to implicate the cartels unless they were caught red-handed, which of course, unlikely to happen.

They had found no way to effectively follow the money trails. The amounts were too great—and the various international banks too protective of their "favored" clients. Also, the cartels' money managers were some of the sharpest financiers Miller had ever seen. Trying to follow their convoluted trail of laundered money remained a painstaking and almost impossible task.

Miller and the DEA had to find a way to follow the drug trail more effectively. They had to indict the cartels for all the drugs found on the street. They needed to convict them with ironclad cases involving the drugs themselves, not just the money.

Numerous conferences on the topic had been held within the DEA, the FBI, US Customs, the Secret Service, the Justice Department, the National Security Agency, the CIA for their expertise in "black" projects, and the US military. Miller personally sat through many of these discussions. Nothing promising surfaced. All the ideas seemed to be a rehash of the strategies already underway.

The president's second-term campaign promised solving some of the domestic issues facing the country. President Osbourne stated on more than one occasion that Patrick Miller, his attorney general, would focus his whole energy on solving the nation's illegal drug problem. The president pledged a "drug dividend" in the future by winning the war on drugs, just as the country shared in a peace dividend stemming from the end to the Cold War with the Soviet Union.

A drug dividend would be a way for Osbourne to finance the domestic problems still facing the country.

Miller focused on helping the president keep his campaign pledge. But right now, they were losing, despite the all-too-frequent reports being issued from his office that the sources for cocaine and other drugs were being dried up. Most of the reports were based on short-term optimism.

Whenever a large shipment of cocaine was confiscated, the Justice Department notified the press of the DEA's success in limiting the quantity of drugs entering the country. Whenever the reported street price of cocaine went up, the Justice Department took the time to point out the administration's strategy of interdiction and eradication of the dealer networks.

However, these positive reports were always refuted by the continued increase in drug-related violence; the Centers for Disease Control and Prevention reports on the rising number of persons using and being addicted to cocaine; and the high-profile stories of celebrity drug deaths.

Miller had to find a better method for winning the war on drugs. He knew the only real answer was to dry up the primary source. He had to hit the cartels, and he had to hit them hard. He had to ensure the court cases against cartel personnel succeeded. He could not afford to place considerable resources against an investigation, only for it to blow up in his face during the trial. *He had to find a way to ensure the convictions stuck and the accused were prosecuted and jailed.*

Chapter 13

Springfield, Missouri

Victor and Hugo Rodrigues had settled into the trip between Los Angeles and Saint Louis. This was their third trip in a month and the sixth since they received their new Crown Vic four months ago.

Under their back seat, they had twenty-five wrapped kilos of pure cartel-quality cocaine. For the delivery, they would be paid $25,000 in cash.

Their instructions were to deliver the cocaine to a certain empty warehouse in East Saint Louis. If they were caught by the police, they would not tell their destination or their starting point. If they were caught and imprisoned, they could well assume they would be killed before the end of their first year.

The stakes were high being a drug mule, but so was the pay.

Their car was purchased with cash by their contact in Los Angeles. It had California tags, and the insurance was in their name, all paid for by their LA contact.

The $25,000 covered their time, meals, gas, hotels, and any entertainment they sought as they made the 4,000-mile round-trip. Since February, they had collected $125,000 in fees for their services. Before the year was out, they each expected a tax-free income of over $100,000 each. It wasn't bad money for a couple of hoodlums living in the Los Angeles slums.

Hugo was a big man with a dark round face, large dark-brown eyes, and a broad girth around the waist. Though on the fat side, he was extremely quick, yet mentally slow.

His brother, Victor, a smaller man with dark darting eyes. He possessed the brains of the two, but he also had a flash temper. His friends called him "Victor Chihuahua" because of his snap.

"Hey, Victor, let's pay a visit to Tokyo Blossom when we reach Springfield. She gives a great back rub, and the blow jobs are good too."

The I-44 stretch of road through Oklahoma and Missouri constituted the worst part of their drive. The flat landscape, few curves, and numerous state troopers. The cops near Springfield were tough and two Mexicans with California tags created a lucrative target for Missouri's troopers.

"Naw, man," Victor said. "I'm tired tonight. Let's just stop at the Quality Inn in Springfield. OK, man? This month has been a bitch, man. We're driving twelve-hour days. Let's get some sleep tonight."

"OK, man," Hugo said, mocking his brother. "You party pooper. We can see her tomorrow afternoon on our return. You know, man. A BJ in the PM, man. You know."

Victor and Hugo had begun to get into a routine with their frequent trips back and forth across the country. Like traveling salesmen, they found locations they were comfortable with and started repeating their visits to the same places. They liked to stay in Springfield at the Quality Inn on I-44. They could park their car outside their room door. The location broke up the drive and allowed them to leave early the next morning to make a 10:00 delivery in East Saint Louis. Then they could make it as far back as Tulsa the next afternoon.

Chapter 14

Washington, D.C.

The spring weather in the invisible part of Washington, D.C., brought on a different kind of activity. This was the nation's combat zone. Ten years ago, people had perceived the area to be poor—very poor. Mothers would work late trying to maintain some semblance of a family. Many of the husbands were long gone, leaving no financial or moral support. For most mothers, the only source of income came from a few menial minimum wage jobs.

For other mothers, the support came in the form of a monthly Social Security check. To ensure the continuation of the checks, these women made sure their wombs were kept full and that a little one was always under the prescribed school age.

This was simply survival.

Gertrude Washington's two sons were over the stay-at-home age. Emmett, age nineteen and Jacob, fourteen filled her government-subsidized apartment on Beeker Street.

Her three children were all born while she and her husband were married. But that ended soon after Jacob's birth, when the man of her dreams left her for another woman and moved somewhere out west.

To support her family, Gertrude worked two jobs. Her first job was a housekeeping position at an attorney's home in Georgetown. She arrived at this job at 7:00 a.m. in time to fix the graying Howard Washer his breakfast. This meant she left her Beeker Street apartment at precisely 6:00 a.m. to catch the Metro, where she then transferred to a local bus that took her into the swanky Georgetown neighborhood.

She would leave this job at 2:30 p.m. to catch the 2:45 bus and then the Metro to the Capitol Marriott Hotel, where she would work as an evening housekeeper until 10:00 p.m.

The two jobs netted her about $350 per week. Because they were both considered part-time positions, she would have to cover any medical expenses or retirement savings. Of course, she didn't have the money to do either.

Her earnings surpassed most people living in her apartment building. It covered the basic needs of her family. However, with her long workdays, her kids' moral choices were left to chance.

Gertrude had no choice. She knew her daily absence left them particularly vulnerable to the negative influences of her neighborhood. *And the neighborhood took its toll.*

They lived in a war zone, fitting the exact description one would have of inner-city government-subsidized housing.

The red-brick, eight story apartment house displayed gang symbols spray-painted across the tile breezeways; broken windows sealed with plywood; a playground with a broken basketball goal; and walkways of chipped concrete with weeds growing through the cracks. The grounds were littered with flurrying newspapers, crumpled fast-food bags, uneaten wedges of pizza, and boxes of garbage lying around the trash containers that had not been emptied in weeks.

As bad as the outside was, the inside was worse—and far more dangerous. The hallways had the putrid stench of aging garbage. Half the lights either were burnt out or had been knocked out by the roving gangs looking to make the hallways better for their business. Every door looked as if the occupant of the apartment tried to enter without the use of a key. And, of course, the elevators seldom worked, though that really didn't matter because no person in a right state of mind would allow him- or herself to be trapped in an elevator with no means of escape. The stairs were much safer.

Over the past ten years, the normal decay of public housing, broken families, and lack of tenant care was compounded by the gang warfare and turf battles for drug dealer supremacy.

Gertrude's oldest son, Emmett Washington, would make it out of the neighborhood in one piece. He had graduated from high school and was currently attending the local community college in the D.C. area. She was proud of her son and especially proud of the boy's desire to become a journalist. All through school, Emmett loved to read and write.

When Emmett had been a baby, she would take him to work. Mr. Washer didn't mind her bringing her young son with her. So, until he was six years old, Emmett spent every weekday at the home of Mr. Howard Washer, Esq. And while Gertrude went about her chores, the young Emmett spent his days in the library of the distinguished attorney, looking at beautiful art books, picture books about exotic faraway places, and a lot of little table-top games would entertain Emmett for hours.

The atmosphere of Mr. Washer's library appealed to the young Emmett Washington who loved to spend the days on the soft leather couch that seemed to swallow the young boy. Even the carpeting seemed as soft as a bed to the boy who slept on an old mattress supported by a piece of plywood.

During Emmett's six years in this wonderful environment, he grasped the importance of reading and innately understood there was more to life than the dark, smelly hallways of Beeker Apartments.

When Emmett had entered first grade, he had a deep-rooted appreciation for learning, especially reading. His teachers at the Grover Cleveland School were extremely pleased to see a young black child so interested in his studies. As a result, the faculty gave him special attention, and his interest in learning accelerated as the school years passed by.

Remarkably, Emmett never wavered or was negatively impacted by the less desirable influences around him. Also, he never suffered the punishment kids would often dole out to children whom they saw as the teacher's pet or who were different. The other kids seemed to leave Emmett alone.

Emmett wasn't a particularly big kid, but he was intense. He had a straightforward, no-nonsense attitude. He never got in the way of or antagonized the other kids. He never touted his intellect or looked down on the others. He was always congenial, but only when they approached him.

Part of this was probably because he didn't play with other children during his early years. His social contact being primarily with his mother, a polite, congenial, hardworking woman who always treated the people with respect and honesty.

After school and during the summer, Emmett didn't allow himself to hang around the apartment. Instead, he headed off to the various museums and D.C. attractions. He only passed through the treacherous environment of Beeker Apartments. He somehow understood his escape from this environment meant not actually living in it.

As a grade school student, Emmett spent his time at the outside monuments, running up and down the steps of the Lincoln Memorial, dragging his fingers along the names on the Vietnam Veterans Memorial wall, or hanging out on the lawn surrounding the Reflecting Pool. However, as he spent more time at these places, he began to read the inscriptions and think about the words written. At school, his teachers would help him find books on the same topics.

Later, Emmett discovered the Smithsonian, the Library of Congress, the Capitol Building, and many of the other free sights open to the public. He literally spent months in the Smithsonian, looking at and reading about the various topics. He toured the White House on numerous occasions, usually by mixing into a group lined up to tour the president's home.

Emmett just finished his freshman year of community college. And because of his strong grades, recognition by his professors, and extraordinary interest in journalism, he earned a junior summer internship at the *Washington Post*. For ten weeks, he would work in the newsroom helping reporters research stories.

Gertrude Washington felt a great deal of pride in her son Emmett. He would become a real success—surpassing any goals she could have possibly set for him. He would get out of Beeker Apartments alive and untarnished.

She only wished the same were true for her other son, Jacob.

★ ★ ★

Jacob Washington headed out of his Beeker Street apartment at 3:30 p.m. His mother still at work, and his older brother, Emmett, somewhere in D.C. soaking up the text of some library or museum.

Jacob had just returned home from school to drop off his books and other props he used to convince his mother he participated in his studies. He made it a point to always attend his homeroom class, where attendance was taken and officially turned in to the principal's office.

But after that, Jacob could be almost anywhere. He would attend classes on a hit-or-miss basis, always careful to attend on the days when tests were given. That way, he would have a passing grade, usually in the B- or C level, to show his mother.

Jacob's successes with his grades could be attributed to his keen eyesight, which allowed him to copy the correct answers from the papers of the better students in his class. The teachers at his war-torn high school didn't care whether the students cheated or not. They knew most of the students would eventually drop out, so they figured being in school served them better than being on the street.

In the afternoon, after attending some of the classes, Jacob hit the streets. For the past three years, he had been a lookout for one of the local drug guys in the neighborhood. Each afternoon, around 4:00, he would report to his station on the corner of Woodrow and Horace Streets. There he would appear to be playing ball, jiving, or just hanging out as most any fourteen-year-old would do.

But, in fact, Jacob was assigned to this corner to watch for police or any other suspicious activity that would concern his boss.

Jacob never really saw his boss. His contact was named Neville, probably a fake name. But every day Neville would ensure Jacob stationed himself on that corner, and every week Neville would bring him seventy-five dollars—in cash—for standing guard.

Jacob knew Neville served as a courier for one of the cartels. This meant he would make pickups and deliveries for his boss. He also knew Neville had been working since he was twelve years old, first as a lookout, then as a runner, and now a courier at age fifteen.

Neville had told Jacob that he made about $300 per week—always in cash, just like Jacob.

The seventy-five dollars Jacob made constituted big money for a fourteen-year-old boy working afternoons 4:00 to 6:30 weekdays; and from 2:00 to 7:00 on Saturday. About five dollars per hour with no taxes or anything taken out.

More importantly, it meant when he got a little older, he could become a courier and make $300 or more per week. Big money for a kid living at home in Beeker Apartments. Also, a future. *The first step in a career that could generate millions of dollars.*

Jacob only needed to do a good job. And he assumed Neville had to do a good job too for his boss every day.

On Jacob's corner, he had to watch for police cars, straight-looking dudes who could be watching the block, or just new people or vehicles appearing on the street. At the end of his watch, he would report his findings to Neville.

If there were an emergency, such as several police cars converging on the area, he was told to kick over one of the garbage cans on the corner and shout out "fuck your mother" as loud as he possibly could. This would alert the armed lookout in an unknown apartment that there might be trouble.

Only once did Jacob use the emergency call. Last spring, several police cars had entered the area at one time, none with sirens. They were preceded by several unmarked cars and a SWAT team van. The vehicles converged on an abandoned storefront one half block down Woodrow Street.

Jacob heard the loud percussion of a shock bomb and saw the SWAT team enter the building and drag out three completely nude women covered with a white dust. Then he saw the police load what appeared to be three steamer-size trunks into the back of a van.

Neville told Jacob the storefront was used by the cartel as a major cutting room where mass quantities of pure cocaine were cut before being distributed to dealers. Neville said he never realized the operation was there and that he was surprised no one saw the storefront being watched. Further, he told Jacob even if he or his boss knew, they would never mention it.

"No one fucks with the cartels," Neville warned Jacob. "If they don't like you, they'll kill you."

Jacob could never tell what house, apartment, or storefront he was guarding. And he never saw which house, apartment, or storefront Neville appeared from.

He also didn't know how many other kids like him were performing the same duties on the block. Jacob had been told early on that any talk, questions, or loose lips would mean trouble. He instinctively knew trouble would mean either a terrible beating or even death. This was not a problem because he continually received positive feedback for the good job he was doing.

Neville had implied the greater demand for cocaine during the summer would give Jacob the opportunity to become another runner for his boss. The most effective runners were boys who were under age seventeen. Typically, a boy worked as a runner for about eighteen months before becoming a full-fledged courier.

At 6:35 p.m., Jacob would leave his post. To ensure he never cheated Neville by leaving early, he always made it a practice to stay for an extra five minutes. From there, he would go down to Doo's to play a few video games, grab something to eat, and hang out with a few of his friends. He never talked about his job, and he never flashed his cash either. Neville had taught him that was the quickest way to get mugged or arrested. Interestingly, Jacob's buddies never asked where he had been or where he got his change. They were possibly in the same business.

Around 7:30, Jacob would return to the apartment. There he would fix something else to eat and watch television until his mother got home around 10:30.

Jacob's scholarly older brother, Emmett, would usually get home around 9:30. He often spent his evenings at the Washington Public Library reading up on some topic or another.

To an outsider, the contrasts between the brothers appeared to be great.

Emmett was an excellent student, attended college, and sure to leave the D.C. poverty behind. He wanted to become a journalist.

Jacob, on the other hand, was a lousy student, had no real interest in school, cheated on practically every test, and basically defrauded his mother with his every move. As with most other black males living in the D.C. projects, he appeared to be destined for a life of crime or poverty.

But Jacob's personal long-term goal was to grow rich and leave the impoverished ghetto via the drug business.

This is here where Jacob and Emmett were very much alike. Whereas Emmett spent his entire day in the library studying, learning, observing, and taking advantage of the cultural and literary fruits of Washington, Jacob spent his day learning the fundamentals of his selected profession. He observed the workings of his selected industry in the same quiet, unobtrusive way Emmett studied his.

And like Emmett, Jacob understood and took full advantage of the cultural fruits of his community. He instinctively knew vice would always yield a lucrative business. And he fully intended to capitalize on it.

Despite their differences, Jacob and Emmett were friends. Their mother had instilled a sense of family among her children. And while they were in the apartment, the family existed. Quite often, Jacob and Emmett would spend time sitting around the kitchen table talking about the family, their own goals, and their futures. For Jacob, he fully trusted Emmett and would tell him things Neville would never approve of.

Gertrude didn't overlook her two sons' individual drives to succeed. Though she was extremely proud of her oldest son's accomplishments—and disappointed in the grades her younger son earned—she did note Jacob's ambition. But she couldn't understand why he was not performing better in school. And she didn't fully understand how he spent his afternoons. But she was thankful she didn't have to go downtown to get him out of jail.

Chapter 15

Upstairs at The White House

The upstairs of the White House has a den and a television set, much like a majority of homes in the United States. And like most American citizens, the president will relax and enjoy a television program.

President Robert S. Osbourne specifically tuned into tonight's broadcast of CBS News's *48 Hours* which dealt with illegal drugs and the street problems associated with them. Exactly the same issue occupying the president's mind for the past several weeks.

The program started by talking about how the warm spring weather brought the commerce of drugs to the streets and more open than during the colder winter months. It covered the alarming statistic how over three thousand drug-related crimes would occur each week during the spring and summer. More than half of the crimes would affect innocent citizens who were neither using nor involved in the commerce of drugs. The crimes included murder, robbery, or some form of gang-related violence.

The program explained how crack houses performed their business; young children worked as lookouts to their bosses' illegal storefronts; and older youths made deliveries, drops, and runs to certain customers. An emergency room of a center-city Saint Louis hospital showed persons who were overdosing, shot, or killed. A Los Angeles police commander responsible for gang-related activities talked about the tremendous cash the gangs were acquiring through the sale of illegal drugs. Further, he discussed how the gangs were taking their commerce into smaller midwestern markets rather than slugging it out with other gangs for a greater share in Los Angeles. In these markets, there was minimal competition, a waiting consumer, and virtually no police experienced in stopping their progress.

The host correspondent interviewed a business professor from Harvard who compared the gangs' exportation of their businesses from the more competitive inner-city coastal markets to the suburbs of the Midwest as the "Walmart strategy." He noted how Walmart grew to the nation's largest retailer by first entrenching itself into the smaller communities where it could beat the prices of the homegrown retailers, rather than fight for a piece of the large market chains.

The program further profiled the typical kinds of users. It started with the stereotypical young black male in the inner city who gathered five dollars to buy a rock of crack. The program used actual footage to show how the user would lurk around the high-rise housing projects, looking for older women to rob. It showed how the gangs controlled the distribution in specific areas of the cities and the bloody battles to maintain the turf.

Next, the program showed a young white-collar sophisticate who usually indulged in a little cocaine. In an interview, a young stockbroker—whose face was hidden by a black dot and whose voice was altered electronically—told of how he viewed the use of cocaine as a reward for his hard work and success at his job. He stated how he worked sixty hours per week to help his clients grow their portfolios and used a bit of coke with his friends as a reward for his efforts—and perceived success.

The young stockbroker told how he was introduced to cocaine by a good friend whom he worked with and how he usually bought his stuff from a dealer working one of the bars he frequented.

The last group the program profiled consisted of an elite group of highly successful professionals who were well placed in society. Though no interview was given, the reporter described how he knew of one cocaine party thrown by a well-known attorney for twenty of his closest friends. The guest list included doctors, other lawyers, lobbyists, business executives, network programmers, authors, musicians, and a few government officials. These parties were common, and their success was determined by the quantity and quality of the cocaine and often the beauty of the prostitutes on hand.

When the program ended, Osbourne used the remote control to click off the set and sat in the quiet of his second-floor den.

"How am I ever going to stop this? How am I going to have a real impact on this country's drug problem?" The program had reiterated facts he already knew.

The problem kept getting bigger, not shrinking. Spreading to the smaller communities. It wasn't just a poverty thing; it now permeated every facet of society. Infused now with big cash from the rich. And people everywhere were being affected. The chances of someone experiencing harm through a drug-related crime or through direct use grew every year. *His friend Clarence Robinson was just one horrific example.*

Plus, it consumed more and more money out of the federal budget. His campaign promise of a "drug dividend" became more elusive every day.

What were his options? What would it take to really stop the growth of this problem? How drastic of measures would be needed to make a real difference?

Osbourne kept turning these thoughts over in his mind. He thought about the different plans already in place and the news program he had just watched; about his campaign promise to tackle the domestic affairs of this country. He considered the good the government could do with a "drug dividend" and his attorney general's frustration as they reviewed various programs at a joint conference.

But foremost, he understood how the ineptness of his war on drugs contributed to the senseless death of Eric Robinson, the son of his best friend.

Taking a pause in the quiet of his den, Osbourne considered the political options where the United States could exert greater pressure on the third-world nations that were supplying many of the drugs to the country. And the educational efforts, where schools, the media, the police, and all the civic groups worked together to stop drug use.

He pondered the new Pentagon strategy to use high-tech military hardware and resources to catch the flow of drugs streaming into the country. That budget alone had risen to $1.2 billion and accomplished only minimal success.

He recalled the added efforts he had initiated over the past two years to seek out and capture the dealers and prosecute them to the full extent of the law.

And last, he reevaluated the approach that focused on the users of cocaine, crack, and other illegal drugs. Should they once again be pursued and prosecuted to the full extent of the law?

The more Osbourne considered the inability of these programs to change anything, the more pissed-off he became. He knew most of these efforts were either underway or had been tried. He knew the courts could not handle the added load that greater emphasis on the user would cause. He knew there wasn't more the South American countries could do, no matter how much pressure Washington exerted. And he knew the media was pouring millions of dollars into public service advertising and even programming showing the scourge of drugs rather than the glamour.

And God knows the schools were trying everything they could to teach the young to "just say no to drugs."

As Osbourne stared at the wall, he wondered what he could do to end this problem, as well as what he could do to keep his promise to Clarence Robinson.

Chapter 16

Washington, D.C.

L uther Gomez looked at his watch. It was 10:37 a.m. American 235 from Saint Louis touched down at Washington National Airport in D.C. right on schedule. His Hertz full-size sedan would be waiting in the Gold Club area with the keys and ready to go. All he had to do was show the agent his driver's license. Luther's real name with a fake address appeared on the California license he used while in the United States. His Colombian address would be a red flag. And, of course, his business card did not say Chief Enforcer, Mendez Drug Cartel.

Unlike his stop in Saint Louis, Luther wasn't sure what his trip to D.C. was going to entail. One of his key customers was way off on their orders. The cartel didn't like it when their gang clients suddenly started ordering less, particularly at the beginning of summer. If anything, the sales should be significantly more. And the Sons of Steuben crew had always increased their business from year to year.

This level of the distribution chain always amazed Luther. As a former small business owner before joining the Mendez cartel, he knew how difficult it was to establish a business. But the gangs in the large American cities had capitalism working like a well-oiled machine.

The average inner-city crack house conducted more commerce than virtually any small retail business in America. Cash and barter ran the enterprise.

The cash of the drug sales maintained the fiscal viability of the house while the barter kept the house's morale high.

Throughout the District of Columbia, crack houses opened, thrived, died, closed, and reopened at some other location. The proprietors of the houses were partners of the highest magnitude. They shared in the rewards, the risks, and the exposure of their business.

However, unlike a normal partnership in the private sector, these enterprises did not operate under the quid pro quo of legal documentation; written contracts; protection from tax exposure; and legal avenues for the resolution of conflict within themselves, suppliers, or customers. This was an honor business built on trust. When it all went well, everyone benefited. When problems occurred, lawyers were not used to resolve them. A knife to the throat or a bullet to the back of the head usually sufficed in ending the dispute.

And if the competition made moves to get a greater market share and adversely affect another's business, then corrective measures were taken to put the challenger back in its place. A "drive-by market adjustment" would close the challenger's doors and likely put an end to the key partners responsible.

For most of these houses, the street gangs were the supporting partnership, as well as the supporting army if "marketplace corrections" were required.

Luther Gomez liked to visit the "Mendez houses" that sold Mendez cocaine. Many years ago, he found the best way to keep the other cartels away from his key distributors was to maintain a personal relationship with the gangs. "Show them a little respect. Don't take them for granted. Let them know you appreciate their business," he would tell his boss, Feliz "Zorro" Herendez, the man in the Mendez cartel responsible for the marketing and distribution of their cocaine.

The code within most gangs, particularly the Hispanic ones, was to appeal to their sense of respect. Luther knew to let them know how important they were to him and to show them he had the power to enforce the rules. Being Hispanic, he didn't care as much for the black gang leaders as he did for the Hispanic ones. But all Mendez gangs were important to the business and therefore important to him.

Besides, visits to local crack houses were fun.

Each house had its special attachment of "buffers," the women who hung around the houses exchanging sexual favors for free coke. "A little blow job for a little blow," was how Luther explained it to Feliz.

THE CAMP DAVID CONSPIRACY

Feliz never joined Luther on these trips, seemingly too sophisticated to consider lowering himself to visiting the street level of the business, much less letting some Black or Hispanic bitch give him a blow job or a little flat back sex.

But to Luther, the streetwise field general, this was one of the spoils of war. Before a trip to one of the houses, he would call the gang leader and let him know he would be in town and wanted to come by. Before the call, he would have a couple of his local operatives update him on the competitive situation and the safety of the gang, the house, and the other marketplace factors that could upset his visit.

Luther also knew the performance of each gang's business. Were their sales up, down, or remaining stagnant? If they were growing, this was a healthy sign. If they were flat or down, this could mean the gang was also dealing with another cartel—meaning trouble. Luther suspected double-dealing at the Son's house on Steuben Street, located in the poorest inner-city section of D.C.

★ ★ ★

He dialed a local Washington number on his cell phone.

"Speak," the Hispanic voice on the other end answered.

"This is Luther."

"One moment," the voice replied dryly.

After a few seconds, there was the click of the call being transferred.

"Luther, amigo, what's happening, bro?" a large voice boomed on the other end of the line.

Luther smiled as the vision of Chico came to his mind. Chico, Mendez' man in D.C. was a large, almost obese, bundle of energy with a large dark baby-smooth face, except for a huge jet-black mustache that covered three sides of his mouth. Luther and Chico had known each other for years.

"Just landed. Still in the Hertz lot. Ready to go to the house on Steuben Street. What's the status?" Luther asked. He and Chico would have plenty of time later to catch up with each other. But right now, Luther had to find out whether there really was a problem with the Sons of Steuben crew.

"Everything is set, bro. I have our best enforcers at each end of the street. Equipped with fully automatic machine guns, percussion bombs, and even tear gas if need be. SOS don't know we are there. Vans have been on the street for the last three days. Doing a little renovation work, you know, man? So far, we haven't seen anything out of the ordinary schedule. No Calis or anyone else that shouldn't be there."

"Why they dropping?" Luther asked, using the slang for why their sales were down.

"This spring has been a bitch, Luther, my man. The crews have been really active. Cutting the shit out of each other. Fighting for every alleyway. Every corner. Every housing complex. Every single space has been fought for and lost or held. It's been a fuckin' war around here. In March, the Sons of Steuben and M+Os shot it out for control of the Ashford Apartments. Five M+Os and four SOS were fucking killed."

Luther knew the M+Os. They weren't as large as the Sons but still large enough to challenge them for turf. "Guess they were going after their flagship store. And it sounds like it didn't go well for either of them."

"Fucking right, Luther."

"The M+Os are still dealing exclusively with Cali?" Luther asked. The Cali cartel had been controlling the M+Os' supply for the past several years. Typically, the cartels did not get into direct combat with each other; they left these unpleasantries to the gangs as they fought for the market. The cartels would simply supply them all the cocaine they could sell. And they didn't mind selling to more than one. It wasn't a problem as long as one cartel did not actively cut into the distribution channels of another. But Luther had heard the rumors that SOS was double-dealing with Cali.

"Yeah, bro. Cali and the M+Os are still tight. Also tight with the Drum Street Boys and the Krafts. We haven't been approached by any of them, and we haven't solicited them, either. Right, bro?" Chico knew Luther did not want to risk an all-out war in Washington, and probably the entire East Coast, by trying to pick up a new crew's business.

"Right, Chico. Who's in charge at Steuben Street?"

"Bosco. Light-brown nigger with arms like fireplugs. Call him Bosco after the brand of chocolate milk. Strongest son of a bitch I've ever seen. Been out of jail for about a month. Served a little time for some petty theft. Judge gave him max because he knew he was a gangbanger. Just wanted to get him off the street.

"He got back the same week as the shootout at Ashford. Blanford Childress was the chief but got whacked in the shootout. Bosco took over leadership that night. You know what he did? The day after the Ashford shootout, he paraded ten Sons through the courtyard and hung their flag for everyone to see. He then posted six guys there for two days to ensure the M+Os and everyone else kept clear. Ashford was his. The man's got balls the size of cantaloupes."

"Fucking inner-city Iwo Jima," laughed Luther.

"Bosco's the meanest SOB I know," Chico said. "Drives a hard deal. Always looking for a way to make a few extra bucks. Smart like a fox, too. Knows he can beat any other crew. He has solidified the Sons behind him. I also hear on the street that the other crews fear him. I heard he would kill a man without even thinking if he got in his way. He was toughened by a few years in the pen."

"OK, Chico, my friend. Nice job. Good info. Bosco is expecting my visit?" Luther was hesitant. This Bosco didn't sound like the typical crew leader he had been used to dealing with. His time on the inside had probably exposed him to many aspects of the drug business most street gang leaders did not know. Luther would have to be cautious, yet firm, with this guy.

"Yeah, bro. The house is real excited about meeting the real Luther Gomez. Fuck, Luther, you're a regular legend to these people.

The Sons love you. They can't believe someone like you would visit the street. He's all set. Told me to tell you he had a special treat ready for you."

"OK, Chico. Tell your men I will be there in about twenty-five minutes. At about twelve thirty. Call Bosco to tell him when I'll be there. I think you told me he was expecting me at noon. I'm driving a white Lincoln. I look like a fuckin' pimp in this white ride. Why the fuck are all these rental companies buying only white cars?"

★ ★ ★

After he hung up, Luther wheeled the Lincoln out of the Hertz lot and to the interstate leading across the bridge into Washington, D.C. The traffic was light, and he knew he wouldn't have any problem being on Steuben Street by 12:30.

These personal visits were key to the business. Saint Louis had never been stronger. On his visit he learned Mendez had picked up a major new distributor running out of Saint Louis to Chicago. This would increase the number of runs needed across the country to keep up with the demand from this new region. Business in the Midwest was good.

But it was the East Coast that made or broke the cartels. Between Washington, Philadelphia, and New York City, over 50 percent of their total shipments ended up in these three cities. Each distributor was important, and each distributing gang or middleman had to be kept happy. Mendez controlled the United States with over a 60 percent share—more of the US cocaine market than the Cali cartel. But Cali had been active during the past year.

Luther turned the corner off NW M Street to a cross street. The look of the area rapidly changed from large commercial businesses to a mix of small retail stores and run-down housing. Kids loitered on the corners. Older boys shot hoops in run-down parks. At the few retail stores, old men sat on the steps drinking wine or beer out of paper sacks. On every third corner, a thin, leggy black woman with tight jeans and a loose-fitting halter top would be suggestively leaning against the corner building waving at the nicer cars moving through the area. Luther's white Lincoln didn't miss a wave. At one stoplight, a big-chested black woman with bleached-blond hair poked her face right in the window and offered a quickie "before the light turns green."

At Steuben, Luther turned right. On the corner was a beat-up light-blue van with the name "L&F Roofing" stenciled on the side. Luther smiled. *Luther and Feliz Roofing*, he guessed was Chico's idea. It looked as if Chico had the block secured for his visit.

Luther parked his car on the curb in front of the house —a small bungalow in drastic need of repair. The light-green paint on the exterior peeling, the yard nothing but dirt, and the pillars holding the front porch bowed. Some of the wide-open windows had missing screens. Luther could hear the bass beat of rap as soon as he opened his car door.

Immediately, three large black men came out of the house. Luther guessed their ages to be somewhere between twenty and twenty-five. Their heads were covered with maroon bandanas, their chests were bare, and tucked into their pants were revolvers.

The larger one with the thickest set of arms pushed his way ahead of the others and greeted Luther. From Chico's description, Luther figured it was Bosco.

"You Luther?" the man asked.

"You Bosco?" Luther mimicked back.

"Well, fuck, man, I'm fucking standing in front of Luther Gomez, the meanest motherfucker from Mendez." Bosco smiled broadly so the gold cap on his front tooth glistened in the noontime sun. "Fucking Luther Gomez. Shi-i-i-t."

"Well, man, you must be fuckin' Bosco I-don't-know-what-the-fuck-your-fuckin-last-name-is Bosco. The fuckin' head of this gang and house. And the meanest motherfucker in Washington, D.C." Luther again mimicked with a broad smile, letting Bosco know he knew all about him and playing to his macho ego.

They raised their fists in a salute and grinned.

"Let's fucking go inside and talk a little business." Bosco motioned to the other two Sons standing at the door to make way for Luther. "A little less fucking traffic inside than out here in the fucking broad daylight. Though the fucking rush hour doesn't fucking start until after three-thirty. But you never fucking know about those fucking M+Os. When they might fucking drive by. Particularly with a special guest like you."

As they walked up the stairs, Luther noticed the two guys at the door relaxed their gaze and seemed to loosen up a bit as he passed the threshold. His instincts told him these guys were not going to be a problem. Their eyes were not guarded at all. They seemed as if they wanted Luther to be there.

* * *

The living room at the front of the house was as deteriorated as the outside. The walls were dark blue, made even darker with years of dirt and abuse. The furniture was the typical assortment of worn overstuffed couches, chairs, and a cheap Formica table with four straight chairs in the corner. Two composite-wood end tables had lamps with torn and bent shades. And a large black flag with "Steuben" in maroon block letters hung on the wall. A few beer cans littered the end tables, and a large ashtray full of butts sat in the middle of a coffee table in front of the two couches. Straight back from the main room was a hallway leading to the two back bedrooms and the bathroom. Luther noticed the bedroom doors were shut.

Seated on one of the worn couches was a beautiful white woman with long blond hair hanging straight down her back. Her long slender legs were pulled up under her short black leather skirt, revealing a glimpse of her upper thigh. Her sheer white blouse muted the definite rise of her pale white breasts and large round pink nipples. On the opposite couch was an equally tall black woman with a huge chest bellowing out of a tight red muscle shirt. Her hair was cut in a short 'fro, and her face was heavily made up with rouge and bright-red lipstick.

Luther suspected these women were hired specifically for his visit. He guessed they were high-class hookers from downtown. It was unusual for a crack house to have women who looked like these hanging around. Most of the buffers were more strung out.

"Business then pleasure? Or pleasure then business?" Bosco asked, nodding toward the couches.

"Business, then maybe pleasure," Luther said, not conceding anything and still weary that this could be a difficult session. *Their shipments were still down significantly.*

Bosco motioned to the women to leave. Each got up from her spot, looked Luther right in the eye, and proceeded to the back bedrooms.

"Sit." Bosco pointed toward the prime couch backing against the side wall. Bosco then sat on the couch whose back faced the front door. Luther noticed that the two men were standing behind Bosco, just inside the door.

Bosco started. "I know why you're here. I know you know our buys are down. I know Chico probably has told you he suspects us double-dealing with you and fucking Cali."

Luther nodded, staring directly at Bosco. Luther had his hard face on. All business. Double-dealing against the Mendez cartel would mean trouble. No exceptions.

"The truth is, we have been. Before I got here," Bosco said.

Luther leaned forward.

"Look it, Luther, let me fucking tell you about this before you fucking get excited and signal those fucking trucks of yours up the street."

"I'm all ears, Bosco. I'm all ears," Luther prompted, with a slight sneer in his voice.

"First, Luther, we're in an all-out fucking war here in Washington. The M+Os have been battling us for every inch of selling space. And we have been kicking the fucking shit out of them for every fucking inch they have. We meet in alleyways neither of us would have given a rat's ass for before. But now, it's a pride thing. We each want to have it all. And we fucking will!

"Second, the slim ass who ran this place while I was in the pen was two-timing your ass. He was buying from the Calis and was setting up to turn a whole lot more of SOS business over to them. He fucking didn't understand what would happen by doing this. He hadn't been on the inside and seen what you guys will do to a man who two-times them. Shit, fuck, I saw some fuckers in there who were fucking maimed, hurt bad by you cartels. Each of these fuckers wished they fucking hadn't tried it. Fuck, we aren't about to get in the middle of a cartel war. Gangbangers think they're tough fuckers; they ain't never seen what you guys will do."

Luther continued the direct stare into Bosco's eyes. Bosco was right. The only way the cartels could manage their business with these street thugs was to meet subversion with single, brutal force. No warnings. And no mercy or care for who might get killed in the middle. And the cartels did it surgically. None of this drive-by bullshit; it made too much noise and raised too many questions. No, the cartel preferred a quieter, more painful approach. It could be a visit in the middle of the night with a shot to the back of the head, only after forcing the double-crosser to write his death warrant. Or it could be a skillful cut across the throat to eliminate the man's voice. And, if the man had a favorite woman, then it could be a brutal elimination of that person from his life, right in front of his eyes. That cut right to the macho and colored him with the rest of his gang.

Bosco was right. The cartel didn't fuck around. And Luther personally conducted the enforcement plans. He knew and he made sure the gangs knew Luther Gomez was not to be fucked with.

Bosco continued. "Shit, man, besides the M+Os, he would have had your fucking ass all over our ass. Against the M+Os, no sweat. Against you and the M+Os, we would have been smeared all over this fucking city. A no-fucking-win for the Sons of Steuben. Word."

Luther didn't want to respond too quickly to the confession Bosco had just made. He wanted him to squirm a little and reflect on how close he may be to doom. He wanted him to think that Luther Gomez was not going to provide absolution on the spot.

"So, where are we," Luther stated, rather than asked. He wanted to hear what Bosco and the Sons were proposing to do to make up for their indiscretion.

"We have one more shipment coming from Cali, ordered four weeks ago. A fucking kilo, paid for, is due here next week. We've ordered since then only from you." Bosco sounded hesitant.

Luther then moved forward, thrusting his large head across the middle of the table, right in Bosco face. He whispered. "Did you, Bosco? Did you place any fucking orders with Cali?" He knew the answer.

Bosco turned pale, and a bead of sweat formed on his bare upper lip. He glanced over toward the door, where the other two men stood. He knew they had not heard Luther's question but could tell he was deeply concerned by the look on his face. Through the open windows, he could hear an engine on a truck start and begin moving down the street.

This could be it, the fucking end, Bosco thought. Did Luther know the truth? Could he finesse the answer because he had been back on the street for only four weeks? Could he say it was all because of the fucker he had replaced? That motherfucker Blanford got his ass killed in the alleyway in the Ashford projects.

Out of the corner of his eye, Bosco could see the light-blue roofing truck stop in front of the house. The side door slid open.

The gangbangers at the door also saw the truck. Their eyes opened wider, and they reached for the revolvers in their belts. *There wasn't supposed to be any trouble.*

A moment later, a second truck pulled in front of the house.

Luther forced the answer. "Did you, Bosco? Did you place any fucking orders with Cali?" His voice was still a whisper, firm and direct. His eyes did not move from Bosco's. He was careful not to humiliate his prey.

Bosco hesitated, with his gaze drifting toward the men at the door.

He motioned the two to place their guns back into their pants. Any shootout would be a massacre. He leaned back into the couch. "Yes," he answered quietly. "Yes."

"And?" Luther asked, dangling the question in front of Bosco, fishing for the proper resolution. Luther knew Bosco would cut a better deal for the cartel than Luther would by making direct demands.

Bosco thought about the different options. He had considered some as bargaining points before Luther's visit. Others came as the adrenalin flushed through his body. He was caught between the proverbial rock and a hard place. He would have to strike the best bargain he could and hope for the best. As bad as this might be, being caught in a war between the cartels and the M+Os would be much worse.

Catching his thoughts, Bosco turned on his best salesmanship. He was also acutely aware his men were watching his every move and listening to his every word. His long-term success in the gang would depend on the deal he would cut with Luther and whether he came across as a winner to his brothers.

"Look, we're going to be getting real fucking aggressive over the summer. We have held our fucking own with the M+Os and other crews so far this spring. It was rougher than shit. Fucking Blanford had things really fucked up. The boys weren't fucking ready for the war. But the past four weeks have put an end to that. We're going to be increasing our business, our turf. We should be able to handle an extra kilo twice per month. That's a half more than we've been buying, even before Blanford's fucking deal with the Calis."

Luther nodded slightly, waving his hand for Bosco to continue. Bosco hesitated, looking to see if there was any sign Luther was buying into what he was saying.

"Four keys each month, including October. Fucking guaranteed! What you gonna charge?"

Smart move, Luther thought. Bosco had thrown the deal into Luther's lap. This was where Luther had to be careful. Four keys guaranteed was good. And Bosco added October. Luther had to give him the going street price. He couldn't use the price as punishment. It would backfire. The Calis would continue to pressure him. These boys liked to make money; there was no reason to create another problem. However, Bosco would have to be handled.

"Bosco, this is what we will do. You buy three keys now. Pay now. And then the four each through October. All money up-front. We will deliver within three days. Chico will handle the rest." The extra kilo made up for the order Bosco placed with Cali. Luther knew the Sons would take a burning getting rid of the extra keys, plus the Cali key, but that was their problem. Then again, if they got real aggressive with the other crews, they might not have a problem. Luther had landed the solution right back into Bosco's lap. And he knew Bosco could not say no.

"Fucking deal, Luther!" Bosco said almost immediately, leaving nothing to chance or giving Luther any time to add additional conditions. His face showed the weight of the world off his shoulders. The Sons liked dealing with Mendez. They didn't like the Calis.

Luther stood up and stuck his head into Bosco's face. With a toothy grin for the benefit of the two bangers near the door, he whispered into Bosco's ear. "Don't you ever think about buying hog from another cartel, you motherfucker. You're fucking lucky I don't blow your fucking head from that pale-ass body of yours. Do you understand?"

"Yes, thank you, Luther," Bosco said loudly. "It's great doin' business with Mendez. I understand." He looked over at the two smiling and relaxed brothers at the door. As far as they were concerned, Bosco and Luther had struck the best deal ever. And they knew they were not in war with Mendez.

"Now, time for a little pleasure?" Bosco asked with a sly smile.

"You mean those two hookers who were sitting here when I came in?"

"Hookers? No fucking way, Luther. These girls live here. Buffers, man! Good lookin' bitches, huh, Luther? Fucking table-grade poontang, Luther." Bosco was proud.

Luther thought for a moment about the leggy blond. Holy shit, she would be quite a puss, rubbing her hands down his sides, covering his head in those big fucking tits of hers. He thought about his hands lifting the sheer blouse and gently plucking her soft nipples, watching them rise and press against her blouse. Then her hands would unbuckle his pants; slowly unzip his fly; and softly pull his cock from his briefs and rub it with slow, gentle strokes as she touched her lips to the end of it. He pictured her lips enveloping his erect penis, slowly and gently moving her head up and down, up and down, until he exploded in the back of her throat.

He shook himself of her sensual image. "Maybe later, Bosco. Got a lot of business while I'm here." He walked toward the door, giving the two guards a chance to move before proceeding outside.

Chico stood next to the light-blue L&F Roofing van with an earpiece in his right ear. Passing Chico, Luther looked over and spoke above a whisper. "I'm leaving town early. Bosco is dangerous. Sometime later, after we deliver the September bricks, waste Bosco and those two Sons at the door. Don't let them know we did it."

Luther got in his white Hertz and headed back to the airport.

Chapter 17

Location Unknown

The pay phone call was quick.

The Beatles' song "Revolution" played.

. . . change the world
. . . a real solution.
. . . what we can.

"If you truly want to start a revolution, I got a plan," said an obviously disguised voice.

The person on the other end smiled and hung up.

Chapter 18

Chicago, Illinois

"Who the hell is this new hotshot yuppie dealer?" DEA Agent Chuck Harding muttered to himself. "This kid is moving some goods."

For the past few years, in addition to the crews in D.C., Harding had also been keeping track of some of the white-collar dealers in the Lincoln Park and Rush Street areas of Chicago, an intriguing assignment for anyone in the DEA. A break from the inner-city areas which usually led to remarkable revelations on how broadly cocaine was used. A short stint of this duty immediately erased the stereotype of drug use by poor, inner-city blacks. On this beat, he would see bankers, lawyers, doctors, professors, financial analysts, brokers, journalists, corporate executives, and politicians participating in the use of "recreational drugs." Crack use was minimal. For this group, white powder up the nose, or a little free on special occasions. Mostly though, just white straight lines snorted off small square mirrors or out of sterling silver snifters.

For the DEA, keeping track of this segment made plenty of sense. Not only were many of these professional men and women users, but also dealers who immediately saw the profit potential in buying extra for resale to their associates. Their education allowed them to see the easy tax-free money of selling on the side. And because they worked with people of position, there was always a user base who would pay extra to buy from a trusted friend rather than from a stranger on the street. Less chance of being caught or getting hurt.

Harding laughingly referred to these groups as the carriage trade. But still asked himself why. "Why do these people throw it all away? These professionals have everything going for them. They already make good money. They work their entire lives to reach the goal, raise a fine family, and then POW! They'll lose every bit of it if they are caught. Or screw up and become addicted." *None of this makes one bit of sense.*

★ ★ ★

The five o'clock crowd began to swarm out of the office buildings and make their way west to the Rush Street area. With the early warmth of this spring, it was a race to see who could secure a nice outdoor table at one of the new eateries with a patio or deck. This European luxury was a novelty in big American cities. It drew patrons like free booze on the first warm spring days. And it was a real coup for anyone fast enough to reserve a table for his or her friends.

Harding positioned himself at the bar. His corner seat gave him a full view of the bar, the hallway leading to the restrooms, and part of the outdoor patio. Glancing in the mirror, he straightened his silk paisley tie. He liked the way the deep maroon in the tie looked against the red pinstripes of his Egyptian cloth cotton shirt. The olive-green suit looked well-tailored, and except for the unusual scar across his cheek, he blended in with the professional urban crowd filling the place.

Whoopee. I'm a yuppie. Always a role to play.

A bottle of Miller Lite sat on the counter in front of him. He didn't drink, but the decorum of the bar set the prop and the brand. No Colt 45 here. The change for the twenty sat in front of him, thereby keeping the bartender from getting restless.

Harding also knew the blond kid had been working this bar for the past two weeks. All he knew was this kid was receiving a lot of coke from the end of the Saint Louis–to–Chicago pipeline. He saw him drive up to a major cartel distributor in a BMW with no tags. In this case, the distributor was a well-run dry cleaner with a good business, something right out of the movies. Cartel deliveries were made when dirty clothes came in with kilo bricks bundled inside. Then, certain customers dropped off dirty clothes with cash and would pick up their laundry with precisely measured packets of cocaine.

Emil's Cleaners was the perfect scam. It had a reputation for its perfect medium-starched shirts. The owners were of European descent. Perhaps one of the best operations Chuck Harding had ever seen; and it probably would have continued undetected if it hadn't been for a chance incident.

One day, a DEA officer with his drug-sniffing dog happened to come by to pick up his wife's dry cleaning. When the officer returned to the car with the laundry, the dog went nuts. Though the wife's clothes were clean, they must have been close enough to cocaine for the dog to pick up the scent. Certainly, that was unusual for clothes straight from the cleaners. Ever since that day, a certain segment of Emil's Cleaners in Orland Park customers had been videotaped and documented in a dossier of who's who in the Chicago drug scene.

Harding followed the BMW. And every time, the tall blond kid ended up in some Rush Street or Lincoln Park bar. Based on the number of friends who met him at each location, and the number of trips to the restroom, Harding figured the kid was either a very popular yuppie with one hell of a bladder problem or conducting business.

He had a tough time identifying the kid. Not only did the car not have tags, but something on the car's dashboard always covered the vehicle identification number. Harding didn't want to make anything seem suspicious, so he opted not to interfere with the car or pull the local authorities in to assist him in its identification. He wanted to keep this blond kid clean. *I might have other plans.*

Finally, at around 6:00 p.m., after about thirty-five minutes of nursing his beer, Harding looked up and saw the blond kid entering the bar. Dressed the part with a pair of khaki slacks, button-down blue shirt, no tie, and a blue blazer. The kid took a seat at the bar, one stool down from where Harding sat. They both nodded and smiled to one another as their glances met.

The bartender greeted the kid. "Let me have a Corona with a lime, Todd," the kid said, laying a ten on the bar. Todd had the beer and the change in place with one smooth motion.

Soon, a young executive type in a vested, blue glen plaid suit pulled up next to the kid and greeted him. "How you doing, Dwight? Everything doing OK tonight? Any action?" The young exec flashed a toothy grin.

The blond kid, Dwight, reassured his inquirer with a friendly smile. "Eh, OK, I guess. Yeah. Got some action. You in?"

"You betcha. Todd, let me have a beer. A Bud. Gonna take it outside. I'll be right back after I take a pee." The exec pushed away from the bar and walked toward the restrooms.

A few moments later, Dwight rose from his seat and followed him, leaving the Corona and change on the bar.

Business as usual. The same routine Harding had been witnessing over the past few weeks. Someone always greeted Dwight, and soon Dwight would follow him to the restroom. It wasn't a particularly original approach but certainly more guarded than openly transacting business at the bar. Harding knew what was going on in the restroom. He had witnessed it earlier that week from a stall. The two would stand by the sink, supposedly primping themselves and saying a few idle words while passing the coke and money back and forth. And then they'd leave. No revealing words, just a short private transaction. Quiet. Discreet.

Harding had seen Dwight make ten or so of these transactions each night at each bar he stopped. Usually, he stayed in a bar no longer than an hour and a half. And usually stopped at two bars each evening. If these transactions were the typical one- or two-gram deals, and the coke was of the normal purity for the carriage trade, Dwight took in about $300 during each transaction and about $3,000 at each bar. Two bars each night totaling ten bars per week came to one hundred grams or $30,000 per week. His take totaled probably $10,000 per week or at least a half million per year. *Nice private business*, Harding thought. *Tax free. Real nice.*

He knew Dwight's game, and he knew he had enough evidence to convict him if he wanted to put it together. But who the hell is he? Harding had never seen the kid before or heard about a hotshot new and pissed on the same tree as his dad, then he could be anything he wanted to be.

All of this worked to instill the value of learning, excelling, and working hard in all endeavors. This reinforced the lessons and values his father spent trying to teach his young son.

In high school, Eric excelled in his studies. He took a college-prep curriculum, including algebra, trig, chemistry, physics, and advanced writing. He did well in the math and sciences, but his passion was writing. He loved working on the school newspaper, and during his senior year, he served as an intern at a small local ad agency.

Outside the classroom, he starred as the running back on the school's football team and served as vice president of the senior class.

The internship, being a class officer, and the incredible references he received from his teachers all led to a full scholarship at Northwestern University, where he studied journalism and business with an eye on advertising as a career.

* * *

It was now just past 7:30 p.m.

Eric completed his section of the Burnett assignment. Although he was late, he knew the gang would still be at the Brasserie.

As he headed toward the door, he realized he would need extra cash to make it through the evening. He also realized he needed cash for the business trip the day after tomorrow.

Eric stepped through the archway of the Leo Burnett Building onto Wacker Drive. Across the drive flowed the Chicago River, with its green water moving west away from the lake. A gentle breeze was blowing down the canal the river cut through the city skyscrapers. Turning right, Eric headed toward Michigan Avenue. It was just about dark, but the cool March evening brought a beautiful change from the frightfully cold months of winter.

At Michigan Avenue, Eric headed north to the Wrigley Building to use the cash machine. Using his Visa card, he withdrew $400. After kid working the carriage trade. *Let's see if he's been around,* Harding thought. The mission tonight was to get some fingerprints to run through the system and determine whether he was new or had an existing record. The prints would be easy to get from one of the beer bottles, a glass, or anything else smooth. In a bar, that would be easy.

Soon, another customer approached Dwight. Like clockwork, the two headed toward the restroom. From his coat pocket, Harding took a clean black ashtray—the standard black plastic type used by practically every bar in the country—and placed it on the bar counter near where Dwight had been sitting. No one in the bar would have noticed the maneuver because during the smooth stretch to place the ashtray, Harding picked up one of the bar napkins neatly stacked next to Dwight's seat.

Within a couple of minutes, Dwight returned.

After another minute, Harding reached in his shirt pocket and pulled out a pack of Salem cigarettes. Glancing around, as if he were looking for an ashtray, he leaned over and asked Dwight if he was using the one sitting in front of him.

"Here you go, buddy." Dwight handed Harding's ashtray back to him.

"Thanks." Harding smiled, fidgeting with the cigarette but never lighting it.

He then grabbed the change off the bar, left a two-dollar tip, and placed the handful of bills and the ashtray in his coat pocket. He walked out the bar with Dwight's prints neatly in his pocket. *Spy versus Spy 101.*

In a few weeks Harding would know this kid's identity.

Chapter 19

Georgetown D.C.

G ertrude Washington had worked for Mr. Howard Washer for close to twenty years. She had started working for him shortly before she became pregnant with Emmett.

She had answered an ad in the newspaper:

Wanted: Part-time housekeeper. Must be willing to work from 7:00 a.m. to 2:30 p.m. Must know how to cook, keep house, and hand-iron laundry. Send name and references to: Box 2222, Washington D.C.

Because Gertrude's husband worked 6:00 a.m. to 3:00 p.m., the hours worked out well. Gertrude had experience as a short-order cook and a housekeeper at a motel before she married. Her former employer provided glowing recommendations.

When Gertrude arrived for the interview, she was surprised to be sitting across from a small, bifocaled gentleman in his mid-forties. Howard Washer was a bachelor and a very successful attorney in a prestigious D.C. law firm with his name on the door. His previous housekeeper recently quit after nearly ten years of service.

The man had a soft voice and extremely courteous to the young black woman. He quietly asked Gertrude questions about herself, her family, her husband, and what she wanted out of life.

He listened intently as she told him about how she grew up in the Baltimore area. Her father had left her mother and her three children when Gertrude was about ten years old. Her mother had worked as a maid in a family's home during the day and stayed at home reading from the Bible during the evenings. Gertrude and her two sisters went to church every Sunday morning and Wednesday night with their mother.

She told him how she had met Herbert, her husband, two years earlier. They had worked together in a small Baltimore motel and restaurant. Herbert was a short-order cook, and Gertrude a kitchen helper. Herbert strove to become an excellent cook so he could leave the small restaurant and become a line cook or assistant chef in a better restaurant.

Though Herbert wasn't immediately interested in Gertrude, she was quite interested in him. She liked his ambition to better himself; his work ethic; and, later, his willingness to teach her how to cook in a restaurant. Besides that, he was tall and handsome and had the cutest grin when she did something that pleased him.

They worked together in the restaurant for about a year when Herbert received a job offer from a fancy white-tablecloth restaurant in downtown Washington, D.C. With hardly any nudging, she followed him. A few months later, they were married.

Howard Washer liked Gertrude and immediately hired her. He liked her honesty and her desire to succeed, and she seemed to be an extremely dependable young woman with strong religious principles. Essentially, she was a woman he could trust to leave alone in his home while he wasn't there.

After working for Mr. Washer all these years, Gertrude still did not know a whole lot about him.

Every morning, she would let herself into the house with her own key. She would hear his alarm clock buzz at precisely 7:15. A note usually sat on the table, stating his breakfast preference of either eggs and toast or hot cereal and yogurt.

At approximately 7:45, he would come down the stairs, fully dressed in a vested suit of gray or blue, a conservative tie, and one of the heavily starched white cotton shirts she had washed and ironed.

Gertrude would serve his breakfast in the dining room on fine china with sterling flatware, per his instruction's years earlier. She always ensured the silver was spotless, the glasses gleaming, and the china shiny with no grease smudges from her hands.

Mr. Washer always asked about her morning, the family, and whether her trip in was OK. He would usually ask a follow-up question to one of her answers, and then he would proceed with eating his breakfast, drinking a couple cups of coffee, reading the paper, and catching the CNN news wrap-up on the small portable television sitting on one of the side tables in the dining room.

Gertrude never asked or knew how Mr. Washer was, other than seeing that he had a cold or was maybe more tired on some mornings. She knew nothing of his family. She knew only where he worked. And if there were any problems with the house, she was to call Maggie Miller, who was Mr. Washer's secretary at Mills, Washer, and Bird.

During the early years, Gertrude brought Emmett with her to work. Mr. Washer would usually say a few kind words to the boy and then proceed with his breakfast. Gertrude was always careful to ensure the young boy did not disturb him.

Only once in all the years was there ever a woman with Mr. Washer at breakfast. That morning there was a simple note telling Gertrude to prepare two breakfasts. The woman who eventually came down from the upstairs bedroom suite was middle aged, perhaps around forty-five, with nicely coiffed graying hair, a professional dark-blue business suit, and a modest amount of makeup.

Gertrude was pleased the woman did not turn out to be some bimbo. But, of course, that would not have matched the Mr. Washer she knew.

Mr. Washer was definitely a gentleman and a well-established attorney. Gertrude had read that the Mills, Washer, and Bird law firm was one of the most respected in the area. Mr. Washer had never made that boast to her; that would have been out of character, too. She had read that some of their work was connected to the government, along with other corporate work pertaining to Delaware and Maryland corporations.

Gertrude's only connection with the law firm was through Maggie Miller, who would call Gertrude if there were any changes to Mr. Washer's plans. She would let Gertrude know if Mr. Washer was called out of town, leaving no need to prepare a dinner for him, or if there would be more than just Mr. Washer and if two or more dinners should be prepared.

The best Gertrude could figure it, Mr. Washer would usually arrive at the house around 7:00 p.m. He would warm the meal Gertrude had prepared in either the microwave or a regular oven. He would usually clean up after himself, leaving a few dishes neatly stacked in the sink. The countertops and table were always wiped off.

About once a week, the dinner would still be in the refrigerator the next morning. Gertrude figured these were due to a last-minute change in plans made after she left to catch her 2:45 bus.

Mr. Washer's home was just about what one would expect a distinguished bachelor attorney's Georgetown home to be. The furnishings were on the masculine side, without going overboard. A tidewater print in the dining room complemented the seventeenth-century Queen Anne style furniture of both the dining and living rooms. All the pieces were fine replicas of the period, purchased from the more expensive boutiques. There were also a few antiques mixed in with the replicas. All the coverings were either fine fabrics or glove-soft leather.

The most interesting part of Mr. Washer's home was his library and study which comprised of a large room with dark paneling and tremendous bookshelves on all four walls. In the center of the room was a large glass-top coffee table covered with neat stacks of journals, books, and recent magazines. Flanking the table were two large black leather couches that would draw a person right into the soul of the covering. Reading lamps were strategically placed so one could read from virtually any place on the couches. A dark oxblood leather wingback chair filled out the triangle of furniture surrounding the glass coffee table.

What uniquely caught one's eye when entering the study were the number of toys scattered about the side tables, shelves, corner of the desk, and anyplace else where there were a few square inches of space. These were not children's toys; they were adult library toys: a

Newton's cradle with the hanging steel balls, magnetic tangrams, a wooden labyrinth, a Rubik's Cube, a pyramid puzzle with white connected balls, and many others.

These toys were not decorations or ornaments. Most days when Gertrude entered the study to clean, she noticed the toys had usually been used the night before. They were never all in the same place.

Years earlier, when Emmett would join her at Mr. Washer's house, Emmett would always play with the wide assortment of toys. However, Gertrude was not aware of any other children who might be frequenting her boss's home. At least, there wasn't any evidence of it.

Gertrude also thought it was odd the glass coffee table was always so clean. Though the magazines and the toys had been moved around, there was never a smudge or a water mark. Gertrude never had to clean or dust it. All of this seemed odd in such a distinguished gentleman's home.

More normal was his collection of books. Each of the shelves contained a different category. One was dedicated to the literary giants and the classics: Milton, Twain, Cooper, Longfellow, Dante, Lewis, Stevenson, etc. Another shelf represented history with books stemming from the Time Life series on the world wars to Kissinger, Nixon, Sandburg's *Lincoln*, Theodore White, and Arthur Schlesinger, as well as the historical fictional works of James Michener, Irving Stone, and Leon Uris.

The modern-fiction shelf was covered with spy and techno-spy volumes, including Clancy, Koontz, Le Carré, Ludlum, Straus, and others. His philosophy section looked like the personal library of a professor with all the works of Plato, Socrates, Kant, Nietzsche, and Confucius. An incredible number of audio tapes and compact discs were also placed on the shelf. Most of the recordings were classical. However, sprinkled in were popular vocalists, including Barbra Streisand, Carly Simon, Paul Simon, Ella Fitzgerald, Cleo Laine, and Bonnie Raitt. Instrumentalists included James Galway's flute, Doc Severinsen's trumpet, the Spanish guitar of Luiz Bonfá, and various Windham Hill new age recordings.

All in all, Mr. Washer's library showed the broad range of interests of its owner. And it was not an aging archive; rather, it was current, having the latest releases in the fictional, historical, philosophical, and business publications.

Gertrude had always admired Mr. Washer's library. She liked seeing the shelves full of books, games, and music. And she loved the fact that Mr. Washer was not selfish about its contents. From the very beginning, he encouraged her to borrow any book, magazine, or periodical she liked. The offer did not pertain to any of the music, though he certainly did not mind her listening to his collection while she worked inside his home.

During the days when Emmett was little and came with Gertrude to Mr. Washer's house, Mr. Washer always encouraged Emmett to spend time in the library. Mr. Washer asked Gertrude to watch her son and ensure he would not damage anything and was always willing to loan her any of the books she thought Emmett would like to take home. For this, Gertrude was always grateful. She knew her son's success in school and deep appreciation of books probably started with the days he spent in Mr. Washer's library.

While Gertrude went about her daily chores, she usually listened to one of his tapes. Over the years, she came to love and appreciate classical music, especially the pieces with the full chorus. Much of it reminded her of the gospel singing in her church as she was growing up. The gospel, however, did swing a bit more than the choir arrangements of Beethoven, Mozart, and Schubert.

Each year, Gertrude would get four weeks of paid vacation. These were the weeks when Mr. Washer would be on vacation, though Gertrude never knew where he went. He typically took two weeks during the summer and a week around Christmas. He never took the fourth the same time of the year.

His summer trip was commonly for fishing. Upon his return, there would be several vests needing washing and ironing. Plus, the garage was loaded with fly-fishing equipment, and many of the magazines on the coffee table were outdoor and fishing oriented. Mr. Washer always looked well-tanned upon his return.

For Christmas, Gertrude figured he went to his sister's home in Atlanta. His sister had two little girls, whose photos were prominently displayed on Mr. Washer's bedroom mirror.

Gertrude liked her job at Mr. Washer's house, mysteries, and all. She knew he respected her and cared about her well-being. Each day, she prayed for his health, happiness, and long life.

Chapter 20

The White House

"Mr. President, Attorney General Miller and FBI Director Hunt are here for their two o'clock appointment," Pat Hayes said through the intercom connecting her office with the working office of the president.

"Please send them in" he responded.

Osbourne looked forward to today's discussion. Miller had called him the previous day to set a special meeting with FBI Director Troy Hunt. Miller had indicated the FBI, in conjunction with the DEA, had developed a beautiful scheme for trapping and later successfully prosecuting illegal-drug sellers, traffickers, distributors and most importantly, the cartels.

Osbourne knew Hunt well and genuinely appreciated his reputation as a capable and dedicated FBI operative. He had nominated him to run the FBI approximately eighteen months earlier when the previous director's term expired. And importantly, Osbourne knew Hunt had the chops to move the war on drugs forward and shared his priority in this one area.

Miller and Hunt entered the office and stood at their chairs until Osbourne graciously asked them to be seated.

Hunt looked the part of an FBI Director: wearing a dark-brown suit, white shirt, solid tie with a bar clip, and slicked hair in a neat part. For a man of fifty-five, he was in excellent shape. Osbourne always thought he resembled Jack Webb's Joe Friday character in the old *Dragnet* series—very matter of fact, straight-forward, a real tight-ass.

"Mr. President," Miller began, not wasting any time on small talk. "Mr. President, as you know, the progress we have been making stemming the flow of cocaine into this country has been limited at best. We are being hampered at every angle. The latest setback was the *Marks* case where a noted dealer was found guilty of only possession because there was not money found during the raid on his home. Despite the large amount of cocaine, the government could not prove he had intent to sell."

Osbourne nodded slightly, staring directly at Miller. This better be the answer. We don't have time for anymore false starts.

"Further, Mr. President, you know the toughest part of our job is trying to follow the money trail and gather enough evidence to convict the seller and certainly the cartels."

This setup was more for the benefit of Troy Hunt than for Osbourne. Osbourne and his Attorney General Patrick Miller had met privately two weeks before and had discussed in detail the lack of progress justice was having in winning the president's war on drugs.

Osbourne's message to his attorney general was damn clear and very frank. He had admonished him for the lack of success the various agencies were having on the situation. Osbourne had just come back from his visit to Camp David, where he had met his friend Clarence Robinson. At this point, the president was adamant about finding a real solution to the drug problem.

He had challenged his AG to take a bold and different step in attacking the situation. "Patrick, if the dog doesn't hunt, then don't take it hunting. Find a new way to spot the prey."

Over the past two weeks, Miller had been in almost constant contact with Hunt. Miller believed that if a solution were out there, then he and Hunt would find it.

As they had worked together to dissect the problem, they kept coming back to one thing: they had to find a way to follow the trail of the drugs themselves—not the money. The money was too easily placed away in a basement or laundered through a bank where being anonymous was not only a virtue but, in some places, the law. As the FBI found with BCCI and their money laundering, many banks believed their best interest was in their clients and their clients' deposits, not in helping the US government.

If they could somehow find a way to follow the flow of the cocaine from the time it entered the US borders until the time it was used, then maybe they would have a better way of catching all the persons involved in the pipeline.

The efforts of the DEA and the FBI could catch the final pushers, dealers, and users all day long. Less often, they were able to snag the couriers, runners, and mules. And occasionally, they were able to capture the cartel shipments as they entered the country.

Miller and Hunt determined it would be a brilliant coup if they could somehow determine the exact flow of drugs through the various supply pipelines and dealer organizations the cartels had established. They figured after a year or so of tracking these distribution channels, they would be able to connect the "big guys" to the "little guys."

Miller spoke proudly. "Mr. President, we think we have just what we have been looking for." He then looked over at the FBI Director.

FBI Director Troy Hunt stood up, straightened his coat, adjusted his collar, cleared his throat, and looked directly at the president.

"Mr. President," he said calmly and deliberately. "We want to share with you Operation Blueprint. This is a completely new approach to winning the government's drug war. It is a twelve- to eighteen-month program designed to make a significant, if not fatal, dent into the entire drug-supply side as it exists today. If Blueprint is successful, then the cartels and the major dealer networks existing in the US today will be caught, tried, and successfully convicted."

Hunt paused to let the thought set with the president.

Osbourne's eyes twitched at Hunt's remarks. He stared at Hunt and then over at Miller, who sat motionless. If these words had come from Miller or almost anyone else, Osbourne would have thought he was being sold. But he knew Hunt was not a man of hyperbole and had carefully chosen his words. And Osbourne knew Miller believed the same thing.

Hunt continued. "The process is quite simple. It's a shame we didn't think of it before. It's not unlike what military security operatives have done for years to catch leaks. If security suspected a compromised player, they planted a seed with that individual to see if it comes up elsewhere. Or they place a unique sentence into each secure copy of a top-secret document to see if a copy of it resurfaces.

"In this case, we plant a unique tattoo into each shipment of cocaine we intercept. But, unlike our interdiction programs where we confiscate the contraband, in Operation Blueprint we will let the contraband continue through the pipeline."

Again, Hunt paused, waiting for a question from the president. There wasn't one. Osbourne seemed to be tracking with him.

Hunt then pulled a tablet out of his briefcase and laid it horizontally in front of the president. Like a basketball coach during a timeout, Hunt drew various circles on the pad. Starting on the president's left side of the pad, he drew two large circles about one and a half inches in diameter. He drew the same-size circles on the bottom middle and bottom right of the pad.

"These circles represent the primary points where drugs enter the US. These circles on your left are Southern California, the circle in the middle is south Texas, and the circle on the right is—"

"Miami," Osbourne said.

"Yes, sir, Miami." Hunt had a guarded twinkle in his eye. He knew the president tracked with him.

Hunt drew slightly smaller circles in the middle of the page and at the top center, top right, and right center. "These represent Saint Louis, Chicago, New York, and Washington, D.C. We know drugs enter the US primarily through the areas marked by the larger circles and are then transported to the main distribution points indicated with the smaller circles." He drew lines and arrows from the large circles to the smaller circles.

"We certainly don't know about all the drugs entering or about all the channels taken to get the drugs to the smaller circles. If we did, then our interdiction programs would be having far better success than we are having now. But we do know about quite a few of the channels, at least enough to get started."

Hunt drew a ring of smaller circles around each of the middle-size circles. "But we are having pretty good luck at this level. This represents the dealer networks, the gangs, the runners, and the sellers of drugs on the street." He placed x's through the smaller circles to indicate the government's ability to interdict drugs at this level of commerce.

Osbourne held his hand over the page for a second to let the thought set in. "Please continue, Mr. Hunt. How does all this work? What's the end benefit? How does this enable us to dry up the supply side?"

Miller jumped in while Hunt prepared his next diagram. "Our goal, Mr. President, is to create a trail of commerce—a trail that may be submitted in a court of law that will show transportation of illegal drugs across state lines, a federal offense; the selling of drugs, large quantities of drugs, certainly another federal offense; and the distribution of drugs from the main suppliers, starting with the cartels and working its way to the smallest street pusher selling on the corner."

Hunt jumped in. "And by doing so, we can light up the entire distribution network and catch and convict virtually every person currently shipping, distributing, and selling cocaine on the streets of America today."

Hunt had taken a red pen and had drawn the arrows on the page, showing the trail of drugs from each of the larger circles (Los Angeles, south Texas, Miami) to the middle-size circles (Chicago, New York, Saint Louis, Washington, D.C.) to the little circles representing the gangs and small dealers.

He continued. "You see, Mr. President, we can tattoo a shipment of drugs entering the country in Miami, let's say, and track its distribution to New York and through the various dealer networks on the East Coast. As we make routine arrests and confiscate the drugs, we can determine exactly where the drugs entered the country and, as time goes on, know exactly through whose hands the drugs were handled. You see, in some cases, we will interdict and keep the drugs. In other cases, we will tattoo the drugs and let them pass to see where they show up."

Osbourne looked up and nodded his head to confirm he understood the map and the concept of tracking the drugs. He then asked, "and this 'tattoo,' what exactly is it?" not in a negative way, but genuinely wanting to understand exactly how the program was going to work.

Hunt and Miller looked at each other and smiled.

"The tattoo was the most difficult part of this problem," Hunt said. "Our challenge was to find a way to place a unique signature in every shipment of cocaine we intercepted. This signature had to be easily applied because our agents would have only a limited time to place the substance while in the field. Also, the signature had to be able to penetrate a large amount of the substance in an easy and efficient manner so that when we intercept a single kilo, our tattoo will survive multiple cuttings all the way down to a single-gram purchase. And we can scale it up for treating even larger containers or down to common one-ounce transactions."

Miller joined in. "Obviously, the tattooing has to be undetectable on the street. It must be invisible to the dealer and the buyer. It can't change the potency of the drug, and it should withstand the normal kinds of street tests for purity."

Hunt nodded. "On the street, cocaine gets cut several times from its 'pure' state. The cocaine entering this country from the cartels is usually pure. As the drug moves from one dealer to the next, the drug is then cut with various substances, such as baking soda, to increase the yield. Sellers base their prices on the level of purity. The best is the cocaine bought by the wealthy upper classes in the large cities. They will pay substantially more for a gram of pure cocaine. The worst is the stuff bought on the street in the poor sections of Washington, New York, and Chicago. To get the price to a pocket-change level, the cocaine is only about forty percent pure. Quite frankly, that's why crack cocaine is so popular in the inner cities; it's a tremendous high, and it's cheap."

Osbourne paused, leaned back in his chair, and reached for the chrome carafe of coffee. As he poured a cup, he motioned to Hunt and

Miller, asking if they would like some. Both waved their hands in the negative.

Hunt continued. "As the cocaine moves through all these people, there are a few common practices used to determine the quality level. The dealers who are off the street will commonly place a small amount of the cocaine in ethyl alcohol. Pure cocaine will melt. The substances used to cut cocaine will not. By examining the fallout in the bottom of the glass, a dealer can determine the level of purity.

"Less sophisticated dealers will use Clorox bleach to do the same thing. Chlorine will also melt pure cocaine. Other experienced dealers will rub the cocaine between their thumb and forefinger. Pure cocaine will melt into the skin, while the impurities will form a gritty texture the dealer will immediately detect."

Osbourne mused. "Interesting. I didn't know that."

"And, of course, the ultimate test for the experienced dealer is the taste or the impact of the drug when they use it." Hunt placed his hand near his nose as if he were snorting cocaine. "Tasting the drug assures them they are dealing with cocaine in the first place. Some will scrape a prime layer off the top of the kilo and snort the drug to see if it gives them the same lift as the good stuff they normally use."

Hunt paused for a second and then continued.

"But you know, Mr. President, the interesting thing about dealers is that many of them are not actual users of the drugs they sell. It's kind of like the ex-alcoholic bar tender; they may serve the public all day, but they never drink. It's only a business. I guess they see the harmful effects too often or something."

"So, again, what exactly is this tattoo if it is not detected with normal street tests and easily added to a large or small shipment by your agents?" Osbourne asked, shifting forward in his chair. The whole notion of creating a means of tracking the distribution of drugs with some sort of secret blueprint fascinated him.

Miller gave Hunt a chance to collect his thoughts. "Mr. President, as you know, the FBI has made great strides in forensic science and the unique signature of one's DNA. Our crime labs can take a semen sample from a rape victim and match it to the blood sample from an accused man and determine if the semen and the blood came from the same person. The same thing can be accomplished with a single strand of hair, a piece of dried skin, or even saliva. Our tattooing process uses the same basic idea. Think about it as crumbling a very small amount of baby powder or dried skin with a unique DNA signature into a cocaine shipment. No matter how much or how little of the tattoo is found, we can identify its origin.

"The entire strategy of using the tattooing process calls for the ability to develop an endless number of 'tattooing codes'—that is, a large number of unique codes that may be added and documented to various shipments of drugs. This could include cocaine, marijuana, or heroin but not crack due to its preparation process. We are recommending tattooing cocaine.

"Anyway, we must be able to add the tattooing substance to a given shipment; document the who, where, and when; and then let the drugs pass on through after taking a small sample for our records. It is entirely possible several tattoos may be found in a single gram of cocaine, highlighting its path from the starting point to the ultimate street pusher and user."

"Sounds wonderful," the president nearly gushed. "Who created this trackable tattoo?"

"Our labs—mostly someone you may know—Dr. Clyde Ostrow, head of the FBI's Pharmacology Lab found a way to essentially create a DNA-style signature in a simple spray mist that quickly evaporates or absorbs but does not dissolve the cocaine. In fact, the whole idea of creating the Blueprint markers was essentially his invention."

Osbourne smiled as he remembered the quirky Ostrow from the Washington World War II History Club meetings they had attended together. What was that? Ten, fifteen years ago. Longer? He had thought Ostrow had retired by now to become a lounge singer on some South Pacific Island.

Hunt continued. "A small amount of this liquid will leave a microscopic signature on the cocaine. Totally undetected under street tests. The only way one could see the signature is with an electron microscope, and then it is as apparent as the Grand Canyon. Electron microscopes are hardly the type of equipment used on the streets, or even in the cartels.

"When one of our agents intercepts a shipment, they will use a small preloaded hypodermic syringe and small needle to mark the cocaine through a tiny hole in the packet. The vial number is recorded and forwarded to the FBI labs for time, place substantiation, and evidence. The empty syringe is then returned to the FBI lab, where its contents will be verified and cataloged. Each agent will be assigned many syringes, each with a different code. On large bricks of cocaine, the agent will insert the needle under the package gusset and slowly withdraw the syringe while applying the marker across the upper edge of the brick. When the kilo is broken into smaller packets, the tattoo will disperse throughout. We need only one molecule for identification. Smaller packets would be injected with smaller amounts. Again, the thin-needle intrusion will be virtually invisible.

"And it really doesn't matter how much is applied—or how little, for that matter. Injecting more just increases the chances of the marker being picked up as the shipment is broken down and cut throughout the distribution process."

Osbourne leaned back in his chair and stared at the ceiling of his small working office. His mind wandered as he thought about the street use of drugs, the setback from the *Marks* case, the crippling effect drug enforcement had on the budget, and the rehabilitation costs involved once a person went straight. He thought about young Eric's death and the look in Clarence's eyes as Clarence pleaded with him to do something about the drugs used in this country.

Would this Blueprint tattooing process really work? Did Hunt and Miller have a successful approach? And how much time would it take?

"Mr. Miller. Mr. Hunt. Do you think this dog will hunt?" Osbourne asked, staring the FBI director straight in the eye. "Do you think this will really work? Will it create a trail to aid in our prosecution of the dealers and eventually the cartels?"

"Yes, sir," Hunt said. "It's an ingenious idea, one we haven't tried, much less thought about. I believe at the end of a year, we will have hard proof and evidence to prosecute the cartels, along with dealers, pushers, gang members, and users. And the state's case will be based on the flow of the drugs, not the money. We will be able to prosecute on charges of possession, intent to sell, trafficking, carrying illegal substances across state lines, and of course sales of illegal substances. The cartel networks won't know what hit them. Their defense will be in shambles."

"Who will you use to implement the plan?" Osbourne asked. Through his years as vice president and the various positions he held in the Senate, he was familiar with many of the top agents in both the FBI and the DEA.

"We're still putting together the activation plan, Mr. President," Hunt said. "But at this point, we're leaning toward Chuck Harding to lead the DEA field agents. His experience and his physical appearance make him uniquely qualified for this operation. We will assign a tight group of our best agents under him."

"Chuck doing OK?" Osbourne asked, looking across the office at no particular item.

"Yes, sir," Hunt said. "He's been back in drug enforcement for the past eighteen months. He's doing fine, sir."

"That's fine. He's a good man. I'm personally glad to hear he's doing so well and glad to hear he'll be one of the key agents on this operation."

★ ★ ★

Osbourne paused, stood up, circled his desk, and stared upward for a few moments.

Troy Hunt followed him with his eyes. He had seen this before.

"Then what?" Osbourne asked. His voice slightly raised and agitated.

"Sir?" Miller asked.

"Then what?" Osbourne turned and faced his attorney general. "Will everyone stop using drugs just because we locked everyone up who is selling? This will stop the supply or at least hinder it for a while, but it won't do anything about stemming the demand."

Miller looked at Hunt. What was the president saying?

"Look, General Miller, Director Hunt. Your tattooing plan is ingenious, all right. In fact, the concept behind Operation Blueprint is superb. I agree it will go far in bringing the selling and distribution network to justice. But I also believe the demand for drugs is so great and the financial reward is so lucrative there will be some other cartel and distribution network preparing to pick up where the last one left off. Then what do we do, Mr. Miller? Then what do we do?"

Both Miller and Hunt were silent. Osbourne's latest remarks were more philosophical and not the type that needed to be directly addressed. Both knew Osbourne's friend had lost his son in a drug-related incident. Both knew the nation's drug problem occupied Osbourne's mind. And they both knew he was also thinking about some way to reduce or even eliminate the nation's insatiable appetite for drugs.

Chapter 21

FBI Headquarters

Attorney General Patrick Miller and FBI Director Troy Hunt received full funding from the president and the Justice Department for Operation Blueprint. The security clearance on the plan was high. They could not chance letting the cat out of the bag on a complex, broad-reaching program with a nine-to twelve-month duration. The number of operatives who would be used on Operation Blueprint needed to be small.

Hunt handpicked the initial agents who would be employed to place the tattoo on various shipments. The agents were his best and most trusted men. He was sure they would not leak anything about the operation to anyone and be thorough enough to ensure the accurate processing of the paperwork required to build an airtight case when this program was finally brought to trial. Any sloppy work could endanger the entire operation.

He selected men from both the FBI and the DEA. He had to have both the proper lab organization and field network.

In the lab, FBI veteran Dr. Clyde Ostrow would be the chief lab agent. He was a trained pharmacologist, microbiologist and an expert in DNA forensics who had been with the FBI for over thirty years. He created the Blueprint idea and Hunt felt confident Ostrow would guarantee the chain of evidence would be bulletproof.

For Ostrow, the mechanisms of Operation Blueprint were not new; he had implemented the idea of the tattooing technique while working on a case to nab grain exporters who were illegally selling and shipping grain to Iran during the time the United States embargoed any food or equipment sales to the country. For three months during the key harvest seasons, the FBI had sprayed a "tattoo" into grain silos across the Midwest. They traced shipments and sales. When a shipment reached a foreign port, field agents confiscated a small sample of the grain. If it contained the tattoo, the source and the exporter of the grain were identified. The operation worked, and the federal government brought the illegal exporters to trial with an iron-clad case.

Hunt had remembered the operation, and when he and Miller were working on an alternative approach to tracking down the cocaine network, Operation Grain Belt came to mind.

Hunt and Ostrow tried the tattooing technique on cocaine. It worked. The tattoo did not color or in any way visually distort the look of the coke or the efficacy of the drug when used. It also remained invisible when the coke was prepared for freebasing, though the tattoo was no longer visible after the drug had been heated. And as he had pointed out to the president, the tattoo was invisible to any field test the dealer network would use to test the purity of the cocaine.

Dr. Ostrow had set up a computer program to keep track of the ten thousand combinations, or "tattoo prints," that would be issued to the field. The substance, approximately one ounce of liquid, was placed into syringes with four-inch needles. To aid the agents in the field, briefcases with space for twenty-five syringes were issued. Each syringe had a number and letter code. Each number was equal to the letter code as an added security. For instance, the number 27 was also represented with the letters *BG*, the second and seventh letters of the alphabet. When the agent placed the total code 27-BG on his status sheet, the lab would be sure the number was correct. This ensured complete accuracy by both the field agent and the lab.

FBI Special Agent Charles Bruce would coordinate the entire operation from inside the FBI. The fieldwork would be coordinated by DEA Agent Chuck Harding.

Harding's assignment to Operation Blueprint was difficult for Director Hunt and Agent Bruce. Five years ago, Harding had been relieved from his field duties because of a tragedy to his young family. His wife and two children had been caught in a gang-related shooting. The police report and FBI follow-up indicated the gangs were heavily involved in drug trafficking and the shooting was related to a turf battle for drugs.

In fear of "unprofessional retaliation by a federal agent," Harding had been transferred to the military security investigation sector for a three-year period. After intensive review by his superiors, he returned to the drug-enforcement area eighteen months ago. Since his return, his conduct has been unquestionably professional, and his abilities to carry out the investigative tasks are every bit as good as before this transfer.

Hunt believed Harding's "history" also would enhance his performance of Operation Blueprint duties. A twelve-month program with no intermediate results took an emotional toll on the investigators. Agents, by their nature, liked to see results from their work. They liked to see raids successfully conducted, people arrested, and convicted. The nature of the Operation Blueprint plan meant no action would be taken until the entire distribution network was "lit up" and the DEA and Justice Department simultaneously indicted virtually the entire drug community in one fell swoop. Hunt believed Harding would be in favor of such a program and would maintain the patience and accuracy necessary to affect the legal "revenge" on the drug community that Operation Blueprint promised.

"Troy," Harding had said to Hunt. "This operation is the best revenge I could ever hope for. This will get all the folks off the street who were in any way connected with the death of my family. I'm in. You can count on me."

"This operation will be very time consuming," Hunt said. "It will mean nonstop, seven-days-a-week. We must intersect the flow at every point. And due to the security, we're placing on this internally, the manpower will be a fraction of the size we would normally employ."

"No problem, sir. I got all the time in the world. It's not like I have to spend the weekend at home with a family or anything." Harding wasn't being sarcastic but matter of fact. The emotion of five years ago seemed to be behind him. This pleased Hunt. He felt more comfortable in his decision.

"Oh yes, Chuck. When we told the president that you would be the field agent in charge of Blueprint, he seemed genuinely pleased."

"The president is a fine man. He cares deeply about people. Did you know he invited me to his home shortly after Peg and the kids were killed? It was during the presidential campaign, but he took the time to invite me to his home and tell me how sorry he was to hear about their deaths. Before that, our only association had been during briefings on our progress in the 'drug wars.'"

Hunt looked at Harding. He did not know the president had met with him after his family's death.

Chapter 22

Washington, D.C.

Jacob Washington was now on track to getting his promotion from lookout to runner. He had been superbly performing his duties on Neville's corner. He liked the drug business. It provided him with more money than any of the other kids on the block. It was his ticket out. He wasn't going to end up like his mother and work two menial jobs each day just to make ends meet. And he sure wasn't cut out to read books and study all day like his older brother, Emmett.

No, the drug business was perfect. And he was good at it.

As with most kids at age fourteen, Jacob grew like a weed and no longer had the small boy looks needed to be a worthy lookout. Bigger black boys standing aimlessly on street corners drew the cops' attention. Jacob's size and proficiency made him ready to be a runner in Neville's group.

As a runner, Jacob's responsibilities included delivering drugs to various sellers around the Washington, D.C. area. He wasn't to engage in any selling himself; rather, he was to deliver the merchandise to those who made the actual "client contact."

Even the most ambitious of runners were not allowed to sell. If a runner was ever caught selling the drugs he was supposed to deliver, he would probably be found dead in some back alley. And to send a warning to others why the runner was killed, two fingers on the right hand would be severed and stuck into his pants pocket.

Like the trucks that deliver Hostess Twinkies or Frito's to the supermarkets, the runners delivered merchandise to the retail sellers who then sold to their clientele.

Runners were to blend in with their surroundings and basically look like any teenager running the streets. They were to have skateboards or rollerblades or carry a basketball or some other toy, so they resembled other poor black teens. They were encouraged to ride their skateboards on the sidewalks, bounce their basketballs, or even have their boom boxes too loud. After all, what better cover could there be than drawing attention to oneself? But they weren't to do anything that would get them arrested or draw the cops' attention.

So, for Jacob, the training to be a runner began. He was buddied up with Nelson, a trusted runner with one year's experience.

Nelson was a tall, lanky, fair-skinned black kid about sixteen years old. Except for his brown curly hair, he could pass for white. His eyes were blue, and his face long. Chances were pretty good he had a white father. He had been a runner for over a year, and if he continued along his current career path, he could look forward to becoming an actual seller.

The organization tried to rapidly promote kids who could fit into a school situation and who looked different from the mainstream black inner-city kid. This helped it expand or create new markets for its goods.

Jacob's training period would last two weeks. During this time, he joined Nelson on his runs to see how deliveries were made.

The runners never came in direct contact with the sellers. Instead, they were directed to leave the merchandise in a specific area described by their supervisor. Often, the directions were to place the merchandise at a specific street corner on top of a garbage can, inside the breezeway of some storefront, or next to a dumpster. After placing the goods, the runner was to leave without looking to see who might be picking up the merchandise.

With this knowledge on how the merchandise was delivered, Jacob better understood his role as a lookout. As a lookout, he stood on a specific street corner and watched for the police. At the time, he did not understand that his stationed corner was probably the drop-off point for a runner. And because the seller had the most exposure, the lookout's job was to ensure no cops were around when the seller picked up the goods.

As a runner, Jacob would make two or sometimes three drops per day. He was usually given the merchandise in different kinds of bags.

However, Emmett did talk to his brother about not taking the drugs. For the most part, Jacob understood this, but the pressure placed on him by others to experiment was great. Although Jacob had not used anything to date, they both knew it would be a matter of time before Jacob took his first hit.

It was like a kid in a candy store never snitching a piece of candy.

Chapter 23

The Washington Post Building

"Emmett Washington, I would like you to meet Geoffrey Wines. Geoffrey Wines, meet Emmett Washington, our intern for the summer." Charlotte Gatty from the *Washington Post*'s Community Relations Department was responsible for assigning the *Post*'s summer interns to specific reporters.

Wow, the famous Geoffrey Wines, Emmett thought. The *Washington Post* reporter who had broken so many stories about events in Washington for their Metro Section. It was Wines who first reported on the arrest of Washington's mayor whom the FBI caught in a drug sting and how the police commissioner had connections with "unsavory characters" in other cities.

Geoffrey Wines, though still under age forty, had earned the reputation as "a reporter's reporter." He had worked for the *Post* for ten years and won a Pulitzer for his daily coverage of the nongovernment parts of Washington. But most of all, Wines had cultivated sources all over the city, from pimps to police commissioners. He knew the answers to questions others didn't even think of asking. And though the editors wanted to promote him to a higher desk, he chose to stay right where he was. "It's a whole lot grittier," he would say.

Wines looked even younger than Emmett had imagined. He had a slender body, a head of dark disheveled hair which was past due for a cut, and a bit of a baby face. Emmett was excited just meeting Geoffrey Wines and ecstatic about the prospect of working with him as a researcher over the summer.

"Good to meet you, Emmett. Hear you know a lot about D.C. That's great. I need all the knowledge of this city I can get. It's a hell of a beat. Shoot, I bet you have seen parts of this city I wouldn't dare go into." Wines wasn't trying to insult Emmett but rather compliment him on being a poor kid from the projects who picked himself up enough to secure a coveted internship at the prestigious *Washington Post*. College freshmen from all over the country would die to be in Emmett's position.

"Well, yes, sir, Mr. Wines. I've seen quite a bit of this city." Emmett was unable to contain his enthusiasm. This was a dream come true. And Wines seemed like an okay dude.

"Emmett, one thing has got to be clear right now: my name is Geoffrey, not Mr. Wines. I'm not the president. Please call me Geoff."

"OK, Geoff."

"Let me show you our digs." Off Geoff went taking Emmett in tow, leaving Charlotte Gatty standing alone.

"Thank you, Ms. Gatty. Thank you," Emmett said over his shoulder as he raced to keep up.

Chapter 24

Georgetown, D.C.

Howard Washer drove his Mercedes 300 SEL up the driveway of his Georgetown home. It was about 7:30 p.m., and the Spring days were getting long enough that he could see his entire yard in bloom with the twelve dogwoods and numerous azalea bushes scattered across his property.

He entered through the kitchen door. On the kitchen counter, Gertrude had left the mail and a note confirming the dinner he had requested. A single place setting of everyday dishes and stainless flatware waited on the kitchen table.

"Gertrude's great. Never misses a beat," he said under his breath. He really liked her.

"Let's see, two barbecue pork chops, green beans with small chunks of country ham, homemade cinnamon apples, and a sprig of parsley all sat on a dinner plate. Perfect. Fresh pitcher of iced tea. Good, good. Lemon in the tea. Perfect. Garden salad with Gertrude's honey mustard dressing. Perfect. Pop it in the microwave. Hmm, sixty percent power, three minutes. Ought to be perfect."

He placed the plate in the microwave, set the power setting to 60 percent, and set the timer for three minutes. He then walked up to his bedroom and undressed, washed his face and hands, and put on a pair of loose-fitting cotton slacks and a knit shirt.

Downstairs, he silently ate his dinner while looking over the mail and the latest *Field and Stream*. The magazine had a particularly good article on fly fishing in the Rocky Mountain streams of Colorado.

"I'll have to go there again this summer. It was perfect a couple of years ago."

After finishing, he placed the dinner plates neatly in the sink and retired to his study. He selected Paul Simon's *Graceland* compact disk, put it on the stereo, and activated the "repeat" sequence. The accordion chords on the first cut started immediately.

He reached in his pants pocket, grabbed a small desk key, unlocked the lower left-hand drawer, and pulled out a small silver cylinder. He walked over to the couch, cleared a space on the glass-top coffee table, and knelt down. *Ah, a little relaxation and entertainment.*

He sprinkled a measured amount of cocaine on the glass tabletop, took out his pen knife, and formed two neat lines about one inch long.

"Perfect. Perfect."

He leaned over the table. After one quick snort, the first line was gone.

Only a small amount of dust remained on the edge of his nose. He worked it into the nostril and sniffed it in. Then snorted the second line.

Falling back into the rich arms of the leather couch, he closed his eyes, listened to the music, and gracefully moved his entire body with the beat.

I'm going to Graceland.

As the song ended, Howard Washer sighed. "Perfect. This is perfect. Now, where's that maze-ball game? I'm going to beat it tonight."

"You Can Call Me Al" started to play with its bouncy beat.

He grabbed the wooden labyrinth from one of the end tables and set it on the coffee table where the line of coke was. Placing the ball in the start position, he furiously worked the knobs. He turned each knob left and right, twisted his shoulder for a little English, and steered the ball through the maze and around the traps toward the home court.

The ball dropped into the first trap on the back side of the maze. He started over, working more furiously.

"Move, move! Left, left, right, left. Damn!"

The ball fell through another hole.

"Last try, then let's try another one. Something creative. Let's try the triangle puzzle. It's always a challenge."

Mr. Washer played on for another three hours, skipping from one game to the other, all while the *Graceland* CD kept repeating itself.

At the end of the evening, he cleared off the coffee table and cleaned the top with Glass*Plus and a piece of paper towel. He then locked the silver coke canister in the drawer.

. . . why we must learn to live alone.

He ejected the CD from the player, placed it in its sleeve, and turned off the unit. "Perfect, just perfect," he muttered to himself as he headed up to bed.

Chapter 25

New York City

"Hey, Brucey, how's it going, man?" Dwight asked over the phone.

Bruce Zimmer sat in his New York apartment with his feet up on the leather footstool. A cold can of Miller Genuine Draft in one hand, and his phone in the other. His old, tattered Michigan T-shirt wet with perspiration. He had just returned from softball with a few of his friends, where his team had lost again. But what the hell, the babes looked great on the sidelines.

"Dwight, you old dog, what the fuck you up to these days? Christ, man, where the fuck you been?" Bruce hadn't talked to his old college roommate in several months. The last time they talked, Dwight had seemed on edge, saying he and his girlfriend, Marsha Tidman, were having a tough time of it. Since then, Bruce had tried calling Dwight at various times but never got through to him. He had even tried Dwight's office at Seaton and Earnst, but they had said he was no longer with the firm.

"Oh, man, been busy as shit the last few months," Dwight said. "Out of the stock biz and into my own business. Beginning to work out pretty well, too."

"What're ya doin'?" Bruce asked, slipping into his college lingo. Whenever he talked with Dwight, he always conjured up the old days of trawling for coeds at the Ann Arbor bars.

"Remember those two girls we met before my last semester? Anita and Holly, the wild redhead who taught you 'blow dicking'?"

"Yeah, you bet. Haven't seen her in a while. But as they say, no time like the present to rekindle old flames." Bruce thought how that girl had turned him every which way but loose that first night. "Why you ask?"

"You still do that shit? You still blow dick? You still…" Dwight began to ask Bruce if he still snorted cocaine but decided it would not be a good thing to say over the phone.

"Yeah, you bet. Damn, we all do it around here. A regular social club. We're not nuts, be we like a little blow once in a while, like once a week." Bruce laughed to himself. Hell, all his Gotham buds were into the shit. It was kind of a status symbol for them. Do good in work. Do good in drugs. Shit, it didn't hurt anyone.

"Need any?" Dwight asked, holding his breath. "Make you a deal."

The other end of the phone went silent. Bruce couldn't believe what he was hearing. Dwight never used the shit. Hell, he was into the financial thing and didn't want to get messed up with anything that could end his career on the floor.

"Dwight, is that your new business?" Bruce asked hesitantly.

"Yipper. A new business with better and safer returns than anything I traded before. Top quality, too. No shit. All good stuff. Pure. I fuckin' guarantee it."

"Well, fuck, buddy, I wouldn't buy from anyone else. Let's get together. Shit, man, I'll even introduce you to a few of my city buds. You can make it a haul. Our man here, well, let's just say he's out of the business and is taking a prolonged vacation at the expense of the mayors finest. Good time for you to have called. Perfect timing. But, of course, you always knew the perfect way to play the market. Timing. Shit, man, it's all about timing."

"How about next weekend? I'll drive over next week." Dwight could hardly control himself. This business might just make it. If he could set up a couple of good customers in New York and maybe get Bruce to do some handling for him, he could increase his volume significantly. At this stage of the game, volume was crucial.

"Hey, Dwight. You using the stuff these days?" Bruce asked, a bit concerned. He never knew if Dwight actually used the cocaine—he only suspected it after his last conversation with him. Dwight wasn't the type who could handle it.

"Not anymore, buddy. Bad for business. Could eat up all your profits. This is business. And Brucey, you know I don't do anything that isn't good for business."

"See you next weekend, man. Friday night?"

"Yeah, Friday night, about eight o'clock," Dwight said. "See you. Bye."

Dwight set the phone back on the cradle. He had made his first purchase from Vinny about five weeks ago. Since then, he had liquidated several buys and had made more than enough cash to get off the hook with the rent and the credit card companies. He was putting his life back together.

He hadn't used cocaine since the night he made the buy from Vinny, which he vaguely remembered. Dwight had been as scared as hell and still shaking from the experience on underground Wacker. Vinny had thought it was first-time nerves.

There hadn't been much in the news the next day about the murder, but it seemed to be directed toward a hoodlum druggie. The investigation still didn't seem to be headed at all in Dwight's direction.

Dwight continued to play the cards as they lay. He wasn't leaving Chicago. He wasn't running from the scene. If he got caught, so be it. He somehow managed to put the thought from his mind. All that was kind of hazy, anyway. He knew he had killed the guy but had no idea how or why he did it. He just knew that after that night, he would never use cocaine again. Besides, the selling of it was a better high for him. He loved developing clients and making money.

Chapter 26

Washington, D.C.

"Cam," the unknown caller said on the other end of the phone. "I think we have the break we've been looking for. We can do it. We can end this crap."

Cam Maggard stood in his pseudo lab in the basement of a small Baltimore house. His name would never be found on any government payroll, but he derived 100 percent of his income from the US government—always in cash.

He supported field agents of the FBI, the CIA, and other "unlisted" government agencies, using his skills as both a chemist and a pharmacist. He provided the tools needed to perform certain *unauthorized tasks*: a little something to make a foreign banker have a heart attack; a potion for getting the truth from a particular suspect; or an invisible substance that would lead the agent to a certain location when needed.

Cam functioned as one of the very few government-supported contractors who supplied the means for the government to execute its less desirable and potentially most embarrassing jobs—if caught. He worked outside the government payroll, stayed invisible to congressional oversight, or any newspaper sleuth who might be curious about his job.

"Cam, I think we can cleanly rid ourselves of every fucker who ever sells, buys, or uses drugs. The same assholes who directly or indirectly ruined our families. And the full might and resources of the federal government will help us. I'll reach you later on the details."

Click.

The caller hung up the pay phone as the D.C. Metro train pulled into the station. The call cost $1.25, paid with five quarters.

Cam knew he would meet the caller at his lab at 8:00 tonight. He wondered what exactly the caller had in mind; or what the man's plan would reveal. He knew only the caller was one of the best men he worked with, and that the two of them had a certain comradeship after the deaths of their families.

Chapter 27

FBI Headquarters

Attorney General Patrick Miller, FBI Director Troy Hunt, and DEA Agent Chuck Harding developed a three-phase plan for the implementation of Operation Blueprint.

The first phase would be to build the ironclad evidence to convict the distributors and dealers whom the FBI and DEA had already identified.

"There is no use in re-creating the wheel," the frustrated attorney general said during one of the first strategy sessions. "We know who a lot of the bastards are. I just want to be sure we can nail their asses in a court of law."

Hunt and Harding agreed with the approach. They could use the trail that had already been identified as an excellent starting point. By working forward and backward from the major dealers already on their books, they could quickly broaden their base of knowledge.

Hunt suggested they begin with the Saint Louis/Chicago and the Washington D.C./Northeast connections. "This will provide an excellent base for us to identify the major I-44 connection; the West Coast entry point; and the Norfolk entry point. Once we have honed our skill in these areas, then we can go to work in the south Florida and south Texas areas. They are a lot more complex but, when we get them, a lot more lucrative."

So, the first stage would begin with the known areas. The second phase to expand their current knowledge pool.

The third phase of the program would be to arrest and try all the participants who could be indicted and convicted using the evidence secured through their new operation. It would be implemented only when all targeted cartels, distributors, and dealers were identified. Then, warrants would be issued, and the FBI and DEA would undertake a massive sweep and arrest literally hundreds within a two-day period. *Blueprint had game-changing potential.*

They estimated phase one would take two to six months. Then Phase two another eight months after that.

And, because of the backlogs of the courts and the challenges the justice department would surely encounter, the trials for phase three would probably last half a decade. This anticipated length of time would be accompanied with a media frenzy they figured would work as a deterrent to others wanting to enter the business.

Chuck Harding totally agreed with the approach. As the fieldman most responsible for making Operation Blueprint a success, he knew he could work faster by exploiting the areas that were already identified. The first several weeks of the program would be like "falling off a log," he told Hunt, Miller, and Ostrow.

Chapter 28

The Thomas Jefferson Memorial

Three weeks after the plan was activated, Dr. Ostrow had the tattoo syringes filled, readied, and numbered for Operation Blueprint to begin.

To try out the system, Hunt had Harding place the Blueprinted drug into some known distribution patterns. The idea was to see if they could read the results after the drug had been "street cut." He had tattooed a few smaller drops and was already getting results.

As the first test on whole bricks, Harding intercepted two kilos of pure cocaine from one of his known D.C. resident distributors. This Neville character had been dealing in the inner city of Washington for years, and Harding pretty much knew who Neville's major clients were and who transported the drugs around the city.

Also, Neville was like clockwork in receiving his shipments from the cartel pipeline. The package was almost always left at a certain trash container near the bottom of the steps of the Jefferson Memorial. This wasn't a stupid idea because there were typically so many people visiting the memorial that it was easy for someone to simply drop a small paper bag near the trash container without ever stopping. And it was easy for someone else to drop a soft drink can next to the receptacle and then stoop to pick it up, along with the paper bag—a simple handoff.

Harding knew there was usually a fifteen- to twenty-minute lag between the drop and the pickup. Wearing an old army jacket and disheveling his hair with a combination of cooking oil and vacuum cleaner dust, he hunkered down on the steps about twenty feet from the trash container.

First, the drop. A well-groomed Hispanic man with a round cherub face and dressed in vacation attire walked past the container, dropping what appeared to be a used white deli bag. Harding slowly got up and rooted through the container and finally the deli bag as if he were looking for scraps of food to eat. Looking in the bag, he knew this was the delivery.

Inside the bag were two tightly formed bricks of white powder in a double wrapped Ziplock freezer bag. Walking slowly to the public restroom at the base of the monument, Harding continued to fumble around inside the bag just as a hungry man might. Inside the restroom, he entered one of the stalls and sat down on the toilet seat. He then reached inside his coat, pulled out a pair of surgical gloves, and put them on, careful not to allow the gloves to snap. He feared at this moment possibly piquing the curiosity of a park ranger or some other police authority. With a couple of kilos of cocaine, he would have a lot of explaining to do, even after showing his federal identification.

On his lap, he gingerly removed the two bricks from the plastic bags and placed one brick on top of the bag cradled in the furrow between his legs. The exposed brick had a slight ammonia smell. Harding then reached into his inside coat pocket and pulled the syringe with the alphanumeric code written on a small label: "CEO-3500."

He carefully nestled the needle below the tight gusset of the wrap, plunged the entire solution into the brick, and slowly withdrew the needle. This ensured distribution across the top of the brick—the prime cut.

He checked over the CEO-3500 brick to ensure it was pristine in appearance. It looked good. *Man, I should have been a doctor. Look at my needle skills*. He amused himself as he placed the treated brick back into the Ziplock bag.

Next, he placed the second kilo on top of the bag. He repeated the procedure. It was another perfect job—fast and clean and left the kilo in perfect shape. *Not even my grandma would notice this*, he thought, remembering how she could spot a tampered package when he and his brothers would unwrap their Christmas presents before the big day.

He noted the code: "ADC-1430."

Two bricks. Two codes. Two chances to catch the bad guys.

He then placed the bricks back into the white deli bag, rose from the toilet, flushed it for effect, quietly removed his surgical gloves, opened the stall door, and exited the restroom. He casually walked past the trash container and dropped the bag next to it in the same manner as the original drop had been made.

Glancing at his watch, he saw it had been twelve minutes since the first drop.

He left the monument, not waiting to see who was going to pick up the bag. He knew it would either be Neville or one of his runners. That wasn't important. But determining whether the differentiated drugs could be identified later was.

If this had been an actual drop, then Harding or someone would have videotaped or photographed the pickup and placed it into evidence for the distribution trail of the drugs tattooed with the CEO-3500 and ADC-1430 markers. By tying the photographic record to the drug's tattoo, the entire distribution chain would be identified. From cartel delivery to the actual street user, a complete linage of the drug could be tracked and submitted into a court of law.

Harding walked off. Before the end of the day, he had written the code numbers from both treatments into his logbook and placed the empty syringes into the "used" portion of the briefcase. When all syringes had been used, the entire case of empty containers would be returned to the FBI lab and Dr. Ostrow's evidence chain.

This would become the key evidence used to convict the cartels, distributors, and dealers.

Chapter 29

Camp David

Three weeks had passed since President Osbourne met Clarence Robinson at Camp David. The plea of his best friend had not been very far from his mind. Over and over Clarence's words echoed: "We need to get rid of those druggies. We need to put a stop to this killing of innocent men."

Osbourne stood at the bank of one of the numerous streams meandering through the naval grounds. Camp David reminded him so much of home and of growing up with his best fishing buddy, Clarence.

Tossing stones into the water, he thought about the plan AG Patrick Miller and FBI Director Troy Hunt had brought forward. Operation Blueprint was a brilliant strategy for pulling a decisive dragnet over the movers and shakers of the illegal-drug industry. At the culmination of the operation, the kingpins and their most lucrative distributors and dealers would be behind bars with an ironclad legal case facing each of them.

Osbourne was proud of the plan. Although he knew it would not put an end to the drug situation in America, he knew it would slow it down—akin to how the world of communism slowed when the USSR gave up its communist doctrine. The likes of North Korea, Cuba, and Romania were left to flounder for themselves. But overall, it ended communism as a major threat. *And it had happened on his watch!*

Was Operation Blueprint the plan that would put an end to the cold war on drugs? Would it end the same way? And put another notch in his legacy?

A fish jumped in the stream, temporarily disrupting Osbourne's train of thought. Osbourne picked up a stone and threw it right in the center of the ripples.

Quickly, his thoughts returned to Operation Blueprint. It was the reason he had invited Clarence and Chuck Harding, the DEA field operative, to Camp David for the weekend.

He wanted to tell Clarence about the plan and introduce him to Chuck. Eight years ago, when Osbourne first met Harding, he had instantly reminded him of Clarence. At the time, Osbourne was vice president and heading the drug-enforcement task force for the president. Since then, he always felt a special kinship to Harding.

This would be a good time to get Chuck Harding and Clarence Robinson together. Like Clarence, Chuck liked to fish. Osbourne figured they could spend a relaxing weekend in the streams and Clarence could see there were some very good people and plans working on solving the nation's drug problem.

And Osbourne thought the two would also form a kinship, given their common loss of loved ones to drug-crazed killers.

It was approaching 7:00 p.m., and Osbourne knew Harding and Clarence would soon arrive at the Camp David lodge. He had scheduled a White House limo to pick up Clarence at Washington National Airport. It was simpler than having Clarence rent a car or try to bring a cab into the compound. While the president resided on the property, it is nearly impossible for a civilian to make it to the grounds. However, Harding's high level of clearance would allow him to enter, but he would need to leave his car in a sanctioned area well away from the lodge and cabin occupied by the president and his party.

★ ★ ★

Just as Osbourne broke through the woods and started walking the path leading to the main lodge, a golf cart with Harding headed up the drive.

God, he reminded Osbourne of a young Clarence, tall, long, and muscular. He had moderately brown skin, closely cropped hair, and a pleasant smile. The key distinguishing feature was a two-inch scar on his right cheek—a bad scar from a DEA bust that ended with a broken beer bottle jammed into Harding's cheek. However, because of his pleasant features and friendly expression, the scar never made him appear thuggish or gangster. It came across as one of those marks that happens by accident.

Harding saw Osbourne walking toward the cart, so he jumped off and started walking to him.

"Mr. President. Thank you so very much for inviting me to Camp David. You don't know how much I really appreciate this. Thanks!"

Osbourne noted Harding's eyes were bright with excitement; he truly was excited to be here. Osbourne often forgot who he was and that an invitation by the president of the United States to spend a weekend of fishing in the streams of Camp David was indeed a privilege.

"Chuck, so good to see you again. It's been several years." The last time they had been in contact was after Harding's young family had been murdered, about five years ago.

"Well, Chuck, are you ready to do a little fishing this weekend? Ready to catch the really big one out of the ponds of this government-stocked resort?"

"Well, Mr. President, I'll try to leave a few of the big ones for you and your friend." Harding flashed a broad grin.

That's what Osbourne liked about Chuck: he was comfortable in a number of settings and seemed to get right into the swing of things. This would be a tough weekend on both Clarence and Osbourne if Harding were stiff and formal.

"I'm not sure you'll have a chance to catch the big ones. Clarence is pretty good at landing the lunkers. Hell, he'll have the big ones out of the streams before we even finish tying a hook. Wait till you meet my old friend."

Harding smiled. He didn't know exactly who Clarence Robinson was. He only knew he was one of Osbourne's oldest and best friends from South Carolina. Harding thought Clarence would be some bubba close to retirement, someone from the country club set. But he didn't care. He liked Robert S. Osbourne. He always liked the way he treated him during all the meetings. And he still remembered the personal phone call and visit from him, then the vice president, a few days after the murder of his family. These types of things meant a lot to Harding. He remembered those things.

"Chuck, before Clarence gets here, let me talk shop for a few moments and ask you how things are going with Operation Blueprint."

"Well, sir, the setup is going well. We have pretty much put the systems into place. I've placed the prototype with several known distributors and dealers. We're beginning to pick up the cocaine off the street and are successfully identifying the source. If this holds throughout the operation, we should be in pretty good shape meeting the operation's objectives."

"Excellent, Chuck. Excellent. Any snags at all?"

"No, sir, not yet. It's running well. But you know the actual fieldwork is going to be much tougher. It's easy when you're just making day trips that are close to your home base. But when you start hitting the road for weeks at a time and the fatigue of the road starts to set in, then things are a little less perfect. But we're used to it. Besides, what do I need to stay around D.C. for? It's not like I must be home for dinner with the family."

This last remark struck Osbourne. It had been five years and still seemed as if Harding had not forgotten his family, nor moved on to a new life. It had to be tough on a young man to lose that much all at one time.

"Listen, Chuck. Things will get better with time. You take care of yourself, and time will heal the loss," he coached, thinking of Emily Rose, his wife and soulmate he had lost to cancer many years before.

"I know, sir. I know, but it still hurts whenever I think about it. And quite honestly, I still get angry at the situation. You know, if the killer had not been captured so quickly following their murder, I would have quit my job and tracked him down myself—*and killed him.*"

Osbourne couldn't believe Harding's openness. But he also knew Harding trusted him and wouldn't let the words spoken in an informal setting like this come back to haunt him. Osbourne knew Harding knew this.

"Let me tell you about my friend Clarence," Osbourne said. "Clarence Robinson is one of my very best friends. While we were growing up, we were virtually inseparable. We fished together, hunted together, and basically hung out together."

"Should be a fun weekend, then. Three die-hard fishermen." Harding didn't know where Osbourne was leading with these remarks but figured the president wanted to get something off his chest.

"Yes, Chuck. And one other thing." Osbourne stepped back from Harding and looked him square in the eye. "We're going to break the rules this weekend. Clarence just lost his youngest son to some drug-crazed hood. A fine boy, Northwestern grad, good job in Chicago. About five weeks ago. No arrests, just some unidentified fingerprints found on the car."

Harding watched Osbourne as he fidgeted.

"Chuck, I promised Clarence we would do something to put an end to the drug situation. He pleaded with me as I'm his old friend and president of the United States. And I promised him we would do something. I think Operation Blueprint is that something."

Harding was about to respond when they both heard a car rounding the last turn into the circle of the Camp David lodge. The medium-length black limousine pulled to a stop. The driver jumped out to open the right passenger door. However, before reaching it, out stepped Clarence Robinson.

At first, Harding thought Clarence was one of the presidential aides. Then he heard the president address the man.

"Clarence. Clarence, how are you? You ready to do a little fishing this weekend?" Osbourne tried to set a good, fun, informal tone for the weekend. "You ready to fish this place dry and cause a federal wildlife disaster that will result in a bevy of *Washington Post* reporters descending on us for their exclusive front-page stories?"

Clarence smiled, briskly walked up to Osbourne, and gave him a big hug. "Bobby, what are you talking about? You already have all the fish out of here. Heck, we fished it dry just a few weeks ago."

Osbourne forgot about how much fun the remainder of Clarence's visit to Camp David had been after they had spent long hours talking about Eric and his death. They had fished like old times, spending all day at the bank of the stream, throwing their lines in, and pulling out a bucket full of fish. The chef had prepared the catch at a huge fish fry for Osbourne, Clarence, the presidential staff members who had been on the premises, and the navy men who kept up the camp.

Harding stared at the two men, in shock to see exactly who Clarence Robinson was. Never in his wildest dreams had he expected the president's boyhood friend Clarence to be a black man. It wasn't because he believed Osbourne was racist in any way; rather, he knew Osbourne was from South Carolina and had grown up during the 1930s, when it was unusual for whites and blacks to have socialized.

"Oh, I'm terribly sorry," Osbourne said. "Clarence, this is Chuck Harding. Chuck, this is Clarence Robinson, one of my oldest, err, my oldest friend."

"Good to meet you, Chuck." Clarence smiled, putting his hand forward to shake Chuck's hand. "Good to meet you."

"Clarence, Chuck here is with the DEA, but more importantly, he likes to fish almost as much as you and me. Let's see if he can keep up." Osbourne was trying to position Chuck Harding to his old friend and didn't want the DEA to be the focal point of their relationship. The discussion would come during the course of the weekend.

The three men walked toward the front door of the lodge. The drivers of the golf cart and the limo had already taken Chuck's and Clarence's bags to their appointed rooms. Osbourne would not sleep in the lodge but in the president's cabin, which was appointed with the necessary communications and security equipment required by his office.

Because the May weather was nearly perfect, the large floor-to-ceiling windows allowed the warm breeze to blow throughout the lobby section of the lodge.

Osbourne led his guests out to the deck that overlooked a large ravine filled with newly leaved trees, yellow forsythia, blooming dogwood, and azalea bushes. This was Osbourne's favorite time of the year at Camp David. The foliage virtually matched South Carolina, just a few weeks later.

The three men sat themselves around a rustic wooden table. A waiter in a white jacket asked each if they wanted anything to drink.

"I'll start, just so you guys don't pussyfoot around," Osbourne said. "Jim, I'll have a Maker's. Clarence?"

"Yes, sir. I'll have a cold beer. Something light."

"And I'll have a Coke," Harding said. He didn't drink alcohol, never had. His father was an alcoholic, and Harding swore all while growing up that he would never drink it.

"So, men, let me tell you about the fishing we have here," Osbourne said.

★ ★ ★

Per the agreement the evening before, the three awoke at 4:00 a.m. to head down to a fishing stream—Osbourne's favorite—well shaded by the new leaves on the trees. The raccoons weren't afraid of disturbing the president, and the rocks along the bank yielded a nice place to sit. Osbourne loved the spot.

The game plan for the morning called for not eating anything at the lodge; they were going to catch their breakfast. They all concurred the taste of freshly caught trout, pan-fried in real butter with nothing but salt and pepper, would be the perfect start to the day.

Because Osbourne was the president of the United States, they didn't have to worry about gathering their own wood or finding dried leaves to start a fire. A nice stack of firewood, a few issues of the

Washington Post, and cedar shingles split into thin strips were sitting next to a firepit.

The place sat hidden in the woods, completely void of any Secret Service personnel or naval caretakers. Camp David allowed the president to have all the privacy he wanted and demanded. The only trapping of this important office was a mobile radio with immediate hookup to the rest of his staff in the compound buildings. He also knew that any number of military personnel and presidential aides could be beside the stream within two minutes or sooner.

Osbourne started building the fire. "I'll give you men a head-start on breakfast. Besides, if I were to throw my line into the stream now, all we would be doing is waiting for the fire to start. Breakfast wouldn't be quite as fresh."

During the evening before, Clarence and Chuck became well acquainted. Each had told the other about his childhood and families, each spending a great deal of time talking about their loss of loved ones. Just as Osbourne expected. He knew the two would get along. In a way, he knew Harding would almost be a surrogate son to Clarence. They were so similar—though Chuck was significantly older than Eric had been.

The fire flamed right up. The oak logs were dry and well-seasoned. The cedar shingles ignited with a touch of a match. Within fifteen minutes, the fire blazed, sending a bright-yellow reflection across the stream. The flames and the shimmer of dawn were the only light.

The fish were catching every fly, and soon six trout lay on a piece of canvas stretched out next to the fire.

"Let's eat!" Osbourne yelled when he caught his second fish.

Clarence had already pulled his line from the water and was fingering the edge of his knife to test its edge. Grabbing one fish off the canvas, he swiftly sliced off the head and had the knife moving under the scales in one fluid motion. Harding placed a scoop of butter in one of the heavy cast-iron skillets and arranged two logs about ten inches apart to rest the skillet over the fire.

A blue-speckled graniteware coffee pot already sat on the hot coals, perking away. Osbourne loved the taste of his "fire-brewed coffee."

The three sat on the rocks, watching the fish sizzle in the skillet.

"You know, Bobby," Clarence said. "Before going to bed last night, I was thinking about that Operation Blueprint you and Chuck told me about."

"Uh-huh," Osbourne replied, his eyes fixated on the skillet.

Clarence continued, "Yeah, you guys were saying it would take about two or more years for the full operation to be completed."

"That's right. To gather all the evidence and light up the distribution network enough to convict the kingpins and several layers of distributors and dealers below them, it will take about two years. Anything less than that will leave the big guys basically intact." Osbourne answered, quite factually, still intently watching the cooking fish and smelling the sweet aroma of breakfast rising from the heavy black skillets.

Clarence continued. "Bobby, I don't mean to be disrespectful, but I really don't think the program will work the way you think it will."

Osbourne's face snapped up from gazing into the fire and looked directly at Clarence. It wasn't a glare but more of a look of quizzical disbelief.

"What do you mean, Clarence?"

"Well, Bobby, let me give you a couple of examples. You know after the end of World War Two, I stayed in the service for several years. I was stationed as an MP in Germany. The country was a mess. We did a pretty good job of destroying the German war machine, eliminating their political leadership, and basically disenfranchising the people from the fascist structures that were in place just a few months earlier. The Nuremberg trials were beginning to take shape, and there was tremendous fear among all persons who were in any position during the war to do anything out of line. They knew we were watching them very closely. As a result, they didn't do anything to risk imprisonment."

Clarence continued, moving his gaze from Osbourne to Harding. "Despite the efforts of the US government to help rebuild the country as quickly as we could, we couldn't provide everything that all the individual people wanted. And the people wanted goods and food and blankets and coal and other necessities."

"I think I see where you're going with this," Harding said, looking over at Clarence with a slight smile.

Clarence nodded. "The black market filled the void. The demand was there, and people figured out how to fill the demand and make good money doing it. Pretty soon, the people could get almost anything they wanted if they had the money. And, as you know, a lot of the food, blankets, and fuel was US government property." Clarence then chuckled, "Hell, there wasn't anything we could do about it. The money was just too good, and there were plenty of Germans and Americans who wanted to make money."

After a long pause, Harding spoke. "Mr. President, Clarence may have a point there. Every time we make a significant score and bust a major player or two, someone else falls right in and fills the void. And the funny part about it, in many ways we were better off knowing the habits of the original dealer than having to figure out the practices of the new player. With a new player, we would always have to start over. Bastards are too creative."

"Chuck," Osbourne said with a controlled edge. "Are you saying you think Operation Blueprint is a mistake?"

Harding did not pause for a second. "No, sir, I don't think it is a mistake. It will be effective in disrupting and eliminating the current infrastructure of the cartels, distributors, and dealer networks." Harding searched for the right words before continuing. "But, sir, I don't think it's the solution—a disruption, yes, but not a solution."

"Please go on, Chuck. I'm listening." Osbourne concentrated on every word Harding and Clarence were saying.

"Well, Mr. President, it's like this. When I was little, we lived in an old row house in a decaying section of Chicago. We rented the house from a slum lord who did nothing with the property but collect the rent. And, as you know, Chicago winters are a real beast. The hawk blows and the temperatures drop, and it is tough to stay warm."

Harding got up and held his hands close to the fire before continuing.

"The back door on this house did not fit well because the house had settled, and there was a large crack along the top of the door. We couldn't seal the crack because it was so big, and we had to use the door. So, during the winter, tons and tons of cold air would pour in. We would wear heavy sweaters, long underwear, and sweatshirts and wrap blankets around ourselves, and we would never be totally warm. We would spend extra money and turn up the old furnace, and we would be warm for a while. But as soon as we set the furnace back, it was cold again.

"You see, as long as that hole was in the door, the cold air would come in, and our lives were affected in many ways. It was so frustrating. Our food got cold, we couldn't study, my father would stay at the bar drinking rather than being in the goddamn cold house, and the extra money we spent on gas and electric to warm the house kept us from saving anything or buying other things we needed."

"So, you're saying the illegal-drug problem is like the hole in the door?" Osbourne asked.

"Well, err, yes, sir. That's what I'm saying." Harding sat back down. "That cold air was endless; until the hole was fixed, we would always have the problems connected with the hole and the cold air."

Harding directly faced the president and continued, his voice quiet and steady. "Cocaine, crack, and many of the other drugs are just like that hole in the door."

He then continued, making points by touching the fingers on his hand. "As long as people are demanding and using the drugs, we will have gangs, gang murders, unstable South American governments, AIDS, unwed mothers, crack babies, degenerating education, absent fathers, overcrowded prisons, lost productivity, escalating health care costs, et cetera, et cetera."

Osbourne stood up, turning the comments of these two men over in his mind. Then we'll be right back where we started. It's the same old crap: do everything you can, and it isn't enough. The cold air is still coming in.

Finally, Osbourne sat down on a rock, so he was directly across from both Clarence and Harding.

"What do you men think we ought to be doing?" he asked simply and directly. "What do you think we should do?"

Harding shifted nervously. As open as he had been with the president, he wasn't sure how totally open he should be now. He felt he didn't have anything to lose. He was committed to personally avenging the death of his family, but he knew he could do it better by being a DEA agent and having the resources of the government than by pursuing it by himself. He sat tight and waited for Clarence to make the first move.

Clarence, the president's old friend, was not reluctant.

"Bobby, I think we've been patient enough. You know I'm never one to rush into a fight. You know I believe patience will pay off in the end. But now it's time." He then mimicked Chuck's hand actions: "Every year we wait, there are another six thousand six hundred sixty drug-related deaths; fifty billion dollars spent on the war on drugs; another three thousand men placed in prison on drug charges; another one thousand crack babies born; countless kids turning to the streets rather than the schools; and further infiltration of drugs into the heretofore safe streets of small- and mid-size towns in the Midwest and South."

He then looked straight into his old friend's eyes. "Bobby, since Eric's death, I've been reading a lot about the subject, seeking the facts that I'm sure you already know, and I'm saying we can't be patient any longer. We can't just fight this war much longer. We need to *win* the war. Win the war. *Now!*"

Clarence continued—animated, exaggerated, and passionate. The bright spark in his eyes reflected the fire burning in his mind.

"Bobby, I lost my son because *they* are winning the war. The longer we wait, more innocent sons will be lost. We need to fight fire with fire. These people are killing our boys."

Clarence sat down and started wiping the tears from his eyes. "These people are killing our boys. Every goddamn one of them. Every son of a bitch who buys, sells, makes, or carries cocaine and other drugs. They are killing our boys. They are killing…" He buried his head into his hands and wept.

Osbourne quietly reached over, pulled the skillet off the fire, sat back, and stared at the dawn sky.

No one said a word for about ten minutes.

Chapter 30

New York City

"So, old Ned is getting married on August 10. Not much of an engagement, is it? God, I didn't think that guy would ever settle down long enough to get to know one skirt, let alone marry it. Well, I guess it's the end of the pussy age, isn't it?" Jesse Smith couldn't believe it; his old friend Ned Sellers was getting married. Jesse took one last gulp of his beer and ordered a round for the table.

Bob Moseley and Doug Quigley had joined Smith at their favorite bar in the Upper East Side of Manhattan near their condos. Moseley, Quigley, Smith, and Sellers usually met at the Crystal Bar on Second Avenue a couple of times a week. It gave them a chance to unwind a bit before they joined their wives for the evening. Sellers had called Moseley to tell him he wouldn't make it because he was getting married and had to cover some bases with his fiancée. Moseley had just shared the news with the rest of their gang.

All three had very successful jobs. Moseley and Quigley worked in the financial district at the foot of Manhattan. Smith worked in the insurance industry as an actuary in Midtown. And Sellers was a buyer for one of the major department stores on Fifth Avenue. They had lived in New York for a little over ten years and on the Upper East Side for about two years. One by one, they had each found their spouse and married. And each time, the others had thrown a bachelor party that made the whole marriage commitment worthwhile.

Now they had the opportunity to plan the fourth and final party—for Ned, no less. Ned, the ultimate skirt-chasing wild man. The department store was crawling with good-looking babes who were all vying for a buying position.

"Well, which way should we do it this time? The city? The country? With or without the babes?" Quigley asked. He was the last one married, close to two years ago.

"Hey, this is a double whammy," Moseley said. "This one must be our best one. It's the last one. After this, there won't be any more. We got to do this one right. It's got to shame all the others. Hell, man, let's go for it."

Moseley was always ready for a good party. And having a good excuse always made it better.

"Checklist!" Smith said. "Hotel? Grand Hyatt."

"Check!" the others said in unison.

"Food? Fully catered. The best!"

"Check."

"Guest list? The usual ten to fifteen."

"Check."

"Bachelor-city security." This meant hookers and strippers, no wives, no girlfriends, and no female associates. Top security meant a week ahead of time. No mention of bachelor party. A fake bachelor party was set for the week of the wedding.

"Yeah, double check-check!" Moseley, Smith, and Quigley said.

"Coke?"

"Check."

"Limo for road trip and blow trip."

"Check. Check."

"OK," Smith said. "The plans are set. Thursday, August 1. I'll get the room and food. Quigley, you line up the girls. Moseley, you get the coke. And we'll each invite the usual crowd. Remember, tell the wives we're traveling on business that night, and let your office know you're taking Friday off. The usual plan. Check and recheck!"

Chapter 31

Upstairs at the White House

Operation Overlord. 1944. Europe. The Allied Forces were closing in on the Nazi Armies and the Axis Powers. For months, the commanders of the Allied Forces, under the direction of Gen. Dwight D. Eisenhower, were stationing men and machines for the assault on the beaches of Normandy, France.

This invasion would be critical to the continued success and the ultimate defeat of the German forces. France had to be liberated at all costs.

Operation Overlord was also one of the most daring plans ever conducted in any war in history. The Allied Forces had to travel across the English Channel in the silent dead of night via amphibian carriers. The beaches were protected by numerous German-placed barriers that would hold the Allies' boats approximately fifty yards off the beach. From there, the men would have to wade through chest-high water to reach the shore. Thank God it was June and not during the cold months.

For those men who were lucky enough to make it out of the water, there were then cliffs to climb to make any forward advancement. German guns were trained on the beach. Men had to dig in once they hit the sand and seek out and destroy the German gun nests.

I was four months into the army and had just finished boot training in South Carolina when I was shipped to the shores of England to begin fighting for America in the war.

I left my family in a great fanfare. My mother and the other women in Greenville, along with their younger children and friends, lined the town square as the regiment of new soldiers marched down Main Street. We were going off to fight in Europe. We were the fresh troops who were going to defeat the dreadful Nazis.

"Bobby Osbourne," my mother said as she squeezed me around the waist, with her head buried in my chest. "Bobby, take care of yourself over there. Do what you think is right. Have courage and faith in General Eisenhower. Remember, we love you."

I remember the look in my mother's eyes as she stared up at me. At eighteen, I stood a good six inches taller than she. The look was one of great pride in her son. In those days, there wasn't any question of a young man's duty to his country. Many boys and fathers were already in Europe. Many had already come back—some wounded, and some dead. But no family grieved for the decisions made. No family felt the sacrifice wasn't worth it.

Mother was proud her son was going to fight. She was also scared to death she might not ever see him again, alive and whole.

We were transported over to Europe in May by steamer ship. Since the ship was a cruise liner that had been shifted over to transporting troops, it really wasn't bad. There must have been ten thousand men, sleeping in three shifts as bunk beds lined the hallways, state rooms, and recreational facilities.

During our training in South Carolina, the sergeant taught us how to shoot, though many of us country boys were already crack shots. We practiced handling a knife and defending ourselves in hand-to-hand combat. I often thought about my friend Clarence and how quickly he had eliminated those tough older boys at the lake with a sudden upward thrust of his knee into the groin and then into the redneck boy's nose. Here we learned more deadly tricks. Of course, Clarence was not in this regiment. He trained with black troops elsewhere.

The last two weeks of our training were spent on the beaches of South Carolina. We were taken out in amphibious personnel carriers and had to wade on to the beach while maintaining dry equipment and keeping a low profile. We were timed on how quickly we would make it to the beach and dig into the sand. A few times, the sergeant would shoot real bullets over our heads to give us a true sense of combat.

At the time, we had no idea why this beach activity had been added to our training. When we learned the reason, we were grateful.

So, there we were on the fifth of June 1944. Our officers had us sleep during the day. "Our mission begins at dark. Get some rest, men," we were told.

The commanders knew what lay ahead. They knew the difficulty of our mission. We were to take the beach. Omaha Beach. We were to "land, wade in, and dig in" as quickly as we could. Then we were to seek out enemy gun nests and destroy them.

Our commanders also had made an assessment on the number of men who would be killed in achieving this goal. They knew hundreds of men would die before they reached the beach. They knew many more would die climbing the cliffs to control the waterline. And they knew countless numbers would be wounded or killed as the Allied Forces made inroads into the heartland of the German Army.

We were awakened two hours before dusk. We were fed a full meal of steak—believe it or not—potatoes, and green beans with lots of bacon fat.

We were then briefed by our lieutenant.

"Men, tonight the Allied Armies are going to start the final assault on the Nazis. We are going to liberate France." These words shook through me like a strong shot of whiskey. Was the war getting that close? Liberate France. The news clips had been telling about Patton's successes, as well as the atrocities of the German Army on the French people.

The lieutenant continued. "Men, it will be extremely tough tonight. You will be transported by boat to within fifty yards of the Normandy beach. From there, you will wade in and dig in as quickly as you can. Our mission is to secure the beach and eventually scale the cliffs. Keep your eyes out for enemy gun nests; they are suspected in the area but not confirmed. If you see one, shoot to eliminate. Immediately.

"Men, your nation is grateful to you and your bravery. This is it. This is the beginning of the end for Hitler. God bless every one of you."

He saluted us.

We didn't know what he knew. Our odds were not good, with us being part of the first unit to reach the beach. But he knew that was the cost of winning the war. And in the scheme of things—of a nation's freedom; of the liberation of Europe; of a rich, free life for our future families, for the defeat of a deadly enemy.

It was a small price to pay.

Chapter 32

The White House

Several weeks had passed since President Osbourne, Chuck Harding, and Clarence Robinson met at Camp David. Soon after their predawn discussion about Operation Blueprint and the need to step up the war on drugs, the threesome returned to their fishing. However, Osbourne turned the words of the other two over in his mind during every idle moment.

Osbourne had promised Clarence he would do something about the drug situation. Operation Blueprint certainly represented the most extensive and creative program ever undertaken by the US government in its war against drugs.

But was it enough? Was it enough to win the war? Was it a solution? Or would everything return to the status quo, except with different players at the conclusion of the operation?

Osbourne also knew he could step up the other programs that were already in place. He knew more pressure could be placed on those little South American countries—but results would be limited. He knew he could place even greater pressure on the inner-city authorities to clear out the gangs—and whether effective or not, the additional federal monies would be welcomed at the municipal and state levels. He knew he could get any one of these programs and the appropriate budgets through the legislature in the name of "the War on Drugs."

But he also knew these things would not truly end the problem. He knew other avenues of commerce would open to meet America's demand for drugs.

Chuck Harding was right. Unless the hole in the door is fixed, the cold air will keep entering. And no matter how much money they spent on trying to stop the supply, the hole would always be there.

The real solution would be to cut the demand for illegal drugs. Osbourne knew programs were already in place to teach people *drugs could kill*. But he also knew the results of this strategy would be at least a generation away.

He needed to find a quicker way to dry up the demand for cocaine, heroin, crack, PCP, and other drugs. He was less interested in marijuana. In fact, he didn't see it as a bigger problem than alcohol. But, of course, he never said that to anyone, in fear his political career would implode with such a statement.

The question was simple: What would make the American public stop using these drugs? Not just the kids in the ghettos and slums, but all people—the bankers, the lawyers, the rich on Park Avenue, the suburbanites in the Midwest, the rural users in the South. Everyone. What could he do as president to get all people to simply stop?

What could he do to create a totally new war on drugs that would affect both the user and the seller? How could he get people to stop doing something they liked to do? *Wanted to do.*

This question had never been far from the president's mind since he and Clarence met. A real war on drugs—what would that be? What would it look like? What would make it different from the strategies already in place?

Then the solution hit him. It was the philosophical answer he had been seeking. It was right there in every news report, every newspaper, and every newscast. The chronicle of every war stressed one thing: Casualties.

A real war *has* casualties, both enemy and friendly. They are a real part of a real war. It was what his mother had feared most when he joined the army and shipped off to the European battlefield. A real war couldn't be won any other way. A real war cannot be won without such a risk. D-Day in World War II could have never been pulled off without the planning generals risking a sizable number of casualties. The first night of bombing on the Iraqi capital of Baghdad would have never been tried if the generals had not decided to risk man and machine.

How would this make a new war on drugs different? How would this affect the drug buyer, as well as the drug seller? Could there be casualties on both sides? Could the user, regardless of his or her social status, truly be considered just an innocent bystander—*or were they also a combatant?*

Could users of illegal drugs automatically be enlisted as participants in an actual war on drugs? Was their demand for drugs sufficient to pull them into combat? Was this the same as when the police battled the gangs and the big-time drug lords? Was it all right for these people to not only be arrested, but to also lose their life in this new war on drugs? *Could the harmless individuals who merely used the drugs financed by their own means be allowed to become casualties?*

These thoughts were chilling to Osbourne.

He contemplated pulling people, who heretofore were considered innocent, straight into the crossfire of the war on drugs—making all users the enemy too. They were enemy combatants because they chose to use the product. It didn't matter whether they were habitual or first-time users.

Osbourne's thoughts then solidified. The answer to the drug situation is to make it a life-or-death decision when one chooses to use drugs. It isn't the fear of being arrested or becoming hooked. *It's the fear of death—instantly—if you use cocaine or any other illegal drug.*

Osbourne knew this is the answer to the problem.

Now he faced the dilemma of whether to mention these thoughts to anyone—much less use the power of his office to implement a plan.

Chapter 33

Washington, D.C.

The crime scene was grisly but in a very different sort of way. For Officers McBee and Dugan, seeing dead gang members in the heart of D.C. wasn't anything new. They were constantly picking up the pieces after the gang fights over turf, buildings, and rights to specific street corners.

But this was different.

As they walked into the house on Steuben Street, they immediately knew something unusual had happened.

The house was a typical single-story bungalow with a sagging front porch. The front door opened into a large living room, with a couple of couches, a coffee table, and a few end tables with lamps. A large black flag hung on one wall with the word "Steuben" in block maroon letters. The dinette was off to the left, with a large door to the kitchen. Even though the D.C. weather had been warm, the windows were closed. The stench of body odor and stale beer permeated the air.

In the living room were five male gang members and three women. Six bodies were motionless on the floor, with another on the couch. One woman sat noticeably shivering and silent in the corner. Scattered around the floor were articles of clothing: halters, panties, T-shirts, jeans, skirts. None were ripped or tattered.

The furniture all upright. Nothing pushed over or broken. No signs of a fight or a struggle, no guns, no smell of gunpowder, and no blood. Just seven dead bodies.

On the cheap Formica dinette table sat a mound of white cocaine powder and several perfectly straight lines.

Quart bottles of Colt 45 sat on the tables next to the well-worn couch. Other empty bottles were scattered on the floor and the kitchen counter.

Dugan recognized a couple of the dead men. They were both well-established drug dealers in the area. Bosco was one, a muscular dude who had recently returned to the street after a stint in prison. Dugan couldn't remember the other's name. Gang members. Sons of Steuben crew members. The women were well-known hookers from the neighborhood.

Juanita, a hooker with bleached-blond hair, lay flat on her back on the floor near the couch, totally nude. Her long shapely black legs were spread, and a moist spot of semen and vaginal fluids pooled at the vertex of her legs beneath the dark hair of her pubic area. Directly to her side laid a lightly colored black male whom neither Dugan nor McBee knew or had seen before.

On the couch lay the second prostitute, known to the police as Gay. She was one of several white prostitutes who worked the predominantly black areas of Washington. On prior arrests, she said her business came from those who liked to "mix their color up." She and Juanita had probably been working as a team on the poor boy lying on the floor. Like Juanita, she, too, lay totally nude and seemed to have been engaged in sex just before expiring. At least, Dugan hoped it had been before she died. Not even these punks could be that sick.

A black woman with long strains of bright-red straightened hair sat shivering in the corner. Also unclothed, she had her legs pulled up into a fetal position, with her hair covering her knees. McBee surmised she had made the call to the police.

This was not a scene of violence, as so often the case. This had been a party—a fun, do drugs, drink, and screw-your-brains-out party. But these people were dead, just plain dead. Their faces indicated a peaceful death.

Dugan and McBee were used to walking into the aftermath of "parties" in this neighborhood. Usually, the radio in their car would crack with a message to investigate a house at such and such address. Bodies would be found on the premises.

Upon investigating these calls, McBee and Dugan would find themselves in the middle of a battle zone. The story was a particular crew would be having a party at some house when a visiting gang would arrive uninvited. The result was usually a house blown to bits with machine gun fire or an incendiary device. Or, if late at night, a few throats would have been slit while one slept.

This was not the case at all here. Sure, there were bodies, but there wasn't any violence.

McBee thought this was still some sort of gang-related "event." But what was it? What happened to all these people? A mass drug overdose wasn't the answer. It didn't fit. Yet these people were dead.

Approaching the redhead in the corner, "Miss, may we have a few words with you?" he asked. He had taken a blanket off one of the beds in the next room and draped it around her shoulders. Meanwhile, the police photographer was busy taking photos of the seven bodies and of the overall scene in the house. When he was finished, the fingerprint experts would dust the entire residence.

"Miss, what's your name?"

"Nicole," the redhead whispered. "Nicole."

"Nicole, were you the person who called us?"

"Yes. Err, yeah…yes."

"Nicole—"

"They all died. Everyone just died, like they were falling asleep. Juanita and Willie were fucking over there, and they just died." Nicole pointed to the couple lying next to each other on the couch. "Billy there just rolled over and died. They all just died. They all just died."

"When did this happen?" McBee asked, touching Nicole's arm. McBee knew these were the times when the most accurate assessment of the situation could be made. No lawyers, no crowds, no nothing to cause the witness to second guess her story. A little compassion would go a long way with this witness.

"We started partying around two this morning. Broke open a new wrapped kilo. Took a sliver from the top—you know, the prime stuff. This was a celebration with our first new shipment from Luther. Just as it was beginning to get light out, everyone started rolling over. Bosco there fell asleep first. We thought he was kidding us. Even the girl he was with thought so at first. Then she also fell back and fell asleep. Dead asleep. We thought it was a joke Bosco was playing on us. But soon everyone was rolling over. Asleep. At first, I tried mouth to mouth, but...they were all dead, all at the same time."

"What time did you call us?" Dugan asked, joining the questioning. He knew the call came in at 8:17, but he wanted to test the witness's sense of time.

"I don't know. I don't know. I freaked when I saw everyone dead. I tried to help one. Tried giving mouth to mouth, but there were too many to help. I tried..." Nicole buried her head into her knees and cried.

"Were they all using cocaine?" Dugan asked.

"Yeah, I think so, I think so," Nicole whispered, looking up into Dugan's eyes as if her honesty would somehow correct the evening's deadly events.

"Did you use any?" Dugan asked.

"No, I don't. I like to drink, but I don't use that fuckin' dope. I don't do no fuckin' dope."

McBee exchanged glances with Dugan. Any testimony received at the scene of the crime was usually weighted, and direct questions were seldom answered. In this case, the woman was freaked. Not the ordinary. This was beyond her comprehension.

Dugan and McBee left her alone as a policewoman took over and helped settle her before taking her to the station for additional questioning.

"What do you think?" Dugan asked McBee.

"She said everyone just died. Rolled over and died, like they were falling asleep. Damn, never had anything like this before. Everyone was having a party, and they just die. Strangest overdose I've ever seen."

"Too strange," Dugan replied. "Too strange."

* * *

Washington Post: Section B: Page 17
Five Gang Members Found Dead in Drug House
By Washington Post Staff Writer

Washington, D.C. (*Washington Post* News Service)—This morning, the police responded to a distress call from a house on Steuben Street in Washington. Upon arrival, they found the bodies of five known Washington, D.C., gang members and two known prostitutes. The dead were members of the Sons of Steuben crew, who use the residence as a drug house and base of their distribution enterprise. Names of the dead are being withheld until next of kin are notified.

Police officers on the scene report there was no apparent violence associated with the overdose deaths; however, they do not rule out gang-related reprisal from the rival crews.

Chapter 34

Washington, D.C.

The caller made two calls from the D.C. pay phone.
On the other end of the first call, the very private cell phone rang.

The man answered.
No words were spoken.
Just this old children's tune sung by a children's choir:

This old man, he played three,
He played knick-knack on my knee;
Knick-knack paddywhack,
Give a dog a bone,
This old man came rolling home.

This old man, he played five,
He played knick-knack on my hive;
Knick-knack paddywhack,
Give a dog a bone,
This old man came rolling home.

This old man, he played zero,
He played knick-knack for my hero
Knick-knack paddywhack,
Give a dog a bone,
This old man came rolling home.

This old man, he played zero,

He played knick-knack for my hero
Knick-knack paddywhack,
Give a dog a bone,
This old man came rolling home.

This old man,
He writes three
He writes five
He writes zero
He writes zero
He plays knick-knack for your wife and children.
Knick-knack, paddywhack,
Give the dogs a bone,
This old man is rolling home.

The second call was not picked up.
The caller left no voice mail.
He would try again later.

Chapter 35

The Washington Post Building

Emmett Washington settled into his "job" at the *Washington Post*. Geoffrey Wines was a fine mentor who truly appreciated Emmett's help in handling the never-ending stories crossing the Metro Desk. Geoff asked Emmett to run down many of the facts and even take a first cut of many of the minor articles Geoff needed to write.

Emmett also knew Geoff was particularly impressed with his background and family. How often would Geoff have direct access to a young black man who grew up in the tenements and still had family living there? He knew that in the back of Geoff's head was a story—an exposé—percolating.

"Geoff?" Emmett asked, looking across the top of the two computer monitors that sat back-to-back on Geoff's desk. Emmett's machine placed there at Geoff's insistence. He did not want to have Emmett in some cubbyhole down the hall, where they usually put the interns. He wanted Emmett right next to him where he could have him run down something on a moment's notice or ask for his insight on a particular manner.

For Geoff, having Emmett in his office was an education and an opportunity. Their backgrounds were so completely different, their perspectives on life were so unalike, and their experiences were so diverse that Geoff was sure he would learn more from Emmett than perhaps Emmett would learn from him. Emmett would get hands-on reporting experience and journalistic skills. Geoff would learn an entire culture.

It was a fair-enough exchange for a few months of sharing his small space and giving up a couple of square feet of desk space. Besides, the paper had agreed to run a second phone for Emmett to use. That phone would remain there even after Emmett's internship ended.

"Geoff?" Emmett asked again. He knew when Geoff was in the middle of a thought, he was deaf to the world. "Geoff, I've been thinking."

"Yeah, what about?" Geoff's thoughts were still on his screen.

"Those gang members and the girls that died in that gang house. You know—that story you had me cover for you last week."

"Yeah, what about them?"

"It just doesn't seem right. That was a well-established crack house. Been doing business for several months, almost a year. Rival gangs attack houses like that in the early months, not once they have been established. Pisses too many people off. And if they did attack it, they would have left their mark. Uh-huh, they need that macho thing."

This got Geoffrey's attention. Things out of the ordinary were usually the beginnings of a good story. That's why the death of a few gang members didn't raise his attention at all—and why he had sent Emmett to cover the story in the first place.

"Uh-huh." Emmett continued. "I was looking at the autopsy report on the dead. Just came through yesterday. Takes about ten days for gang deaths. No one is usually interested in the results. No insurance to be paid. No wills or the rest of that stuff."

"Yeah, so?" Geoff coaxed, beginning to get itchy. "Come on, Emmett, get to it."

"Well, uh, the report said they died of a drug overdose. Seven people don't just die of a drug overdose in one night at one party. Gang members know about overdosing. Sure, one will freak out and go nuts. But not an entire group."

Emmett had stood outside the house while the officers were looking over the scene. He hadn't heard what the sole survivor said to the cops, but it had been bad. Seven bodies without any marks of violence and with no rival gang calling card seemed strange.

"Maybe it was just some bad shit," Geoff said.

"I thought about that, too. On the street, maybe." Emmett smiled. He loved it when he got Geoff's attention, and he had thought about the same things Geoff asked. Maybe he was getting a nose for this business.

Emmett continued. "But bad shit in a crack house doesn't make sense either. Too early in the distribution channel. Bad shit happens when a dealer wants to stretch his take further than it should. Adds impure substances that are not detectable to the user until after they use it. But in a crack house, they will use the good stuff. In fact, they may not even cut what they have. Certainly not what they use."

"So, what do you think?" Geoff's full attention was now on Emmett.

"Uh, I don't know. Haven't gotten that far yet. Just doesn't seem right."

"Who were the cops?" Geoff asked.

"Dugan and McBee."

"Did they have anything to say about the scene?"

"No, they were pretty quiet. Said it was 'strange,' but they were sure it was gang related somehow."

Geoff knew the team of Dugan and McBee well. They were both good cops in the Narcotics and Gang Warfare Division. They certainly had seen their share of drug and gang violence. He also knew they were open to the press and would not try to cover up anything. *Maybe there really isn't anything*, he thought.

"Keep thinking about it, Emmett. Maybe there is something else there." Geoff wanted to keep Emmett encouraged, though he didn't think there was anything. If there was, then Dugan or McBee would have said something.

Emmett pondered, "Right. Maybe something else. What could that be?"

★ ★ ★

Geoff kept thinking about Emmett's concerns.

Maybe Emmett might be on to something. He wasn't wrong. Deaths without violence meant something killed the gang members and their girls. *But to get to the heart of the story meant getting to the reason for the deaths.*

This might be a long shot, but it might be worth pursuing. Perhaps he could convince his police buddies Dugan and McBee to share forensic information with him, such as a small sample of the crack house cocaine. What could he give them in return? Maybe a theory would be enough. But that would need to come later.

Geoff called and the phone was answered more promptly than he had anticipated. "McBee here."

"Officer McBee. Geoffrey Wines here." His voice was genuinely friendly. He had a great rapport with McBee; his partner, Dugan; and even their boss. It came from years of working the same beat, exposing the same bad guys, and mutual respect.

"Mr. Wines! What can I do for you? Haven't heard from you since the last mass killing of Steuben boys at Ashford Apartments. What? Two months ago? Not a lot of them left."

"Exactly right, my friend. I want to ask you about the crack house case. I believe my young reporter, Emmett Washington, was there. But maybe it sounds like I should have come, too. Seven deaths with no violence is indeed strange."

"What can I say? The force can't do a decent job, the kids have no respect for the law."

Geoff smiled. McBee was always interspersing musical lyrics into his banter.

"No, Geoff, it *really* was odd. Five bangers are dead. No overturned furniture or blood. No gang tags. And an awful lot of cocaine was left on the dining room table, nearly a kilo. As my grandpa used to say, 'Ain't going to see that very often.'"

"And one live buffer who described the scene," McBee continued. "And I just learned this morning—this is off the record—that the cocaine was spiked with some mysterious substance. Weird. Still trying to figure it out."

Keeping quiet, Geoff scribbled this information on his pad.

McBee continued. "Now, we don't know how to release this latest finding. This was certainly a new kilo, probably straight from one of the cartels. So, it wasn't going to have the usual street shit added to it. Our theory is it was somehow intercepted by another cartel or crew, fucked with, and then sent onto the Sons as retaliation."

"Retaliation?"

"Yes sir, that's what we're hearing from the street. It seems this house had been a Mendez house and then briefly switched over to Cali by their leader, Blanford Childress. Well, as you know, Blanford was killed earlier this spring at Ashford Apartments, and the old leader returned to the street from eighteen months in prison. Name is, or was, Bosco; he took over. And then, he was one of the poor bastards who snorted his last breath at the house last week."

"So why aren't you releasing your findings?

"War. Say it again. What is it good for? Absolutely nothing. All-out war. Gang and cartel warfare. This city would become a total war zone. They'd be flying fucking surplus Russian MIGs over Washington while fighting each other. Remember, Geoff, this is all off the record. I don't need to be reading this in tomorrow's *Post*."

"We're good, McBee. No issues at all."

"You know, Geoff, I often thought one strategy to win the war on drugs was to prod the cartels and gangs against each other and sit back and let them have at it. But seeing how this situation could unravel, I'm thinking we, too, are good."

Geoff let this sit for a few moments. McBee had probably told him more than he had intended.

"Hey, McBee. Do you think there is any way I could get a sample of the cocaine from the house? I promise you I won't use it. I hear it's way too potent."

"Whoa, Geoffrey, old buddy. Pushin' it a bit, aren't you?"

"Yeah. I know. I just have a gut feeling about this. I'm not sure where it will go. I promise you that neither the sample nor this conversation will ever see the light of day."

"Let me look into how I can help, old buddy."

Chapter 36

Washington, D.C.

When Chico answered the phone in his D.C. apartment, he heard Luther Gomez's voice, straightforward and non-emotional: "Luther here."

"Luther, my man. How you hang'n bro?" Chico was always glad to hear from his boss.

"What, you drinking too much espresso? Getting hyped up?" Luther asked sarcastically.

"Luther, man, what're you saying to me?" Chico was now serious.

"Man, I said to waste Bosco and the Steuben muscles after the September shipments, not the next fucking week."

"Shit, man. That wasn't me. Jesus as my witness. Not me. Not us. Shit, man, we had just delivered two keys to the house. Next thing we know, Bosco and his homeboys are fucking dead. Police and paper say it was an overdose. Fucking no way those dudes are overdosing."

"How then?"

"Luther, I don't know, man. Cali could have heard we were shipping to them again. The M+O crew might have fucked with the load. Fuck, I don't know. Ain't no one around to talk to, either. Everyone is fucking dead."

"Do we know who the runner was?"

"Neville and his runners handled it."

"Find out who touched the load and let me know."

"Will do, Luther. You got it."

Click.

Chapter 37

Dallas, Texas

The voice was muffled over the phone. The caller didn't offer a greeting. "Cam, did you see the blurb in the *Washington Post* on May 28? The deaths of the five gang members and their buffers?"

"Yes," Cam Maggard answered simply.

"Police reports state the witness saying it was like they all just fell asleep. What do you think?"

"Man, you should have seen them before they fell asleep. I bet they were humping like there was no tomorrow. They fell asleep because they were exhausted. This shit will kick in like a turbo jet and send these people on a ride like they have never had before. If it's pure, the results will be almost immediate. If the stuff has been cut several times, then it will take a while. But it will have the same effect: a racing heartbeat, high adrenalin flow, exhaustion, and then a sleepy death."

"Except I never treated their bricks," the caller said.

"This wasn't you, err, us?"

"Nope."

"Hmm, interesting. Who do you think—"

"Don't know. My money is on another gang."

"Should we operate our plan?" Cam asked.

"Don't know. Haven't used it in the field yet. But let's stay with it."

"Remember, don't let the stuff touch any skin on your body. And for God's sake, don't inhale any fumes, either. If it works OK, we'll roll with it."

"OK." Click. The phone call came to $1.75, paid in quarters from a pay phone in the American terminal of DFW International Airport.

Sometimes it would be in a burger bag, such as from McDonald's or Burger King. Other times it would be in a Fritos or Ruffles potato chip bag or a grocery bag. He never carried more than one drop at a time, and the locations always varied. He would deliver to a certain street corner only once or twice during a three-week period. This ensured he was not drawing any attention to himself by covering the same path and leaving something in the same area day after day.

Jacob, and all runners were instructed to make the drop, no matter what. He was never to dispose of the merchandise himself. This worked as a safeguard against a runner keeping the goods for himself while claiming he had to dispose of the goods because of the heat.

Quite often, Jacob was required to take the subway into other areas of town. He was given appropriate tokens to use for these deliveries because the organization did not want to risk losing the merchandise while some runner was busy digging into his pocket for the right amount of change or taking a chance in jumping over the turnstile and getting arrested. These entrenched procedures ensured no stupid stuff hindered deliveries or caused unnecessary arrests.

On occasion, Jacob was asked to make deliveries right to the plaza near the Capitol. He would place or pick up an old grocery sack with the merchandise next to a trash container near the entrance to the Vietnam Veterans Memorial, the Smithsonian National Air and Space Museum, or on the thirteenth step of the Lincoln Memorial.

★ ★ ★

In the evening, when Jacob and his brother, Emmett, met at home, they would often discuss what they had done that day.

Emmett was familiar with the way Jacob spent his afternoons. He knew his brother was working with drugs. He knew he would never be able to talk his brother out of the business. The money was just too good for a kid his age. And while he was a minor, the risk was minimal.

Chapter 38

Upstairs at the White House

A real war on drugs? President Osbourne again found himself pondering this and his experiences during World War II.

Toward the end of the war, after D-Day, the German Army began to retrench itself in the motherland. Allied Intelligence determined all the German troops had to pass through the Deutsche Reichsbahn railheads.

It was up to the US Army Air Corp to bomb these rails and clear the route for the advancing infantry, who would effectively cut off the German supply lines.

It was the middle of the last winter of the war. On the morning of the bombing run, freezing rain coated the wings, engines, and fuselage of the B-17 bombers. This coating of ice on the planes could not delay the mission. All morning long, the crews of the B-17 crawled over the twelve bombers in the squadron and chipped away the ice. The men had to be careful not to damage the planes' fragile skin.

Each plane was fully loaded with bombs, flak shields, fuel, crew, reaching the maximum weight designed by Boeing, the manufacturer.

It was time to begin the raid. The twelve planes were standing ready in taxi formation on the airport turf. Snow still fell. The mission still at hand.

The first plane rumbled to the head of the runway, and the pilot put the throttle forward as far as it would allow. The plane slowly began to increase its speed as it headed down the runway. The pilot took the plane to the end before rotating, thus allowing the broad wings to provide the lift necessary for the maximum payload.

The plane began to lift off the ground—hovering, not climbing. The engines and men strained with everything they had to coax the plane upward to 100, 150, and 200 feet.

Suddenly, the plane lost its lift and fell straight down, nose first. It burst into flames, leaving a large black spot about one quarter mile off the end of the runway. The weight of the payload and of the ice still on the wings was too much for the Grumman engines to handle. The men—unable to jump or parachute on such short notice and at such a low altitude—met a fiery death.

The second plane made it to the end of the runway. Given its position, only the pilot knew of the first plane's fate. After all, such things happened. He had been on twenty-five of his thirty allocated missions, and he knew the fate of war—his responsibility to follow the plan. Men's lives depended on it.

He placed the stops all the way forward, and the plane made for the distant end of the runway, slowly gathering speed into the wind. The plane rotated upward, leveling off at one hundred feet before also dropping to the ground, its fuel tanks exploding into a massive fireball.

The third plane rolled out. Its entire crew had witnessed the unsuccessful takeoffs of the first two planes, for they were on the turn with all side windows facing the far end of the runway. The men prayed to themselves as the captain pulled the plane into position. The orders blared over the radio to continue. Without the mission, many more American men would die in the fields surrounding the target. This was war. Men die during war, but the objective had to be met with success.

The captain radioed his commander for instructions.

"Go, go, go. We must meet our objective," was the emphatic answer.

The men braced themselves. In their hearts, they knew they would follow the fates of the first two planes. The payload, with the added weight of the ice yet to melt from the fuselage, would be too much for the engines.

They sat at the end of the runway. Unlike the captains of the first two planes, this captain fixed the brakes and revved the engines to full throttle. The plane shook from the vibration and bucked. Wind force succumbing to the mechanical constraints, not allowing the plane to move from its position for over a minute, yet violently vibrating everything and everybody on board. The men onboard glanced at each other, thinking about the ice outside and the unpredictable acid bombs inside.

As the plane threatened to fall apart, the captain yelled out a violent scream. "Let's go, honey! Give us all you have!" Each member of the crew joined in; if they screamed loud enough, perhaps the takeoff would be successful, and the plane would remain airborne.

The plane shook and rumbled down the runway, gaining speed from the standing start. The captain kept it on the ground until the very last inch of the runway and then hopped it off the earth's surface and yanked its wheels out from under it.

Ever so slowly, the plane rose into the sky. The lift of the wings overcame the forces of gravity. The men strained to see out their windows, seeing ice fly from the wings.

The plane rose one hundred, two hundred, and then three hundred feet. The blotches below them seemed to drift farther behind. At five hundred feet, the plane got a second wind and pulled itself free of the earth, exclaiming its victory with a sudden rev in its engines. The crew cheered. They would make it off the ground. They would make it off the ground. *They made it off the ground!*

The immediate danger was over. Soon, plane number four followed suit, vibrating the ice off its wings and successfully pulling itself into the sky. In fact, the last ten planes made it.

In a couple of hours, the elation of their miracle takeoff would be replaced with the terror of the close-in bombing run. The Germans would not freely accept their payload without first sending fire their way. Odds were that one-third of them would not make it back.

* * *

The last of the invincible German Army held on to what they firmly believed their birthright: the domination of Europe. The high

THE CAMP DAVID CONSPIRACY

command had convinced each soldier of his duty and privilege to serve the führer.

None, however, would have ever believed the strength the Allied Forces gathered each day. The US Army troops were all over Europe, and the easy days of the initial blitzkrieg successes were well behind. France was no longer theirs. The German soldiers were now fighting in the motherland. And they were fighting for their lives.

Yankee ingenuity had also taken on a new dimension. There was the immediate kill, and then there was the residual kill of their weapons. It wasn't enough that the railheads were destroyed as scores of B-17s dropped their bombs. But now the Allies were including acid bombs that would explode at any time, from an hour, a day to a week or two, after the bombs were dropped. No one knew when they would explode, not even the damned Yankees.

The acid bombs were an ingenious invention. The propeller firing pins usually attached to the front of the bombs were replaced with a vial of acid. When the bombs were released, the acid would eventually explode the bomb. Sometimes soon. Sometimes later. Acid bombs were a crapshoot.

The threat of these explosions made it a devastating mind game for the German soldiers enlisted to start repairs on the bombed railheads. The wreckage needed to be cleared and the rails rebuilt to begin resupplying their men on the front lines.

The acid bombs made this chore unexpectedly deadly. They would explode without anyone touching them. And they would explode when touched. Or they would not explode at all.

The acid bombs were no picnic for the Air Corps, either. The ground crews would place the bombs on the B-17s at the last moment before takeoff. They didn't want them around any longer than necessary, and the flight crews certainly weren't excited about their presence on the plane either. The damn things could go off at any minute. And they often did. No one knew when. That was part of the design—and part of the danger. Sure, the weapons engineers wanted to give them several hours or more of shelf life. But the controls were in the strength of the acid, its temperature, the amount of agitation, and countless other factors.

This scared the shit out of every B-17 crew, as well as the German troops assigned to remove the unexploded bombs from the railyards.

It was war. In a real war, there are casualties on both sides.

Chapter 39

Springfield, Missouri

"It's showtime. It's time to see if this thing really works. Tonight, I'm Bruce Willis playing DEA Agent Charles Harding," Chuck Harding said to himself as he readied for a typical drug-enforcement operation. *Well, almost a typical operation.*

One fact about a steady supply line is that it's predictable, with the same vehicles, same drivers, and same personal habits followed by those charged with moving drugs from Texas and California to the central parts of the United States. For the drug trade, moving merchandise through Saint Louis via I-44 provided an invaluable link.

Although there was no doubt the authorities were missing more than they were getting, the number of mules successfully interdicted on I-44 was good. In cooperation with the Missouri State Police and the DEA, several drug-laden autos were pulled over for routine traffic violations each week. By amazing coincidence, the drug-sniffing dogs would be with the officers and often picked up a scent, thereby giving the authorities enough suspicion to conduct a legal search.

Harding had set up the I-44 interdiction plan over five years ago, before being temporarily shifted out of the drug-enforcement area after the death of his family. Springfield, Missouri, was the perfect place for such a plan because of its location between Tulsa and Saint Louis, and the basic drive time from either California or Texas put it in the middle of the second or third day. "Good lax points for the mules, where they would be more apt to make a driving error. A legitimate reason to pull the car over," Harding had said in his recommendation. "Also, the southwest portion of Missouri is basically white, with few minorities. Blacks and Hispanics will stand out from the local traffic, making the spots easier to make."

It was nearing early evening. Harding knew his best odds of intercepting one of the mules was by stationing himself near the

Quality Inn at the intersection of I-44 and Business 44 in Springfield. This hotel seemed to be a favorite stop for many of the runners he had tracked over the years. The low room rates, free breakfast, and the proximity to an Asian massage parlor with benefits made the Quality Inn the choice stop for drug mules. Harding mused the hotel probably would not feature the last amenity on their welcome sign.

He waited in the parking lot, listening to the radio. Out of the corner of his eye, Harding spotted a Crown Vic pulling into the parking lot, with a pair of Hispanics in the front seat. It was a little past 7:00 p.m., about two hours before dark.

The car appeared to be relatively new, and the California license plates showed it was a long way from home. Hispanic occupants, late-model car with California tags—Harding thought they might as well have hung a neon sign saying, "Drug Runner."

The pair got out of their car. The driver had a dark round face, large dark-brown eyes and overweight. The passenger, smaller with dark darting eyes and jerky movements. Harding overheard them as he fidgeted with his car's rearview mirror.

"Yo, Victor, let's move on. I want to make it to Tokyo Blossom before this night is out," the larger man said to the smaller man.

"Yeah, Hugo, your fuckin' blow job, man. Don't you think about anything else? Blow job here, blow job there. Every place we fuckin' stop, you get a fuckin' blow job. I'll drive your ass there after we check in, but you ain't using the fuckin' car to get a blow job. That's all the fuck we need is for you to get your ass busted at some whorehouse and this whole business gets fucked up."

★ ★ ★

This one was going to be tough, Harding thought. He needed to keep from being detected by these men—and the local authorities since this interdiction would be outside the standard protocol.

He waited as the two checked in at the desk and then returned to their car. They pulled around the corner to the back of the third building and parked outside room 179—a typical MO. The first-floor room would allow them to keep an eye and ear open for any sounds that might indicate their vehicle was being tampered with.

Harding figured the stash would be in a false panel under their car's back seat. It wouldn't be particularly difficult to get to, but it would involve him being completely inside the car, with his head practically under the seat. If spotted, he would have virtually no means of escape. He had a way to provide an early warning against the owners of the car surprising him, but he did not have a way to protect him from any innocent passerby's or a hotel rent-a-cop.

★ ★ ★

Harding's plan would be to enter the car at 2:00 a.m. Most guests would be sound asleep, the late check-ins were done, and most rental cops were beginning to relax or perhaps catch a few winks. Harding figured it best to dress normally and have his DEA identification on him. That might give him an out if the unexpected happened.

From years of conducting stakeouts, Harding needed little sleep to make it through a twenty-four-hour operation. He would spend the rest of the evening checking out the surrounding area and taking down a few license plate numbers from other suspicious cars. He looked for California, Louisiana, Texas, Alabama, Florida, or Pennsylvania plates.

About a half hour after they checked in, Victor dropped Hugo off at Tokyo Blossom. He immediately returned to the motel after grabbing a sack of burgers from the Hardee's sharing the parking lot with the hotel. Through the crack in the curtain, Harding saw him undressing, as if getting ready to settle in for the night.

Guess Hugo's going to walk back tonight, Harding mused. He'll be back in about ninety minutes. About a half hour for the massage and BJ, and about a half hour to walk back to the hotel. He figured Hugo would also stop someplace and grab a bite to eat, using another thirty minutes. A Mexican restaurant and several Chinese takeouts were on the way.

Harding saw him return almost on schedule, walking with a spring in his step and a shit-eating grin. *Ah, nothing like the rewards of the road, eh, buddy?*

If all went according to plan, this shipment would travel to a connection point in East Saint Louis. There, the cocaine would either stay in the Saint Louis area or travel on up to Chicago via another set of drivers. Chances were good it would end up in Orland Park, outside Chicago, at a small dry cleaner's that would then distribute it to local dealers in the Chicago area.

All of this was run by the Mendez cartel.

After the dry cleaner's, the street business would be handled by the targeted multilevel selling organization the illegal-drug industry had fostered and grown. Major dealers would divide, sometimes cut, and sell the drugs to smaller dealers. These smaller dealers would then cut and sell the drugs to even smaller dealers or right to their final users. Some of the purer stuff would end up in the hands of prosperous and successful individuals, whereas the cheaper cuts and recuts would end up in the tenement housing projects or transformed into crack and sold to a growing and completely addicted audience.

This final user group, the addicted crack user, was the real problem Harding was having with his own plan. He would stop the demand of cocaine because he would scare the shit out of people not to use the drug—people with a choice. But the poor junkie crackheads on the street would still demand it. To them, there was no choice. They had to use it. A death scare would not slow them. If they used the drug after Harding treated it, they would be gone.

Harding justified this as just speeding up the inevitable. The growing use of crack had to be addressed, anyway. He might as well harvest this user group and keep new ones from entering the market. Besides, these were the ones who were directly responsible for the death of his family.

The thought of his family brought a lump to his throat. Peg his beautiful wife, had been a tall, slender woman with intelligence, spark of wit, and a beautiful smile. She had been the best wife a man could ever have. She had also been a wonderful mother to Chucky, age four, and Beth, age two...

He had been married all of six years before the murders. They were going to meet him at a restaurant outside the Washington, D.C., area. A safe area—a nice Italian place where the kids were welcomed. As Peg was getting Beth from the car seat, a gangbanger strung out on drugs approached her from the back and demanded money. As she backed out of the car and rose to her full height of nearly six feet, the kid panicked and shot her in the stomach. Immediately, the children started screaming, and he shot both to quell the noise.

Other people on the street witnessed the entire incident. After about a day, the gangbanger was caught, positively identified, later tried, and was now serving a life term in prison for the murder of Margaret "Peg" P. Harding, Charles S. Harding Jr., and Elizabeth P. Harding—the wife and children of Charles S. Harding of the Drug Enforcement Agency.

Harding would get his revenge.

★ ★ ★

The clock approached 2:00 a.m. The Quality Inn parking lot quiet. Harding had been keeping tabs on the rent-a-cop's movement, who made his rounds on the half hour. He had last come by at about 1:30 and soon would approach from the right side. He was on foot and walked only the first-floor corridor outside the rooms. He was unusually alert in watching the cars. On the past three rotations, he had been carrying a Styrofoam coffee cup. Apparently, he was diligent about his job. Most of the time, the cheap-rate rental cops were practically worthless, watching television or sitting in their cars with the radio blaring, nodding off to sleep. Harding knew he would have to be careful. This robo could be a problem.

The two mules were sound asleep in room 179. They had turned off the television at 11:30.

Silently, Harding exited his car. He had positioned it on the outside of the parking lot, facing the hotel and directly opposite room 179. The darkened windows gave him the privacy he needed during the lookout period. Now, he was flying on only guts and luck.

His biggest fear were the two mules waking up and checking their car while he was in it—facedown under the back seat—or with the bricks of cocaine spread out as he treated each with his solution.

In his hand, Harding carried the universal key set commonly used by used car dealers in repossessing autos. The trigger device would slip into the door lock, and with a few squeezes, a custom key was formed, allowing Harding to open the door without the slightest sound or damage to the locking mechanism. He wore a small earpiece hooked to a receiver in the back pocket of his dark coveralls. This receiver was on the same frequency as a small microphone he would attach to the doorframe of room 179. If the mules fidgeted with the security chain or turned the lock, Harding would hear it and have time to react. It would also pick up the footsteps of anyone walking down the outdoor corridor. In this case, it would let him know if the rent-a-cop made an unexpected round along the first-floor rooms.

Harding crept up the corridor, listening intently to every sound. His rubber-sole shoes were silent on the concrete walkway. As he passed by room 179, he stopped for a moment and stuck the highly sensitive mic to the upper portion of the doorjamb on the hinge side. This would be harder to see than on the other side. With a click of the switch on the receiver, he could hear his own movement through his earpiece. The system appeared to be working properly. There was no static. And because of the cooler weather, there was no damn hum of the room's air conditioner.

It was now time to go to work.

With a few clicks of the universal key, he had the driver's door open. He reached over the seat and unlocked the back door. Then, he relocked the driver's door and pushed it until it latched.

Next, he crawled into the back seat. *Thank goodness these boys are using a larger American car. This would be a real bitch in a small car*, he thought as he folded his six-foot-two frame on the floor of the back seat and pulled the door closed until he heard it latching, both through the earpiece and through his open ear.

He lay on the floor while waiting to see if there was any outside reaction to the door latching. It also gave his eyes time to adjust to the ambient light from the parking lot and walkway illuminating the back seat. This was both good news and bad news. The good news was he would not have to fool with a light that could be seen from outside the car. The bad news was if there were enough light for him to do his job, then someone outside the car could probably see him inside.

With his hand, he felt around the lip of the seat where it met the floor. There he found a small latch. He felt to see if there was any sort of seal. Often, the newer runners would have their merchandise sealed to discourage any tampering. If the seal was broken when the runners got to their destination, there would be big trouble. In other DEA interceptions, no one cared whether the runners got in trouble or not. That was their tough luck. But on Operation Blueprint, the idea was not to raise any suspicion that could result in any of the cartel operatives or dealers examining their merchandise more closely than usual. The *same concept applied tonight—for Operation Chuck.*

There wasn't a seal. In fact, this latch was fairly worn. This car had made a few deliveries. *Trusted mules. Now that's an oxymoron.* This would make slipping the seat out of position a little easier. New shippers were tough because the spacing hadn't broken in yet. No problem on this car.

Harding rose to his knees, with his feet forced under the front seat. With a firm jerk, he lifted the seat from its locked position, raising it parallel to the back of the seat. In the dim light, he could see the outline of a seam in the felt under the seat. He lifted the felt, revealing the false-compartment door.

Just as he started to lift the false door, he froze. Through his earpiece, he could hear footsteps on the walkway outside the car. The footsteps stopped. Harding bent over the back seat, forcing himself below the line of sight. This was a dangerous position to be in. He couldn't move with his feet under the front seat, and he couldn't see out, either. He could hear his heart pounding in his chest. Unfortunately, he could not tell the direction of the footsteps.

Slowly, Harding rotated his feet out from under the front seat, allowing himself to be more in a sideways position so he could peer over the front seat and out the driver's side windows. It would also give him mobility if he needed to exit the car.

The rent-a-cop stood just three cars down on the left side. *Hmm, the robo reversed direction.* He shined his flashlight into the back seat of a car. Harding could see the light through the windows of the adjacent cars and the brownish color of the man's form in the sodium parking lot light. Harding sank again below the line of sight. He could not allow himself to be seen in this car. Even though he had his DEA identification in his pocket, the questioning would be too much. Robo would go all out to tell everyone he had outsmarted a Fed.

After a few seconds, robo returned to the walkway and Chuck could hear his footsteps again through the earpiece. They were getting closer to the mic on the door of room 179—and this car.

Then, the steps stopped again.

What the fuck is this guy looking for? Harding started sweating profusely through his coveralls. He counted; this would keep him from exaggerating in his own mind how long the rent-a-cop stood there. After a ten count, the steps resumed and trailed off around the corner.

Harding breathed deeply, concentrating on collecting his composure and continuing his mission. He started counting again, taking a deep breath with each count. By the time he reached seven, his nerves were intact, and he pulled the first trap door open.

★ ★ ★

There in front of him in the secret compartment lay twenty-five kilo bricks of cocaine, each wrapped in a clear cellophane wrap. This was an exceptionally big load. Twenty-five thousand one-gram portions of pure cartel-quality cocaine. At $100 to $150 per gram, they had a value of well over $2,500,000—maybe closer to $3 million. *Trusted mules, indeed.*

Each block had a logo sticker indicating to the receiver this was high quality cartel cocaine. Even though the stickers were not trademarked signatures for each cartel, knowledgeable buyers knew who manufactured the contents. Just like seeing Joe Camel or Tony the Tiger. *Damn cartels are so brash, they even sticker their own illegal products. Let's see what they think about this shipment in a few weeks. It will drive them crazy!*

Harding planned to treat five kilos on this stop. Five would have an incredible effect with the treatment he was about to give. If this had been cut in the usual manner, it would result in about thirty thousand to forty thousand street doses. This could afflict about five thousand to ten thousand people. *Maybe too many*, he thought. *Especially for the first time out of the block. Maybe I should only treat two kilos on this run.*

He lifted one of the blocks out of the compartment—a perfect white brick about six inches by two inches by three inches—nearly the size of a construction brick. It was wrapped in much the same manner as a Christmas gift, with the ends double-flapped and gusseted against the sides. A small piece of adhesive held each flap down.

Harding reached into his coveralls and pulled out a small roll of tape, exactly like the tape holding the sides of the brick. He laid this on the floor beside him. He then reached into his other pocket and pulled out a small black plastic drop cloth about nine inches by twelve inches. The same black plastic homeowners would use in the crawl space to keep the moisture level down. Harding found the heavy plastic made an excellent work surface for the treatment of the cocaine—either the FBI's Blueprint *or the Maggard-Harding treatment.* The black surface would allow him to see any fall-off from the bricks he was treating; and determine whether he had to add it back to the brick or simply dispose of it.

He spread the black plastic over the top of the other bricks and opened the first one he had set aside. His surgical gloves were still intact, even after feeling around under the seat for the latch and pulling the seat forward. No need to change them.

He unwrapped one end of the brick, opening only the end surface. He did not disturb the logo sticker. This would be a sufficient opening to treat the entire brick. The pungent smell of ammonia sprang from the cocaine as he exposed the substance to the air. The first whiff knocked him back from his hunched-over position.

With the edge of the brick exposed, he reached into his pocket to pull out the vial prepared by Cam Maggard. Instead, he accidently grabbed one of the FBI-prepared syringes.

He had applied Operation Blueprint over fifty times in the past two weeks. Its application was simple.

However, Cam's potion would be more difficult. To apply, Harding needed to open the edge of the brick and pour the contents on the top edge. He would then need to wait about sixty seconds before rewrapping the cocaine in the cellophane. The liquid had a super-quick evaporation factor because it reacted immediately with the cocaine to form a substance that was incredibly lethal and virtually undetectable to the user—except for the extra buzz it would give before the user passed out and died. And because of its potency, Cam had warned him to wear gloves and not breathe the fumes.

Better not use Cam's. The car already seems stuffy.

He folded the end gusset back in place, retaped it, and then inserted the FBI Blueprint needle. *Easy, breezy.*

Harding examined the syringe number: CEO-3500.

Wasn't that the same code on an earlier syringe?

Per Operation Blueprint protocol, he would keep careful track of the numbering sequence. He always listed the exact location and time; and a photo of the area, the car, and any legal documents to provide an evidence stream for building the Operation Blueprint case. This included license plates, any mail, or any other items that would show possession. In many cases, he would also stay around and take a photo of the person or persons who eventually picked up the drugs. All this immediately sent into the FBI, where the data would be compiled and cataloged.

Suddenly, a sound in his earpiece about ripped his head off.

The mic on room 179 picked up the rattling of the safety chain being slid out of the slot and the loud click of the security bolt.

For a brief second, Harding froze. He would be OK. Then he realized he had not placed the restraining cable on the door. In many interceptions like these, he would literally chain the runners in their own room with a cable that would lasso on the doorknob and the doorjamb. Although the runners in the room would know they were being messed with, it would be virtually impossible for them to flee, thus giving the Fed plenty of time to escape.

But in this case, Harding had opted not to use the cable. It could be visible from the outside, and the rent-a-cop was much too active for Harding to take this chance. *One right decision and one wrong decision. I need to improve my odds.*

Harding knew he was in a jam. He was undercover in a top-secret operation where he was also under deeper cover with his and the president's own operation. But he had to avoid this turning into a bust, especially with *Cam's BP-D in his pocket.*

Just as he heard the turn of the doorknob, he reached inside his coveralls and pulled out his Glock. He could now hear the door open and the hoarse breathing of one of the mules.

Harding shifted back into the sideways position. He could not let his 210 pounds shift or bounce the car, but he could also not allow himself to be pinned down facing the back of the car with his damn feet under the front seat. He would be too easy a mark.

He switched his gun's safety off. If need be, he would shoot the bastard and get the hell out of there. *Just another drug-related murder.*

Harding moved his eyes just above the seat level, careful to keep his line of sight even with the obtrusion of the rearview mirror. *If I can't see them, they can't see me.* He could not see the face but recognized the obese body of the larger man, Hugo. *Hopefully, the little one is still sleeping.*

"What the hell are you up to, Hugo my friend?" Harding mouthed to himself. "Checking out the load or just getting a little exercise? How 'bout some jumping jacks or something to get your fat, ugly, blow jobbed body in shape for prison?"

Hugo stood directly in front of the car, facing out over the parking lot. Harding still could not see his face, but his body was clearly facing over the roof of the car. Through his earpiece, Harding could hear Hugo's heavy breathing and piercing smoker's cough.

Harding watched over the seat as Hugo stretched up on his tiptoes. Up. Down. Up. Down. Each time Hugo landed on his heels, his bulging stomach shook under his tightly stretched T-shirt. Almost comical seeing just the fat midsection of the man moving up and down through the front window's narrow line of sight.

"C'mon, fat ass, move it. Move it!"

Harding shifted slightly. His legs were killing him. He was much too tall to be crammed in the back seat of this car. And Hugo was merely hanging out, with no reason for him to go anywhere. Harding glanced down, saw exactly where his legs and feet were, and tried to get a better handle on the positioning of his gun.

The car bounced.

Harding caught the bile of his gut forming in his mouth. He instantly froze, afraid Hugo would notice any movement. Harding dared not move a muscle, even his eyes, though he knew better than to think his eye movement would have any effect. He forced himself to look back out the front window, straining his eyes downward because his face was looking upward.

Son of a bitch. Harding gasped quietly. The muscles in his face slackened. The fat ass was sitting on the front of the hood, facing his motel room door. And nothing but *butt crack* was as far as the eye could see.

Harding almost lost it. Here he was on one of the most important missions of his life. Two missions, really. And here he was pinned in the back seat of the car of some Mexican drug runner who decided to spend the early hours of the morning displaying *his* moon over Springfield.

"How long are you going to stay there, Hugo? How long? Maybe rent-a-cop will come by and chase you back into your room." *Isn't it just like a cop to never be around when you most need him?*

Harding settled into a more relaxed position, though he was careful not to shift his weight. Hugo, right on the hood of the car, would feel any movement.

Through the earpiece, Harding could hear Hugo's breathing. He mumbled something to himself about "being back through Springfield the following day and perhaps another trip to the massage parlor."

Finally, Hugo lifted himself from the car. A moment later, the same sharp sound of the chain and bolt erupted in Harding's earpiece. This time, the sound was welcome. Hugo had left the hood and now locked safely inside his room.

Harding returned to his work. He left the other bricks alone. Between the insomniac Hugo and the rent-a-cop, he wasn't going to chance staying in the car any longer.

The BP-D operation would start slower than planned, maybe at the next stop. There's time. The operation was just a few weeks old.

Originally, he'd been thinking of starting with a major splash by treating several kilos of coke with Cam's formula and sending them on their way. By the time the drugs would be broken down on the street, he figured a couple of thousand users would be terminated. That would almost instantly put a scare into the drug using community. *He would do that, just not tonight.*

Harding placed the single treated brick and the others back into the hidden compartment and slid the seat back into position.

Like a gopher, he stretched his neck above the window line to see if the coast was clear. He didn't see anyone in all four directions, and there wasn't a sound coming through his earpiece.

He figured he had better get the hell out of Dodge.

Cautiously, he opened the door, crawled out, and closed it with only the slightest sound. He grabbed the microphone off the room door and retreated from the hotel parking lot without taking photos. Soon, the rent-a-cop would be around, and only God knew what Hugo would be up to.

Harding would record CEO-3500 in the log and send the empty syringe back to the FBI. However, there would be no accompanying photos or evidence.

Chapter 40

Saint Louis

St. Louis Post-Dispatch: Metro Section: Page 2
Ten Die in Cocaine Overdoses This Past Weekend

St. Louis, Missouri (AP)—The East Saint Louis Police Dept reported a sudden surge in cocaine-related overdoses over the past weekend.

A spokesman for department reported a total of ten overdose deaths, all occurring in East Saint Louis, Sauget, and Belleville, IL.

"This time of year, illegal-drug usage climbs as summer approaches. However, we have never had a concentration of overdose deaths, such as these, in such a short period of time," said the spokesman.

Confounding police is the fact that these deaths appeared in separate areas of the Saint Louis eastern suburbs. Five deaths were recorded in the inner-city portion of East Saint Louis, three near the casino in Sauget, and two in the more affluent suburb of Belleville.

Police suspect the cocaine may have been laced with some form of barbiturate used to cut the cocaine. Federal authorities are also checking into the possibility of gang sabotage.

"Something widespread would indicate a problem with the initial shipment from the cartel, as multiple distributors and dealers would have distributed the drugs to the users," the spokesman explained.

Names are being withheld until the police complete their initial investigation.

Chapter 41

Location Unknown

The caller again tried to get through to the person. This time, the government-issued cell phone was answered.

The caller once again played this musical message and hung-up:

This old man, he played three,
He played knick-knack on my knee;
Knick-knack paddywhack,
Give a dog a bone,
This old man came rolling home.

This old man, he played five,
He played knick-knack on my hive;
Knick-knack paddywhack,
Give a dog a bone,
This old man came rolling home.

This old man, he played zero,
He played knick-knack for my hero
Knick-knack paddywhack,
Give a dog a bone,
This old man came rolling home.

This old man, he played zero,
He played knick-knack for my hero

Knick-knack paddywhack,
Give a dog a bone,
This old man came rolling home.

This old man,
He writes three
He writes five
He writes zero
He writes zero
He plays knick-knack for your wife and children.
Knick-knack, paddywhack,
Give the dogs a bone,
This old man is rolling home.

Chapter 42

Georgetown, D.C.

Gertrude Washington unlocked the back door to Howard Washer's home at 7:15 a.m., exactly as she had done for nearly twenty years. She headed through the mudroom and kitchen pantry into the large kitchen.

A note was on the counter, as there was every day:

Good morning, Gertrude. Hope you had a nice train ride in this morning. Please prepare eggs, fried, sunny side up; crisp bacon; rye bread toast; coffee; and a double orange juice for me this morning. I will be down at 8:00 a.m. Thank you, Gertrude. ~ Howard Washer

Though each day's note was similar, she felt appreciated because of the nice salutations and thank-you at the end. Mr. Washer didn't have to do this. He could just write down his breakfast preference. But he had never been that type of boss. He always seemed to appreciate her and the work she did for him.

"God bless you, Mr. Washer." Gertrude always said this after reading his notes. "God bless you."

She pulled the eggs and bacon from the refrigerator and the bakery rye bread from the freezer. She placed the bacon in a frying pan and turned the gas on medium. She would turn it up right before placing the bacon on the plate so it would be crisp and sizzling hot. Her husband had taught her this trick.

She grabbed four fresh oranges from the bowl on the counter, sliced them in half, and used the hand squeezer to extract the juice without any of the rind. Then she placed the juice in the freezer so it would be thoroughly chilled.

"He must be running a bit late," she said to herself, noting she had not heard the alarm go off, footsteps into his bathroom, or the toilet flushing.

The clock read 7:45, and still no sounds from upstairs. The coffee brewed. The juice chilled. The bacon cooking on the stove. Gertrude wouldn't start the eggs and toast until she had given him the morning paper and coffee.

She headed down the short hall toward Mr. Washer's study. *Strange, the door's shut.* She could faintly hear the CD player through the thick door.

She tapped on it, thinking Mr. Washer had gotten up early to do a little work before breakfast.

No answer.

She tapped again, slightly louder. He might have fallen asleep on the couch. He had never done that, but she had not heard his steps.

Still, no answer.

She pushed the door open and stuck her head into the study.

"Mr. Washer?" she whispered.

As she looked around the room from the doorway, she jumped and let out a short gasp. Mr. Washer lay sprawled out on the couch. She was right, she thought; he must have fallen asleep and spent the night there.

She then noticed he was exceptionally still—and his face a pale gray.

"Oh Lord" she shouted, realizing her boss was dead. "Lord, help me and Mr. Washer. Please. Please. Don't let this be."

Her first thought was that he had a heart attack while relaxing in his study. Then she noticed on the glass-top coffee table a single white line of cocaine and the crumbs left from another.

"Oh Lord." Her mind raced. "What should I do?" *He's dead. A heart attack? Did he overdose?* She knew she had to call 9-1-1. She would, but not yet.

"Nobody is going to see Mr. Washer dead in his study with cocaine on his coffee table. This good man deserves more than this," she pleaded to herself.

Gertrude ran into the kitchen and grabbed a Ziplock sandwich bag and a rubber spatula. She ran back into study and used the spatula to carefully move all the cocaine into the plastic bag, ensuring nothing was on its outside. She then ran back into the kitchen, double-wrapped the bag in aluminum foil, crimped the edges tight, and placed it into her purse.

"No sir. No sir. Nobody is going to see Mr. Washer with cocaine."

She then grabbed a bottle of Glass*Plus from the utility closet and two large sheets of paper towel from the roll under the cabinet.

She raced back into the den and cleaned the glass-top table, checking it from every angle to ensure not one speck of anything remained on the surface. She did not see a razor blade or a straw of any sort. She also examined Mr. Washer's face for any signs of cocaine, being careful not to touch him.

She then ran into the small bathroom off the kitchen and flushed the paper towel sheets down the toilet, waiting long enough to give it a second flush.

It was now 7:58 a.m., and she called 9-1-1.

She also called Maggie Miller, Mr. Washer's secretary, and left a message on her phone for her to call the house as soon as possible.

As Gertrude thought about Mr. Washer's kindness over the years to her and her family, she started to cry.

Soon the police would arrive.

Chapter 43

Chicago, Illinois

The results from the fingerprints lifted from the ashtray the blond yuppie had touched came back much faster than expected.

Well, kind of.

DEA Agent Chuck Harding had a match. And the results were fresh and active. Apparently, the match was from the murder scene recovered by the Chicago Police Department last March. They were the prints of the suspected "junkie" killer of a young advertising executive on Lower Wacker. Police were actively seeking any information connected to the crime.

The prints yielded no name, just "John Doe." Yet Harding instantly remembered from the bar his name was "Dwight" but no last name. And apparently this blond hot shot dealer was also the murderer of Eric Robinson, Clarence Robinson's son—President Osbourne's best friend.

When the FBI asked where he had lifted the prints, he fudged by telling them "from the Tango Bar on the South Side." The DEA knew the Tango was a spot with considerable illegal-drug activity. Harding did not want the FBI to be screwing around with his latest target working the carriage trade. *Harding might have other plans.*

Because no name or address was available, Harding decided to follow the young man. It wasn't hard. He could either wait at Emil's Cleaners and tail the BMW or hang out at one of the Rush Street bars until he showed up.

"This kid certainly is not trying to hide his tracks," Chuck recounted to himself. "He drives his own car to and from Emil's. He parks it near the bars where he conducts drug deals. His only precaution is there are no plates on the car, and he keeps a restaurant menu over the windshield's VIN."

Harding decided to nab him the old-fashioned way. He followed his car from Rush Street to a Bucktown three-plus-one building. From there, he waited outside and watched as lights went on in apartments. And being a lucky DEA agent, he actually saw Dwight close the drapes on the east-end apartment on the second floor.

Given Dwight's schedule, Harding figured this would be a short stop, probably to load up more merchandise and hit another yuppie hot spot in the Near North Side.

"Mission Control," he said out loud, speaking into an imaginary microphone. "This is Agent Charles Harding. Stand by for apartment insertion." He patiently waited in his car, fooling with his CD collection, and checking the clock on his dashboard.

Soon enough, Dwight pulled his BMW into the street and headed west toward Clark. This left a parking spot in the garage. Harding would take it. Finding one on the street would be a bitch. Plus, the garage had fewer eyes, and if any of the residents saw him, he would look like any other tenant in this integrated neighborhood.

Harding grabbed his small bag with the Operation Blueprint vials, key chain, and driving gloves. Getting through the main door was a cinch as he headed to the second floor using the steps.

At Dwight's apartment, number 2-G, he shuffled to the pick on his key chain. Within ten seconds, he jiggled the lock and entered the apartment.

It looked newly remodeled with a brand-new white leather sofa, glass-top dining table, white throw rugs, and a new large screen Sony TV sitting inside an entertainment center that covered the entire wall.

The bedroom had a king-size bed and again white-finished furniture.

The bathroom had a large walk-in shower. Harding thought it odd to see a TV table and plastic chair pushed against the tile inside the shower. On the wall length vanity sat a roll of Saran Wrap, a stack of pre-made plastic pouches, and a gram scale. All items expected, *but in a strange location.*

The dining room table also appeared odd, with a stack of the current month's *Cosmopolitan* and *Playboy* magazines—all brand new—along with a cutting board, a razor knife, a steel straightedge, and a stack of plastic CD cases.

Harding started to search the apartment for drugs. He found none in any of the cabinets nor drawers. He then searched the couch cushions. Still, nothing.

Then . . . Chuck heard a key inserted into the front-door lock, and the door swung open. Dwight suddenly stood there facing him.

Neither said anything.

Harding reached for his service revolver but did not pull it as Dwight lifted his hands even with his head.

"Hey, man, take whatever you want and leave."

Harding was about to complete the world's first DRUG UNBUST.

Calmly, he moved toward the kid. "We're good. I just want to talk with you a bit. Seems we might have a deal we can put together."

Dwight froze with his hands up, not moving a muscle and keeping his eyes on Harding's every movement.

Harding stepped behind him and closed the door.

Kid probably thinks I'm with one of the cartels or the distributor that owns this street. Harding let him sweat a bit in his thoughts.

After about ten seconds, Harding motioned Dwight to sit on the plush white sofa while turning one of the dining room chairs around. The sofa would make it hard for Dwight to make any sudden aggressive moves, and the dining room chair gave Harding higher ground. He waited another twenty seconds before saying anything. Dwight never shifted his gaze away from him.

Harding flashed a toothy smile. "I know an awful lot about you, man. I know you take your laundry to Emil's Cleaners in Orland Park. I know you hang out at several Near North bars and seem to have a bladder problem because you head into the restroom more often than anyone I know your age. And I know from a positive fingerprint match that you were at the scene of a murder last March on Lower Wacker."

He made sure he did not accuse Dwight of anything—mentioning only circumstances to ensure he understood Harding knew what the kid was up to.

"Now, here's the funny thing, man." Harding continued with a knowing smile. "I know all of this about you, yet I do not know your last name."

Harding could see the wheels turning in Dwight's head as he maintained his gaze on Dwight's face. "And what *that* means is that the company I work for also does not know your name; have your identity; or know where you live."

Harding paused again, giving Dwight a chance to think about his situation. He then broke the silence. "Your name *is* Dwight. Right?"

"Dwight. Dwight Jones" the blond man replied, still looking Chuck straight in the eye. "And I sell cocaine. I'm a pusher, a dealer. But I'm not a junkie. Not anymore." Dwight said quietly as his head drooped lower to his chest.

"Well, Dwight Jones, cocaine pusher, drug dealer, former junkie. Good to meet you. My name is Chuck. And I am a DEA agent."

Dwight looked back up and directly into his eyes, bewildered.

Harding thought he heard him say "thank God" under his breath.

"Yupper. Today is *your* lucky day. Because today and today only, this DEA agent is willing to let you continue doing what you have been doing. But with one small catch."

Dwight's eyes narrowed.

Harding continued. "Show me what you do. You're new to this, and from my observation, you use a few tricks that we have not seen before."

He rose from his dining room chair and walked into the kitchen. "Any beer, Dwight?"

"Cold Miller Lite in the fridge."

Harding grabbed one can from the fridge and tossed it to Dwight, who caught it with his right hand. Harding noted the reflex and returned to his seat.

"OK, Dwight. I know from video footage that you're fairly popular in your business. Move some stuff. A lot more than just selling one person to another. Seems you supply other dealers, too. And given this place, I would say you're burning through some cash, too."

Dwight grinned at this last statement. He then laid his head back on the couch, looked straight at the ceiling . . . and laughed.

* * *

"You want to hear how I got here and what I've been doing? And in return, you and the DEA will not interfere with my dealings, and the Chicago Police Department will not learn of my identity?"

"That's the deal."

Dwight shook his head and laughed again. "All righty, then. Where to begin?" He pictured the Monopoly man rounding Start and getting $200 and a Get Out of Jail Free card. *Unbelievable*, he thought.

He told Harding of his success trading stocks while in high school and college and about his trawling days at the University of Michigan, including the night he and Bruce Zimmer met two coeds from Florida: Holly Hagen, a sexy drug-loving redhead, and Anita Mendez, a beautiful Colombian.

He continued telling about his success at Seaton and Earnst, his yuppie lifestyle, and his incredible Lincoln Park apartment overlooking the zoo. He also detailed his decline into using drugs, his loss of his girlfriend, and his need to sell all his possessions. That led to the night he tried to rob a young man on Lower Wacker and, in his drug-induced panic, thrust a knife into the man's rib cage. He told Harding that when he saw the blood dripping from the knife, he permanently quit using any sort of drugs. Light beer was his only personal vice.

And then with the pride of any true entrepreneur, he explained how he saw a niche in the "carriage trade" of drug dealing; how he made it easy for folks like him to buy cocaine without visiting the wrong side of town; and how certain customers could create a significant business of their own.

Harding listened intently and interrupted him only one time during his monologue.

"Dwight, do you know how lucky you are that you did not bonk that Anita Mendez back in Michigan?"

He stopped, gave Chuck a puzzled look and asked, "Huh? You know her?"

"Yessiree," Harding answered with a broad smile. "That Anita Mendez is none other than the daughter of Juan Pablo Mendez, leader of the Mendez cartel out of Colombia. You're selling his shit. And I know for a fact that a few boys like you have been erased for trying to manhandle his daughter. You must have been a perfect gentleman."

Smiling, Dwight told Harding about the warning Holly had given him not to be aggressive. "She's a devout Catholic, or so she said. She's from a strict family." *Not a word about any cartel assassins.* "Wow!"

Chuck then turned serious. "Now continue. Tell me about how you do business today."

"Well, I pick up all my stuff from Emil's Cleaners. But you know that. Usually a whole brick. Uncut. And I never cut it myself. I give my customers only pure stuff, straight from the cartels. No ghetto cut shit. Pure. Clean. Safe. Prime. I do all the portioning, repacking, and sealing here in the apartment. Inside the shower. Butt naked. Then I rinse any residual spill down the drain."

"That explains the plastic chair and TV table in the shower." Harding grinned. "Makes me feel better. I thought maybe you were a pervert or something."

Dwight then stood and walked over to the dining room table where Harding sat. "Here's my incredible invention for distributing significant quantities in plain sight." Harding did not move, but he did prepare himself for any aggressive move on Dwight's part.

"*Cosmo,*" Dwight said proudly. "Beautiful women and cleavage on the cover. Big, thick, perfumy ads on the inside. *Cosmopolitan* magazine. I can mail it. I can Federal Express it. I can hand it off in public. I can leave it sitting on a reception room table or on a bar seat. I portion, wrap, and seal the cocaine. Then I hollow out the inside of a *Cosmo* and fill the cavity with the cocaine packet. Lord knows they are almost thick as a brick. Then I rewrap the magazine in its plastic cover. And all the perfume-scent samples make it virtually impossible for a dog to pick up any scent of the cocaine. Plus, I have my own special low-oxygen transfer wrap, so not even a drug dog can pick up the scent through my added package. And did I mention that each package is double washed by a nude white guy in his very own shower?"

Harding laughed. "Fucking crazy. Fucking crazy ingenious. No wonder you have so much cash to burn. And you've separated the money from the drugs."

But he was thinking Operation Blueprint would negate this advantage. And some Blueprinting before Emil's and again here at the apartment would light up this pathway to other dealers and users.

"Thanks, Dwight. I think I'll leave now and give you back your parking space."

"Anything else?" Dwight sounded confused, considering how quickly this encounter had come to an end.

"Oh, yes, one more thing," Harding answered, nonchalant. "Where do you keep your stuff? I might need to see it, and I sure don't want to have to toss this place looking for it."

"Bricks. They're holding my bedroom door open. Rewrapped and sealed in my own film in case someone decides to inspect my apartment. Packages ready for distribution? Sitting on my coffee table with all the other magazines."

Harding smiled. Nothing was more hidden than something in plain sight. Even he had missed the stash by looking in the usual hiding places.

"Thanks. Nothing more—for now, anyway. Keep on doing what you're doing." Harding headed out of the apartment.

I have other plans for you, he thought.

Chapter 44

Washington D.C.

The five overdoses at the gang crack house continued to gnaw at Emmett Washington. And now Mr. Washer had also overdosed, or so the police autopsy reported. Geoffrey Wines had asked Emmett to write up the story for the Metro Section of the paper.

Funny thing, though—Emmett's mother had never mentioned the drugs when she came home early that day and told him and Jacob about her finding Mr. Washer dead. In fact, she had never said or even hinted her boss had a drug problem.

She had said she thought it was a heart attack. So sad. Mr. Washer had been an unusually kind man who certainly had made a huge difference in Emmett's life. He loved Mr. Washer's study and the hours he, Emmett, had spent looking at the books, listening to the music, and playing with the games while his mother kept house and cooked for the man.

And now Emmett had to write the *Washington Post* story about Mr. Washer's death due to an overdose of cocaine. It wasn't fair. But he had completed it like an objective reporter should.

"Geoff," he said as he handed over the text of the article on yellow *Washington Post* draft paper. "I believe there's a connection between Mr. Washer's death and the Steuben crack house deaths."

"How's that?" Geoff asked with a bit of amusement.

"Well, Mr. Washer was really rich and fastidious. My bet is that he bought only pure coke, nothing cut. And he was a user, a functioning attorney, not some junkie. So, his overdosing would be a real long shot."

"And?"

"And at the crack house, we learned from Dugan and McBee that the group was celebrating with a new kilo brick from the Mendez cartel. And they had scraped the prime primo slice from the brick.

Again, not cut. And again, these guys were not junkies. Not the bros, anyway."

Geoff stared without saying a word. Then he asked, "So where should we go from here?"

"Well, you always tell me to get closer to the story, to track down leads where there might not be leads, to talk to people . . . hmm . . . to talk to people." Emmett's eyes lit up. "Let's go talk to my mama and my brother, Jacob. They could be close to this story. And they might be home right now."

"Do you want me to go with you?" Geoff asked.

"You bet. Let me call my mama. We can be there by one o'clock. She won't have to leave for downtown until three. Besides, you can give her a ride if we run late."

"You call your mom while I go over your story. We can leave here in about fifteen. Looking forward to meeting your family, too." Geoff committed.

★ ★ ★

By 1:00 p.m., they had transitioned from the bright, shiny, affluent downtown D.C. to the poverty-ridden broken side. Geoff's Olds Cutlass was mechanically sound but a bit of a junker, so it fit right in. But there weren't many white boys in the Emmett Washington family hood. But then again, Geoff's rumpled look was pretty nonincriminating. He could be a cheap family attorney or some rental-agency dude.

They walked up the five flights of steps to the apartment. The hallways dark, smelly, and in bad need of paint. But the Gertrude Washington apartment looked spotlessly clean and neat with plenty of lamps and open blinds for light. A couple of plants made it more natural, as did photos of family and a few books and magazines on the coffee table. The galley kitchen small, with a simple Formica table, and four chairs in the area between the kitchen and living room.

Gertrude and Jacob sat in the living area when Emmett and Geoff arrived.

"Mama, I want you to meet Geoffrey Wines, the reporter who is my mentor at the paper for my internship. And, Geoff, this is my younger brother, Jacob."

Everyone smiled and nodded. Emmett had told his mother he was bringing his boss with him, but she didn't know why. Yet Emmett knew she would be okay with anything that would help him. He also knew Jacob would be less encouraging.

"Ms. Washington. Jacob," Geoff said, acknowledging Emmett's family. "I appreciate your meeting with us on such short notice. This is actually Emmett's idea because of a story he's working on, and he thought you might be able to help."

Gertrude and Jacob smiled and nodded.

Emmett began. "This is a story I'm working on. Geoff here came along, but I don't think he thinks there's anything to it. But maybe you know something that neither of us know. I also want you to know that anything you tell us will not be on the record. It will be used for background information. Your names, your locations, your relationship to me or the subject—none of this will be referenced in any article, now or later. We'll keep this conversation completely confidential."

He looked at his brother. "Jacob, I also know how important this is for your safety."

Emmett continued. "I've been working on this story about the situation that happened a couple of weeks ago at a crack house here in Washington, where five gang members overdosed on cocaine. This struck me as odd because these bangers were not junkies; they were dealers and users. And the cocaine they were using was a new kilo brick, reportedly from Mendez, so there was no chance some pusher cut it with something."

Jacob nodded, as this seemed right to him.

"Now," Emmett said, looking at his mom. "I'm really sorry we learned today that Mr. Washer's death was definitely due to a cocaine overdose."

She lowered her head, catching a sob. She apparently had not heard about it being a drug overdose. Emmett looked down at his own hands as he thought about the kind man and the horrible news.

"I'm sorry, Mama. I thought you already heard this." He didn't realize the *Post* would normally get information well ahead of the public.

He paused for a moment while Gertrude calmed her emotions, and then he resumed. "While Mr. Washer must have been a user, he, too, was probably not a junkie. And he probably used only really good stuff.

"Mama. Jacob. The story we're pursuing is not about the deaths of Mr. Washer or the five gangbangers—but rather the notion that somewhere, somehow, the supply of cocaine in Washington, D.C., and other places may be tainted with some sort of lethal concoction. Because it seems to be happening high up in the food chain, it could probably be at the cartel level."

This revelation seemed to make Gertrude feel better, but Jacob thrust his hands into his pockets, jabbed his chin into his chest, and looked past his brother.

Emmett noticed his reaction but continued. He knew Jacob would eventually open up. He just needed to get him talking.

"Jacob. Geoff here knows how you spend your afternoons after school. And you know Mama knows, too. Is there anything out of the ordinary at your lookouts and deliveries? Anything over the past few weeks that you would say is not normal? Anything whacked that you have seen?"

Jacob glared at Emmett and shifted his eyes over to Geoff. Emmett picked up on the silent communication.

"Jacob, it was my idea to bring Mr. Wines over today. I trust him. And I trust the paper. If there is a story here, we can use any information you share to help track it down. I promise both you and

Mama that everything you say will not be shared with anyone else. I promise."

Geoff nodded. "Nothing. Your brother thinks he has a story. And it would be a huge story if true. But the only way we can get it is by piecing together various seemingly unimportant facts. Anything you can tell your brother will help him determine what was behind Mr. Washer's death and the other overdose deaths in the news. And if his idea is right, he will have broken one incredible story."

Jacob relaxed. Emmett gave him a reassuring smile and looked over to his mother. She nodded and touched Jacob's hand. "Go ahead, Jacob. It will be all right."

"I make p-pickups and d-drops on a weekly basis near the Lincoln Memorial. Jefferson Memorial, too. I'm given the delivery in a b-burger sack—sometimes McDonald's, sometimes B-Burger King. Always looks crumpled. I never look into the sack. I could get killed for doing it." He flashed his eyes over to his mother. "I'm c-careful, Mama.

"I drop or pick up a bag next to a trash can. Not in it. Next to it. Then I split. I never look back because we ain't s'pose to see who's picking up the stuff." Jacob paused, looking at both Geoff and Emmett.

"C-Couple of Wednesdays ago, I'm asked to p-pick up a bag at the Jefferson Memorial and b-bring it right back to Neville. Says it's urgent. So, I gets over there as quickly as I c-can.

"There's nothing by the trash can, so I hang out, keeping my distance from the can so no one s-sees me.

"Then some round-face, fat M-Mexican dude with this huge mustache drops a burger bag right next to the can. I wait for him to c-clear the area; just like Neville tells me to do.

"Wells, before I get over to the bag, I see a tall gnarly looking nigg—uh—black dude rush to pick it up, almost like he was t-trying to get it before someone else. It's like when I grab the last piece of chicken b-before Emmett gets it.

"Anyway, this dude takes the sack into one of the nasty toilets next to the statue. I thought he was a junkie look'n for leftover food. And he wasn't going to steal Neville's shit, so I s-stick around, not s-sure what I s-should do. Runners don't lose deliveries or pickups. Man, I was scared.

"About ten minutes later, he's b-back out with the same sack and places it exactly where it was before. It didn't even look like it had been messed with. Odd. Really ate up. He s-steals the shit, and then puts it right back! I figure I'm good, so I wait about five minutes and don't take my eyes off that bag. Then I grab it and heads back to Neville."

"Jacob, did you get a good look at the guy?" Emmett asked.

"Fuck yes, man. Sorry, Mama. Yes. Had to know who's messed with my drop. Had to tell Neville 'bout it. Dude was 'bout the same color as you and me. Clothes were dirty, but he looked more clean than his clothes. It's almost like Halloween makeup—you know, where we p-paste stuff to our face and put Mama's t-talc in our hair. Thought maybe the dude was a n-narc or something, but he had this big-ass scar on his cheek that made him look like he's been in some gang fight."

"How tall was he?" Geoff asked.

"Oh, over six feet. Maybe six two. Ripped. But a nasty scar."

"Anything else you've seen?" Emmett asked.

"Nope. Just wouldn't want to run after this dude. He looked like he could outrun a horse."

"Was the drop delivered?" Geoff asked.

"Yes, sir. And I guess Neville really was in a hurry. There were two bricks in the bag. That was whack, too. He quickly grabbed one, unwrapped the c-corner, and removed a big eight ball. He put the eight-ball package into a gym bag and told me to run it to downtown to where all those law offices line the street. I gave it to a young white dude wearing a b-blue blazer. You know what? I never told Neville about what happened with the dude with the scar."

Geoff was searching for something to say, something like "Well, that's good." But his thoughts were on the man with the scar and on Howard Washer's death. *They were somehow related.*

* * *

Emmett turned his attention to his Mama.

"Mama, was there anything at Mr. Washer's house that could give a clue to us about what might have happened to him?"

She leaned forward. "Emmett, tell me, how do you know Mr. Washer died of a drug overdose?"

"Well, Mama, the *Post* has contacts within the coroner's office and makes follow-ups on high-profile cases. Mr. Washer's death was high profile. If it were due to some illness, then the next of kin would have to release the autopsy results. But when the police are called and the results indicate something illegal like a drug overdose, then the information is public and can be released directly to the news media."

"Was his death due to cocaine or something else?"

Emmett knew the answer was going to be painful for his mother to hear. "It apparently was connected to cocaine, as they found cocaine in his system. But the coroner's report also indicated some other drug played a role, but I'm not sure what."

Gertrude looked over at Geoff. "What could that mean?"

"Ms. Washington, drug-related deaths come in a lot of different forms. Some people just plain overdose on too much of one type of drug. These are usually the junkies, who also die from a lethal mixture of drugs. This is what killed John Belushi; he consumed a mixture of cocaine and heroin. Rarely do a couple of lines of pure cocaine kill someone. That's why Mr. Washer's death is so puzzling. Did you ever see any signs that Mr. Washer was a heavy user of cocaine or even heroin?"

Geoff instantly saw Mrs. Washington felt uneasy with answering this question. She looked around the room. Then she stood up and walked over to the sink, adjusting one of the planters along the way.

After a moment, she sat back down and began spilling everything she knew about Mr. Washer, including how she had discovered him dead in the study; the shiny, clean glass-top coffee table; and how the table always looked as if it had been cleaned the night before. Considering the circumstances of his death, she said she now understood the connection between the coffee table and Mr. Washer's cocaine habit.

She said she had never seen any cocaine or drug paraphernalia around the house and how Mr. Washer had always looked refreshed each morning when she prepared his breakfast. He had never been tired or strung out.

"The morning you found Mr. Washer in the study, was there any evidence of cocaine there?" Geoff asked. "The police report indicated there was no evidence of cocaine in the home, and they surmised he had used the cocaine before returning home. I assume the police asked you the same question."

Gertrude looked around the room and at her two children. Then she whispered. "Nothing I say here will be reported? Nothing I say here will go beyond you three?"

Geoff nodded. "Ms. Washington, I promise you that everything you say is privileged, which means I will not tell anyone, and no police, judge, or court can make me reveal anything about this conversation."

Gertrude again looked at her two children.

"I cleaned it up," Gertrude said, still whispering. "There was a line still on the table and a few specks from another line, too. I carefully cleaned the top of the table and used Glass Plus. I put everything back in place and checked his nose for any dust. I just could not have the police find Mr. Washer with cocaine. He was a fine gentleman, not some ghetto junkie. There was no way I was going to let him be found with blow on his nose. No, sir, he was too fine a man. No, sir. He had been too good to us."

"No, he wasn't a FINE MAN!" Jacob blurted out. "He was just a rich white man who you made breakfast for. What, he paid you two hundred a week? You got up at five each morning, hauled your ass to the bus stop to get a bus to take you to Georgetown, and then caught a bus back just so you could work another job? No, Mama, he was not a fine man. He was a junkie just like the people in this ugly ass building."

Gertrude's eyes burned with rage. "Jacob, you shut your mouth! He was good to us. He shared his stuff with us. He paid me more than most housekeepers get. He gave me vacation time and paid me for it, too. He gave Emmett books to bring home. If you hadn't broken his toys, he would have done that for you, too. Instead, look at you: a big ghetto man selling drugs."

"Mama, I already make more than you. I'll make big money soon, more than you. More than Emmett. And more than Mr. Wines here."

"Jacob! You're my son. I love you. Always will. But you're just wrong about Mr. Washer. Just wrong." Gertrude buried her head into her hands.

"I'm sorry, Mama. I'm sorry."

Emmett got up and hugged his mother and flashed a stern look at his little brother.

"Jacob, it's all my fault. If I had just watched you closer playing in Mr. Washer's library...it was all my fault." Gertrude tearfully surrendered. "It was all my fault."

The room became very quiet. After a moment, Gertrude reached over to her two sons and held them tight.

"We'll be all right," she whispered. "We'll be all right."

Drained, she looked over at Geoff. "Anything else you need to know?"

Geoff looked up with a sorrowful expression and his shoulders slumped. He did not want to cause any problems for Emmett and his family. "I completely understand, Ms. Washington. Completely. But...I have just one more question. What did you do with the cocaine from the coffee table?"

She answered Geoff, slowly recalling the situation. "I took a spatula and moved the cocaine into a sandwich baggie. I made sure I got all of it, cleaned the table, and flushed the paper towels down the toilet."

"And where did you put the actual cocaine?" Geoff followed. "Did that go down the toilet, too?"

"I kept it" she answered very slowly, with a tinge of regret in her voice.

"You kept it?" Geoff's voice cracked in disbelief. "You kept the cocaine from Howard Washer's house?"

"That's right, Mr. Wines. I wrapped it in tinfoil and put it in my purse." Then she pointed toward her bedroom. "Right now, it's in my dresser drawer over there."

Chapter 45

FBI Headquarters, Washington, D.C.

Inside the FBI sat a cordoned-off suite of offices dedicated to Operation Blueprint, restricted to only a few agents and technicians.

One entire wall of the windowless conference room had an exploded map of the United States. But unlike most maps, it was not sectioned into states and topography. It resembled a subway or mass transit map showing color coded pathways and stops.

Knowing the importance of this operation, FBI Director Troy Hunt had asked the key staff working the operation for a weekly update. This included Charles Bruce, the agent in charge of Operation Blueprint; and Dr. Clyde Ostrow, the chemical pharmacologist handling the Blueprint coding and analysis. Also attending today's discussion was Attorney General Patrick Miller, who would update President Osbourne on the operation.

"OK, gentlemen. Where are we?" Hunt asked the group to get things started.

Agent Bruce began. "We have intercepted and tattooed one hundred twenty-three shipments comprising five hundred ninety kilo bricks of cocaine. We concentrated on two key corridors: Saint Louis and the East Coast shipping into Charleston, South Carolina, and Jacksonville, Florida."

On the map were three areas marked in bright red that approximated the location of the three cities. Thin red lines extended from cities such as Springfield, Missouri, and Brunswick, Georgia, to indicate the locations where the shipments were intercepted. Dotted red lines pointing to the sites were extended from various places where the FBI suspected the drugs entered the distribution channel. When these routes were proved with positive IDs of the tattoos, these lines were then changed into solid red lines as the entire distribution chain would be defined and documented.

Agent Bruce continued. "We are actually learning a great deal and have been able to pinpoint exact routes for drugs that have been picked up at the street level through either drug busts or undercover purchases, just as we designed the operation to do."

He paused for a moment, grinned, and turned the discussion over to Dr. Ostrow.

Ostrow stood and immediately began. "One area that we thought would be squishy in this operation was whether we could trace things all the way back to each of the cartels. It would be nearly impossible to infiltrate a cartel lab. But as we began analyzing the various tattooed samples and recording our unique markings, we have also started to see three distinct compositions to the cocaine itself." He then smiled, "which means we have a unique signature for each of the major cartel's cocaine. We can precisely identify any sample and tell you whether it is from Mendez, Cali, or Medellin."

AG Miller jumped from his seat and jabbed a fist in the air. "Holy crap! We can build a watertight case against the cartel leadership itself!" Dr. Ostrow followed the AG's excitement with a few bars of the *Rocky* theme song.

"Right?" Miller asked.

"Right-o," Dr. Ostrow said.

Miller recomposed himself. The satisfaction on his face was obvious. "Really?"

"Really." Ostrow repeated as reassurance.

Miller then looked at the map again. This time, he noticed something else. "What are those?" He pointed to a place on the map where the drugs were tattooed—but with no lines extending beyond the point of interception. There seemed to be about five of these on the map. But unlike the others, there were no tattooed lines extending from these points and breaking into multiple dealer network lines.

Agent Bruce looked at Dr. Ostrow, who gave him a slight nod.

"We are calling those 'Christmas checks,'" Agent Bruce said. "You know, when you were in college and your great-aunt sent you a check for Christmas, and you tucked it into a drawer without cashing it. Then, a few months later, you discovered it and ran out to deposit it because you needed the cash. We believe that is what those are. But as of right now, these are uncashed checks—maybe lost checks— though it would be odd for someone to misplace a kilo of cocaine. And none of these missing checks have turned up in any drug busts, either."

"Isn't that odd?" Miller asked.

"Yes, odd," Dr. Ostrow said.

"Anything else odd?" Miller asked.

"Hyperspace," Agent Bruce said. "I love the video game Space Invaders. In the game, when the enemy is surrounding you, you can hit the hyperspace button and show up in a totally new universe."

Miller frowned as if his agent was crazy.

Agent Bruce cleared his throat. "Oh, um, yes. Never played the game, huh? Well, one would expect some geographic adjacency. Drugs are shipped to one city, and then suddenly, the shipment appears half a country away. At first, we thought we had miscoded something. But when Dr. Ostrow went back and double-checked, we found that all our controls were in line."

Agent Bruce stood and went to the map and pointed to Chicago. "We have a tattooed shipment that landed here in Chicago; tattooed in Springfield, Missouri; and transported to Chicago via Saint Louis. But then suddenly the same cocaine ends up in New York City. It wasn't one small user amount but a dealer-size amount that was distributed in both New York and Philadelphia. Like hyperspace. As for the Christmas checks, we just need to be patient and see if they are cashed. Maybe we'll learn something else from this."

Though FBI Director Hunt had heard about the hyperspace shipments and uncashed checks before this meeting, his brain made a leap that put the shipments together in a way he had not considered. His eyes arched for a split moment before relaxing into their normal passive state.

A.G. Miller had noticed. "Troy? Is there something you want to add?"

"Oh. Nothing. Just a thought that I'll check into later."

Miller dismissed it. "Gentlemen, if there isn't anything else, I'll leave you to the rest of the review. I'll fill President Osbourne in on the status. Thanks for your time and effort on making this program even stronger than we could have ever imagined."

He shook hands with Hunt, Agent Bruce, and Dr. Ostrow and left the conference room with a new sense of progress in the war on drugs and the eventual conviction of the major dealers and cartel bosses.

After Miller left, Hunt turned to Agent Bruce and Dr. Ostrow. "We see where the attorney general is headed. You can almost start writing the Justice Department case against the top cartel bosses. But this Christmas check and hyperspace thing is puzzling. Clyde, please ensure the coding is ironclad, because when my boss and the Justice Department start building the case against the cartels, nothing can be vague or possibly picked apart by their counsel."

"Will do, Boss. I will triple-check everything."

Hunt continued. "Also look at the two in tandem, as they might be related somehow. When I think about the two together, it seems odd."

But what Hunt was really thinking was that there might be a rotten apple in the barrel. Though few, these uncashed checks were most troubling, particularly considering the number of overdoses occurring in precisely the same areas.

Chapter 46

Greenville, South Carolina

If nothing else, Clarence Robinson was persistent. His buddy at the Chicago Police Department, Dan Murphy, had given him a set of prints lifted from the top of Eric's car.

And Clarence had sent them to everyone he knew in the private corporate security business throughout the Midwest. "Keep it on the down-low," he would say to his buddies. "Check to see if there's a hit and let me know what you learn."

Clarence knew businesses were always fingerprinting and drug testing applicants for jobs, particularly in law enforcement, finance, restaurant management, and myriad other sensitive jobs. They kept these files somewhat confidential unless the prints were needed for one reason or another. In other words, this information was not forwarded to police databases unless they had cause to bring the police in on something.

After several weeks he got a call from one of his buddies in Chicago. He had a match for a "Dwight Jones, a new employee at Seaton and Earnst Brokerage in Chicago." The prints had been taken three years earlier. No other information available.

"Well, having a name is better than nothing." This was more than his old buddy Dan Murphy had.

A trip to Chicago to search for a Dwight Jones was in his immediate future. Besides, he wanted to meet with a few of Eric's work friends. Several had sent heartfelt notes of sympathy, and he thought meeting with them would ease his sorrow.

Chapter 47

Chicago, Illinois

L ike any corporate sales VP, Luther Gomez kept close track of his major sales regions and top distributors. Something began to stand out in the Chicago market.

Product velocity through Emil's Cleaners showed a greater-than-normal bump. Kilos of pure cocaine were up over four per month, quite significant.

He grabbed his phone and dialed a 312 number.

"Vinny. Luther here."

On the other end listened Vinny, his sales-development manager working in Chicago. He had hired Vinny a couple of years earlier for the specific purpose of more fully developing the young upscale business moving into the gentrified sections of Chicago. Vinny's role was no different from the sales-development managers employed by other franchisers; he was to find persons who were interested in running their own business; and flip them toward his business model and income potential.

"Hiya, Luther. Haven't talked to you in a long time."

"Well, Vinny, when things go well, a manager just stands back and lets his sales guys do their thing."

"Something wrong?"

"No, sir, Vinny, quite the opposite. You've been doing a great job in growing the new white-collar business in Chicago. It's up over twenty percent this spring alone. In fact, it appears to be doing so well, I want to learn more."

"No prob, man. What d'ya need?"

"Tell me what's driving this growth. The Cleaners alone is shipping four additional bricks per month."

"Man, I hit the jackpot about two to three months ago. I had this customer who was killing it in the brokerage business. He kicked ass.

Then he got hooked. I showed him how he could supply his own needs and make money doing it. He wasn't interested. But then he bonked out at his financial job, got straight, and then got serious about selling our stuff."

"And then what?"

"Interesting dude. Smart. Knows how to make money. He started like everyone else and made lots of one-gram sales. But then he realized it was just as easy to sell a few ounces than one gram at a time. He rapidly moved to Big Eights, and then quickly to Quarters and Halves. He's like a guy in the insurance business who targets only group policies. Fewer calls. Less exposure. But major cash. He deals only in pure, with nothing cut. Guaranteed quality. Safe. His hedge against the nasty news going around the country."

"He sounds interesting," Luther inserted.

"Right, he is. Anyway, based on his volume, we keep giving him a better cost structure. He calls it 'arbitrage.' And he exploits the shit out of it. He fits right in with the rest of the yuppies throughout downtown Chicago. Tall. Blond. Good looking. Looks like the people these peeps work with. Buyers are comfortable with him. They no longer need to make trips to the South Side. Like you said, overall volume is up.

"And, Luther, you're going to love this. He's devised a way to make handoffs in broad daylight. He packs the stuff in those big, thick issues of *Cosmo* magazine and *Playboy*, too. He hands it off at bars, except when the buyer is paranoid, which is when they retreat to the restroom routine. Man, the smart son of a bitch also leaves deliveries at reception desks. Just brilliant, Luther. Just brilliant."

"What's his name, Vinny?"

"Dwight Jones. You need his address?"

"Not yet. But where might I see him in action?"

"Few bars here in town. He's at Shenanigan's on Rush Street many nights. Let's see, he just picked up a key at Emil's yesterday. My bet is you'll catch him at the Pelican Bar in the Leo Burnett

Building on East Wacker during lunch this Wednesday. Look for a tall
blond kid sitting alone at the bar, near the restroom."

"Thanks, Vinny. Keep up the good work."

Chapter 48

FBI Headquarters, Washington, D.C.

D r. Clyde Ostrow was a skillful pharmacologist and pharmacological researcher. He had essentially devised the Blueprinting system and the creation of the unique tattoos being applied in the field to track the distribution of the drugs.

He liked and respected FBI Director Hunt—and was also a fan of President Osbourne. He knew the president from years ago when they both were members of the *Washington D.C. World War II Historical Club*. Both had served during the war, and the club gave them a chance to view the war's legacy in a more intellectual perspective than soldiers' war stories of being cannon fodder for some German combatant. And he had worked with Director Hunt since Hunt joined the bureau twenty-five years ago. Dr. Ostrow had his thirty-year pin and was planning retirement.

As with Osbourne and Hunt, he also wanted to win the war on drugs.

After the meeting with AG Miller, Hunt had asked Dr. Ostrow to specifically investigate two issues: First, the hyperspace phenomenon of Blueprinted drugs suddenly turning up half a country from where they were expected; and Second, the blank checks where Blueprinted drugs did not turn up anywhere. Kilos of cocaine just did not fall off the face of the earth.

Dr. Ostrow's review reinforced the disciplined procedures and double-check system he put in place. Everything was working exactly as he had intended. There was nothing out of line. He could not explain the hyperspace situation, other than some distributor had business in a galaxy far, far away. It happened.

And the blank checks? In all but one case, those interdictions were handled in the field by DEA Agent Chuck Harding—*exactly as he had intended.*

Chapter 49

Chicago, Illinois

President Osbourne had warned DEA Agent Chuck Harding something like this could happen. Clarence Robinson was a man of action, and there was no way he was going to allow the authorities to handle the investigation of his son's death by themselves.

When Harding heard Clarence just landed in Chicago, he placed everything else on hold to follow him to a restaurant on the first floor of the Leo Burnett Building. Clarence took a seat at the large oval-shaped bar in the center of the restaurant. The clock across the river on the Wrigley Building clanged "noon" as the bar filled with the office lunch crowd, many also seeking a place at the bar for a sandwich and beer.

Harding managed to find a small two-top table in the dining room, where he had a clear view of the right side of Clarence's face. Clarence sat talking with a well-dressed young executive in a pinstriped suit and wire-rimmed glasses. Harding guessed this was a friend of Eric, Clarence's son. He could see the president's old friend listening intently to the young man.

Sitting opposite Clarence, near the restroom door, was another familiar face: the tall blond kid wearing casual clothes whose apartment Harding had visited a few weeks earlier. *Dwight must be here for a big-time drop*, Harding thought.

Did Clarence know Dwight? Probably not. Not even the Chicago Police Department had connected the prints to a name or even a face. From Harding's vantage point, it did not seem Clarence gave Dwight any attention.

But a heavyset Hispanic man sitting a few seats over also actively observed Dwight with sideward glances.

Lions and tigers and ghosts, oh my. Harding almost gasped. Fucking Luther Gomez from the Mendez cartel. Luther's face was not widely known outside the DEA. Holy fucking shit! *Who invited all these people?*

Clarence seemed deep in conversation with the young executive when they both glanced at Dwight. At first, a casual glance, as if the young exec were merely pointing out a friend. Clarence nodded as he took in the information, but then his posture jolted military straight, his jaw clenched, and his eyes riveted on Dwight. If looks could kill, Dwight Jones was a dead man. Harding figured Clarence had just learned his son's killer's identity.

A young man with an open plaid shirt and blue blazer approached Dwight, said a few words, and headed toward the men's room. About thirty seconds later, Dwight headed in the same direction. Almost immediately, Luther Gomez decided it was time for a potty break.

When Harding's gaze shifted back to where Clarence was seated, Clarence had excused himself and seemed to be heading toward the same restroom.

"Fuck!" Harding mouthed to himself. "What happens when a white drug dealer, a Colombian cartel enforcer, an angry father, and a DEA agent converge in the middle of a drug deal? Not a friendly round of golf, that's for fucking sure," he said to himself as he hurried to the restroom, hand-checking his service revolver under his coat.

As Harding approached the restroom door, the young man with the plaid shirt and blue blazer slammed into him, pivoted, and dashed away, muttering, "Don't go in there."

Another young man was also getting the hell out of there, still hitching up his pants so he could run.

Upon entering the restroom, Harding was relieved no one else seemed to be in there other than Luther, Clarence, Dwight, and himself. And Clarence had Dwight pinned in one of the stalls as Luther quietly leaned against the wall, arms folded, watching the encounter.

"You fucking killed my son, you motherfucker! I will flush you down this fucking toilet. I will break every bone in your body. I will, I will . . ."

Harding grabbed Clarence by the neck and yanked him off the terrified Dwight. "Clarence! Clarence! We need him. Let him go. We need him to finish our business." He pushed Clarence toward the door as Luther studied both of their faces.

Dazed by what had just happened, Dwight looked around. The older black man and the recent visitor to his apartment were gone. He noted the presence of the heavyset Hispanic man with the pocked face. Something was frightening about him.

This is not going to turn out well, he thought. This is not good at all. He wasted no time and exited the restroom.

Luther walked over to one of the urinals and took a piss. There on the floor lay a wrapped issue of *Cosmopolitan* magazine. After washing his hands, he picked up the *Cosmo* with the wet paper towel, placed it into his pouch, and left.

Chapter 50

Chicago, Illinois

Dwight made his way back to his apartment. It was all a blur now, not because of his mugging inside the Leo Burnett restaurant but because he realized his time on this earth was potentially quite short.

First, there was the DEA agent who had visited him a couple of weeks earlier. He had clear evidence of Dwight's involvement in the murder of the kid in the underground. And he knew everything about his drug dealing. Chalk this one up to a life in prison.

Second, there was the crazy black man who almost killed him in a public restroom. He knew Dwight's name and knew he had killed his son. He'd show up again and would probably kill Dwight if he got a chance.

Third, and most terrifying, the Hispanic man in the restroom. Who is he, and why was he there? If he's cartel, he could have been there for two reasons. One, he wanted to see how a single dealer could generate so much business in a very short period. Or two, it was PDA, or a public display of association. Dwight had identified the DEA agent with the scar on his face and his visit to the apartment. And then the same agent was in the middle of a drug deal that went sour. Cartels eliminated anyone who they thought could be a security risk. And the odds were two out of three that Dwight Jones was now a marked man by the cartel.

What should he do? What could he do? Even prison would be unsafe for someone on the outs with the cartel.

Dwight figured the safest thing he could do was stay inside his apartment. He had to think of a way out of this mess.

Chapter 51

Chicago, Illinois

The phone rang and startled Dwight. He must have dozed off into a deep sleep. In the three days since the episode at the Leo Burnett Building, he had stayed in the apartment, eaten very little, and spent endless hours watching ESPN.

The thought of the Hispanic man sent shivers up his spine. He looked like the type of guy Vinny had warned him about when Dwight had entered the drug trade.

"Don't fuck up," Vinny had said. "Don't let anyone think you're in contact with the police or DEA. Play it safe. If you don't, you are dead. It is that simple."

Dwight reached for the phone. Now on its sixth ring.

Before he got the phone to his ear, he could hear a voice screaming on the other end.

"Dwight! What the fuck, man?"

Dwight recognized Bruce Zimmer's voice instantly; in fact, he had heard him say these exact same words but never with the anger and vengeance that was causing Dwight to hold the phone well away from his ear.

"What the fuck are you fucking doing? Fucking killing my business by fucking killing my customers? What the fuck, man?"

"Bruce, what are you talking about?" Dwight tried to calm him enough to find out what had set him off.

"Haven't you heard the news today? It's all over every fucking channel in New York. CNN, too. Maybe Chicago—"

"What news? What are you talking about? I've been out of it."

"That last shipment you sent. The special stuff for the big bachelor party."

"Yeah, I sent you the first cut, the sliver right from the top of a brand-new kilo. It's the best there is."

"Well, your 'best there is' just fucking killed all four of the bachelor party hosts: groom, best man, and best friends. Fucking dead! Thank God it must have happened before the festivities; otherwise, there would have been some fucking hookers dead, too, and some pretty unhappy in-laws. Housekeeper found all four of them fucking dead this morning in the Hyatt at Grand Central Station. Fucking presidential suite. The cops are saying the cocaine was laced with some sort of poison that killed these guys."

Dwight listened, trying to comprehend Bruce's words.

Bruce continued, still agitated. "Papers are reporting the DEA and the FBI think it was some sort of retaliation among the New York street gangs selling blow. Some sort of Crips-Bloods feud, that they had somehow confiscated a shipment and poisoned it in order to put the other gang out of business. Makes sense, right? Except that was my blow. It was the shit you shipped directly to me from Chicago. Not even local! Fuck, man!"

Dwight thought for a moment. His mind raced. "Someone confiscated the shipment and poisoned it," he repeated Bruce's claim to himself.

Laced cocaine? From a wrapped cartel kilo? He thought about the DEA agent who had paid him a visit and told him to keep doing what he had been doing. That same agent had just happened to be at a major drop downtown as well. That was the only way. Whole kilos directly from the cartels were never cut with other shit. And Dwight damn well knew that cartels would not be fucking with their own stuff. But would a rival cartel fuck with another cartel's shit? Fuck, he didn't know.

The Leo Burnett stuff came from the same brick as from Bruce's bachelor party shipment. Dwight had sold some onesies from the end of the same brick. But with Bruce's and the Leo Burnett order, he had exhausted his supply. And he hadn't heard anything in the local news about cocaine-related deaths in Chicago.

He cradled the phone and grabbed his satchel. He blindly shifted his hands through inside of the bag. Shit! The *Cosmopolitan* magazine was not in there. It must have fallen out during the bathroom scuffle.

"Bruce. Bruce. Listen to me. Do you have any more of the stuff I sent you?"

"Yeah. Not much. About a gram. Why?"

"Don't fucking sell it! Hold on to it for a bit until I figure something."

Dwight's mind still raced. He had to find out what was in the shit he had sent to Bruce. But it wasn't as if some former stockbroker in Chicago could go to his neighborhood pharmacy and ask them to review tainted cocaine. He needed a chemist to analyze it. A thought hit him. Who? Whom could he have look at it? He didn't know anyone in Chicago who could—much less would—analyze dope.

"Bruce. Are you and Holly still at it?"

Bruce's tone instantly changed. "Man, best fucking sex I ever had. And like a dog with a good steak, I try to get that stuff whenever I can."

"She in New York?"

"Jersey. I looked her up after you reminded me of her a few weeks ago. Get this: she works with a damn pharmaceutical company." Bruce laughed. "She's a chemist. She makes drugs by day, uses drugs by night. And I see her whenever I can—if you know what I mean."

"Brucey, you haven't changed a bit since Michigan. Do you think you could get Holly to look at the shit you have left over from my shipment? She might be able to spot something."

"Dwight, she *loves* me and would do anything for me . . . and *to* me. Sure, she'll check out the stuff. I need to make sure she doesn't use it. In fact, I need to convince her not to use anything if this shit is all fucked up. I'm going back to good beer and whiskey. Fuck this cocaine stuff. In fact, until further notice, I have fucking left the business."

"Bruce, get her the stuff, tell her what you suspect, and let me know what she learns. In the meantime, I'm closing down too." Dwight then paused, took a long breath adding, "Oh, Bruce, one more thing."

"What's that, Dwight?

Bruce thought again, "Eh, never mind. Give me a call after you and Holly talk."

"Will do, old buddy. Will do."

Chapter 52

The Washington Post Building

The phone rang on Geoffrey Wines' desk at the *Washington Post*. Geoff was on a deadline and let it ring. It stopped for about fifteen seconds and started ringing again.

Geoff picked up the receiver and immediately placed it back down.

"They'll call back," he said to himself.

It started ringing again.

Geoff picked up and spoke without listening. "Hello. I'm on deadline, can you call back in thirty?" The call appeared to be from an inside line at the *Post*.

"No," a man with a Hispanic accent said from the other end of the line. "Fucking no, I am sure you will want to talk to me right now. I am in your lobby."

"Whom may I say is calling?" Geoff asked in as snobbish an English accent as he could muster.

"Luther Gomez."

Geoff caught the bile in his throat. "May I put you on hold for just a moment? I will be right back within thirty seconds."

"No. I don't like hanging out in your fucking lobby. Too much traffic. Come right down and take me immediately to your editor's office. Agree now, or I leave."

"Be right there. Taking the stairs." Geoff put urgency in his voice, so Luther knew he had his attention.

As Geoff rushed past the city editor's office, he thrust his head inside the glass doorway. "Get Downie. In Downie's office. Pronto. Bradley, too, if he's in the building. Code Red. This is going to be a friggin' journalistic coup. A top cartel enforcer is here and wants to talk."

Within three minutes, Luther Gomez, chief enforcer for the Mendez cartel; Leonard Downie, executive editor of the *Washington Post*; Nan Green, city editor; and Geoffrey Wines, reporter, and Pulitzer winner, sat down in the *Washington Post* boardroom. The only conference room without a glass wall. Luther took position on one side of the oval table so he could see all the doors leading into the room. His pocked face looked relaxed and amused. The three bewildered *Washington Post* journalists faced him, with their backs to the inside wall.

Luther began. "Well, lady and gentlemen, I bet you never thought you would see me invite myself into *your* office." A wide grin covered his face. "I think I can help you and at the same time help our business."

"It's your meeting," Downie said, opening his palms toward their guest.

Luther continued, scanning the faces of all the reporters as he spoke. "Look, we are all in the entertainment business. You sell newspapers. But as tough as your competition is, you don't fucking manipulate your competitor's product to blow up and kill the reader. Movie theaters don't firebomb other theaters to garner more business. Starbucks doesn't poison McDonald's coffee. And I am fucking sure none of the cartels are fucking with competitive cocaine. We may pressure and fuck with their sales and distribution people, but we don't fuck with the product." Then he looked directly at the paper's top editor. "And you can quote me on this. Just don't use my name."

Downie answered with just an edge in his voice. "Mr. Gomez, thanks for that quote. But the *Washington Post* is not in the habit of supporting illegal causes. We're not the cartel's PR firm. Why should we publish your quote?"

Luther answered, with an equal edge and warning in his voice. "Sir, because I can give you more background and a huge lead on the whole drug business and the poisoning of cocaine that Señor Wines here has been writing about. And I believe I can give you the inside track that these poisonings may actually be the work of the US government." Luther paused for dramatic effect. "How's that?" His broad grin returned.

"Interesting," Downie said. "Well, sir, let's talk. Are we 'on the record' or 'off the record'?"

"Mr. Downie," Luther said slowly and clearly, "we are completely on the record. But again, do not use my name or the name of my cartel. Everything you print can be attributed to a key source inside one of the major cartels. Unfortunately, I am not sure you will find another corroborating source as open as I am right here, right now." Luther then laughed, stood, and left the room. Wines raced to catch up and escort him to the front lobby. Luther said nothing else.

★ ★ ★

Washington Post:
Front Page (Above the Fold)
Cocaine Deaths Continue Nationwide—
Cartel Claims DEA Is Cause
By Geoffrey Wines
Metro Staff Reporter

Washington, D.C. - As overdose deaths continue to mount, stemming from the illegal use of cocaine, there is striking evidence the Drug Enforcement Agency (DEA) is involved in the lethal tainting of cocaine and subsequent deaths.

Our investigation now includes an extensive on-the-record testimony from a top lieutenant of one of the three drug cartels supplying and distributing cocaine inside the United States.

We at the *Washington Post*, through many avenues of investigation and sources, believe this claim by the cartel source has merit based on unpublished information we have obtained. While making this type of assertion against a federal agency is serious, we have chosen to expose it now to alert the general public and hopefully stem any further deaths.

The accusation of federal government involvement was presented to the *Washington Post* during a sit-down interview with a top-level member of the one of the major drug cartels. The source spoke totally on the record with the provision that neither this person's name nor the cartel affiliation be used.

As broadly reported in this and other news media, since April, there have been over one hundred deaths associated with the illegal use of cocaine. In the Washington, D.C. area we have experienced a handful of lethal incidences surrounding the use of cocaine. We at the *Washington Post* have been investigating these events over the past several months and have reported on each event. In our reporting, we have chosen to withhold certain details because of non-corroborating sources. However, this most recent interview with the cartel began to pull some of these events together.

In one instance, we secured an actual sample of the cocaine and, upon spectrographic analysis, found it contained a small amount of a heretofore unknown and exceptionally powerful sedative.

We also have eyewitness accounts of a man who matches the description of a DEA agent intercepting a drop-off of cocaine in the Jefferson Memorial area. This cocaine was later tracked to a shipment associated with one of the cocaine-related deaths in the D.C. area.

The cartel source also corroborated the

multiple deaths of key gang members, who were known distributors of cocaine, found in a single crack house. An eyewitness to this event described all the dead as being very active and then simply falling asleep and dying. The cartel also noted the usual flow of drugs through this house ended up in the hands of another distributor. Customers of this distributor were also found dead.

Lastly, the cartel source independently described the same DEA agent present during the Jefferson Memorial incident was also present during a cocaine transaction in a downtown Chicago office building. This transaction was interrupted by a man yelling that his son had been killed by the drug dealer. The description of the scene by our cartel informant seems to indicate that the DEA agent knew the man and pulled him off the dealer. The agent was quoted as saying "leave him alone, we need him" as the two rushed from the scene.

The cartel source provided a sample of this drug to the *Washington Post* and asked that we conduct the same analysis as used on other drugs the paper secured. This drug was enclosed in a unique package that would make the drug transaction easy to make in full public view. (We are withholding a detailed description of this package for both security and possible source corroboration purposes.) This drug sample also contained the same lethal substance found in other samples obtained in Washington, D.C.

Although we at the *Washington Post* know the identity of the DEA agent described in these events, we will not report the agent's name or description until absolute indisputable evidence

is collected directly
implicating   the
suspected dealer, the
individual DEA agent,
or the US government
collectively.

Until then, we feel
there   is   enough
correlation of events
to publish this story.

Chapter 53

Location Unknown

The anonymous person made the call to one of the two cell phones he had called earlier. This time it was a musical snippet from the reggae artist Samuel Emmanuel Brown.

So long, my friend
I've left for the islands (islands)
Where the water is blue sea
Where no one will bother me
And I will be left to be
Left to be.

So long, my friend
Life is a long journey (journey)
A path that leads to destiny
Where no one will bother me
And I will be left to be
Left to be.

So long, my friend
I have always loved you (loved you)
Together we shared time and deed
Where life's a force we must heed
And we will be left to be
Left to be.

So long, my friend
They will learn you know me (know me)
They will know our mystery man
They can't catch who they don't see
And we will be left to be
Left to be.

And like the other calls, the phone simply clicked as the caller hung up.

Chapter 54

Chicago, Illinois

Dwight needed to leave his fortress or die of starvation. Over the past week, he had literally consumed every bit of food in his apartment.

He wasn't taking any chances being seen leaving the apartment. But he needed food.

He grabbed an old sweatshirt and ball cap he hadn't worn in a few years. Then he took the stairs to the rear fire exit, avoiding any sight lines from the garage or the front of the building.

"This is crazy." He muttered. "I deal drugs, use my real name, use my own car, and send shit through the mail and FedEx. And here I am sneaking off to the grocery. Crazy."

He cut through the buildings to the next block north and then headed directly to the Jewel store on Clark Street. Though hot, the fresh air—something he hadn't had in several days—felt good. It cleared his head and gave him a weird sense of security.

Once in the store, he grabbed a cart and four canvas shopping bags and stocked up: beer, bread, peanut butter, milk, three pounds of deli ham, two pounds of sliced cheese, four pounds of hamburger, taco seasoning, Triscuits, chips, eggs, bacon, plus a *Chicago Tribune* and a *Washington Post* from the newsstand near the checkout.

He paid with cash and hurried home, taking the same route. He lucked out when one of the other tenants of the building was leaving through the fire exit to walk her dog.

Once he was inside the apartment, his paranoia returned. He put the groceries away and decided to see what the latest Washington scandal was in the *Post*.

Before he had a chance to turn to the inside sections, there on the front page was the headline:

Cocaine Deaths Continue Nationwide—
Cartel Claims DEA Is Cause

He speed-read through the article, sucking in each and every point of the story. "Holy fucking shit! Here it is, on the fucking front page like I suspected. My God !"

Corroborating evidence from the investigation…

The Washington, D.C. crack house…

The cartel source…

Reference to the botched deal at the Leo Burnett Building and reference to his DEA agent friend…

My God, I was there!

There was also a reference to the lost magazine and a sample of the drugs from it, which had been tested and identified as being laced with an undefined sedative.

Dwight read the story again just to make sure he did not miss anything.

He then stopped, slouched into his white leather couch, and stared at the ceiling. Thinking. Thinking. How could he turn this information into a transaction that would save his life?

It hit him; the Hispanic guy had to be the *Washington Post*'s cartel source.

He thought.

He couldn't go to the police. *I'm wanted for murder.*

He couldn't go to the FBI. *They could be part of this.*

He could go to the cartel. But they would deny everything and probably kill him.

He couldn't go to the press; they would turn him in.

Or would they?

Dwight turned this thought over in his mind.

What did he have to offer?

Would they keep his identity confidential?

Would his information change anything?

His mind raced. Could he save his life from the cartel by offering facts that would strengthen their claims and confirm the participation of the DEA in these poisonings and the identity of their agent?

He picked up the phone and dialed.

Bruce answered after the first ring. "Hello?"

"That was quick. You expecting a call?"

"Oh, it's you. I was expecting a call back from Holly. I left a bunch of messages but haven't heard back from her."

"Does she have the cocaine results?" Dwight asked.

"Nope. I never got it to her. She's been in some sort of training and has been completely out of touch. I was hoping this call was her."

"Bruce, that's great news! Hold on to the sample. Keep it safe. I'll have you send it to the *Washington Post*. It will literally save my life."

"What??"

"Just hold on to it. I'll call you back with instructions on who and how to get it to the *Post*."

"Dwight? What aren't you telling me?"

"Bruce, just trust me. It's best you do not know the details. But know if this doesn't work, I'll probably not be around much longer."

"Dwight?"

"Bruce, no time. I'll call you with instructions. Bye."

Dwight hung up.

Chapter 55

Chicago Illinois

Dwight wasted no time after talking with Bruce. Because of this *Washington Post* article, there could be a knock on his door at any minute.

The cops. The FBI. That deranged father. The cartel. Or my DEA friend wanting to silence me.

Dwight scanned the article again: Geoffrey Wines, Metro Staff Reporter.

He flipped through the *Post* to the section with phone numbers: General number, Advertising, Classifieds, Inquiries, and Got a News Story?

He dialed the last number.

"Mr. Geoffrey Wines, please."

"One moment, please," said the woman who had answered.

Hurry. Hurry. Hurry.

After an eternal minute, the line was picked up.

"Wines."

"Geoffrey Wines?" Dwight asked.

"Yes, this is Geoffrey Wines. May I help you?" Geoff asked dryly.

Dwight's heart pounded. "Sir, my name is Dwight Jones, and I'm calling from Chicago."

"And how may I help you?" Geoff asked, this time in a more comforting voice.

"Your article in today's paper, about the DEA, that's about me."

"Slow down. Slow down," Geoffrey said calmly. "Slow down and tell me your story. Are you the DEA agent?"

"No. Hell no! My name is Dwight Jones. I live in Chicago. I deal drugs. And I was the guy you wrote about in today's article. That was me!"

He could literally hear the reporter scribbled notes.

Dwight pushed. "I'm afraid we don't have much time. I'm in my apartment at 644 West Surf here in Chicago. I was there. The DEA agent was there. And I believe I saw the cartel guy you interviewed was also there. And the cartel does not like their dealers associating with the DEA. They kill guys like me. We need to hurry!"

"Dwight? Can I call you Dwight? I need to record this conversation. Is that OK?"

"Yes, but you cannot use my name."

"OK, we are recording. Tell me your name again, though I will not divulge your identity, and please repeat what you just told me. Then I have questions to validate who you are and what you saw in Chicago."

Perspiration now coated all of Dwight's forehead. "All right. We need to hurry."

"First," Wines asked, "where exactly did this event take place?

"The men's restroom inside the Pelican Bar restaurant at the Leo Burnett Building in Chicago."

"And how was the cocaine packaged?"

Dwight smiled. "In an O2-barrier heat-sealed pouch hidden inside the August issue of *Cosmopolitan* magazine. Pretty clever, huh?"

Bingo, Geoff thought as he recorded the answer. "And what was the quantity in the pouch?"

"Precisely two hundred eighty-three point five grams. Ten ounces. A very big haul."

Geoff noted the perfect match.

"Now, you said there was a DEA agent in the restroom. Please describe him and tell me how you knew he was a DEA agent."

Dwight described Harding, including his race; the scar on his cheek; his build; and how he had entered his apartment, told him about his fingerprints being found at the scene of a murder, asked where he kept his drugs, and then told him to keep doing what he was doing.

"You also said there was a cartel guy in the restroom. Describe him."

Dwight described the same Luther Gomez who had visited the *Washington Post* editors and given them the *Cosmopolitan* package with the cocaine.

"Was there anyone else in the restroom at the time?"

"Hell yes. There was a crazy black dude who yelled that I had killed his son. Wiry son of a bitch of about sixty, maybe older. The DEA agent called him Clarence and pulled him off me. He would have fucking killed me if it wasn't for the agent with the scar."

Bingo again. "Tell me what you think is going on here."

"I think this DEA agent planted some sort of lethal substance in my cocaine. I shipped it to New York, and it is what killed the dudes at the Grand Central Hyatt bachelor party. And if he did this to my cocaine, he probably planted it elsewhere around the country, as you reported in your story today. I buy kilo bricks directly from the cartel. Uncut. Pure. There would be no reason the cartel would fuck up their own stuff. So, my guess is this DEA agent did something here. He snuck into my apartment, poisoned some of my stuff, and left. I ship it to New York and downtown, and—bam!—they knock out a whole bunch of people."

"Why would they do this?" Geoff asked.

Dwight paused. He hadn't asked himself that question.

But then it dawned on him. "To stop people from using it and to stop people from selling it. Holy shit. Both me and Bruce, my dealer in New York, said we were out of the selling business. And he said he was also going to stop using it, too. I believe usage is down across the country, as you reported. But until now, my business was thriving because…because…that's the answer! Because I sell pure stuff. Pure stuff is never cut and therefore thought to be safe. And now, it's not. Holy fuck. *The government just beat the cartels!"*

Dwight continued. "Look, I can send you a small amount of the cocaine that was at the New York bachelor party. It will come from Bruce Zimmer, one of my best friends and the dealer in New York that I supply. This dealer must not be associated in any way with this story and what I am telling you."

"We can promise that. We have a New York bureau, and I can give him a name and location where to meet to deliver the drugs. Or I can have him bring the sample to Washington and hand-deliver it to me if he chooses. Or I can meet him in New York."

"Why don't you meet him in New York, maybe at his apartment tonight at nine." Dwight then told Geoff the address.

It was clear to Geoff that Dwight had defined the story—the who, what, where, when, and possibly how.

"One last thing," Geoff asked. "Why would you tell me all of this? You are admitting to murder. You are admitting to drug dealing. You are accusing a specific DEA agent of purposely poisoning drugs, maybe the whole government, too. You are telling me that your drugs were part of the New York City bachelor party event. And you are confirming your associations in such a way that the cartel guy you described knows who you are. Why do you want to go public with all of this?"

"It's simple, Mr. Wines: self-preservation. Either I'm going to jail for murder and will probably be killed by a cartel assassin in jail, or I'll be killed by the DEA agent I'm implicating, or the boy's father."

Geoff started to interject something, but stopped as Dwight took a quick breath and continued.

"Or I'll be killed by the cartel in my apartment because they think I'm a snitch. If you tell my story Mr. Wines, then I become a witness who supports the cartel claim that the DEA is behind these poisonings, and they will not want to harm me whether I remain on the street or in jail. They may even protect me."

Dwight then sighed, "And at the end of the day, I fear the cartels more than I fear the DEA or the US government. Plus, I trust you and the *Washington Post* will keep my identity secure from the government. Whatever happens, my life is going to take a big turn."

Chapter 56

The Washington Post Building

and New York City

Geoffrey Wines had just ended the phone conversation with Dwight Jones. Geoff had Bruce Zimmer's New York City address and would be there at 9:00 p.m. as agreed. If Bruce was not available, Dwight would call Geoff back and leave a message on his voice mail.

The train would leave Washington Union Station at 4:30 p.m. and put Geoff at Grand Central Station before 8:00 p.m. That would give him plenty of time to make it to Bruce's Fifty-Seventh Street apartment. It was 3:00 p.m. now. He could leave by 3:45 and be at Fifty Mass Avenue in plenty of time—less than a thirty-minute walk.

Before leaving, he thought he would follow a hunch.

He walked down to the second floor, where the national reporters had their offices. This was a good group of guys; they were sometimes a bit full of themselves but never toward Geoffrey Wines, Pulitzer Prize winner and totally respected journalist.

Geoff approached Jack Fetterman, the White House correspondent for the *Post*. "Jack? You got a second?"

"Sure thing, Geoff. What's up?" Jack smiled.

"I need you to check out the White House visitor logs for a couple of names."

"That would be no problem at all. From day one, Osbourne made all visitors to the White House and even Camp David available. White House policy. Hell, he even put it on an Excel spreadsheet, so I can literally find it with a touch of a button. No more leafing through endless pages and scribbled names."

"Unbelievable." Geoff handed over a piece of yellow draft paper with two names. "Thanks, Jack. Gotta catch a train to New York. I'll be back tomorrow morning."

★ ★ ★

Like clockwork, the train left Washington Union Station at 4:30 p.m. and arrived at Grand Central at 7:45. It even gave Geoff a moment to grab a quick bite before heading uptown.

Bruce answered his apartment's intercom and rang Geoff up immediately.

The drugs were in a hollowed-out issue of *Cosmopolitan* magazine slipped inside a clear plastic wrapper.

It was obvious to Geoff that Mr. Bruce Zimmer was extremely uneasy about the handoff. Geoff reassured him this transaction was completely off the record and that he would protect his identity. But he did have one question.

"Bruce, do you mind if I ask you one question? It may be extremely important."

"Nope. What do you need?"

"Bruce, is there anyone who would know that you supplied the cocaine to the bachelor party?"

"Well, the four guys who put on the party. But they're dead." His voice trembled. "Would Bob Moseley have told anyone else that I was supplying the drugs? I would say probably not. It just isn't talked about. Would they have referred me to one of their friends? Who the fuck knows? But I did call everyone I've sold to in the past month and warned them not to use any cocaine they purchased from me or anyone else. I fucking don't want to kill myself or anyone else. I'm done."

Chapter 57

The Washington Post

Washington Post:
Front Page (Above the Fold)
DEA Agent Involved in Drugs Used
at NYC Bachelor Party

By Geoffrey Wines, Metro Staff Reporter

The sudden increase in cocaine overdoses continues to plague cities across the United States.

Over the past six weeks, ever since overdoses were first reported in East Saint Louis, multiple overdose deaths have occurred in Washington, D.C.; New York; and Chicago.

Authorities from the FBI and DEA believe the overdoses are due to a tainting of the illegal cocaine supply by rival cartels and their gang distributors. These authorities believe certain cartels and their gang distributors are seeking to build sales and share by creating doubt that the cocaine supply from competitive distributors is unsafe.

This paper recently reported on an interview the *Washington Post* conducted with a key cartel member who refutes this accusation by claiming that any cartel, his and the others, would never place the safety of their product in doubt by poisoning competitive products. He stated this would simply be bad for business for all cartels. He also said he believed the DEA was involved in the actual tainting of the cocaine supply, thereby causing the high number of overdoses.

This cartel member supported this claim by providing eyewitness information from a Chicago drug transaction that went sour when a DEA agent saved a dealer from being killed by a third party. During this action, he tore the aggressor off the dealer while stating "leave him alone, we need him." This cartel eyewitness provided the *Post* with the actual package containing the drugs.

As we reported, the drugs were found to contain a lethal substance that would have certainly led to many deaths in the Chicago area.

Since this report, the *Washington Post* interviewed the actual dealer involved in this same episode, who called this reporter after seeing the August 9 article. This dealer confirmed all the unreported evidence we withheld from the last article.

In addition, this dealer volunteered that he was the source of the cocaine that resulted in the overdoses of four men at the Grand Central Hyatt bachelor party in New York. This ran counter to the NYPD's assertion that the tainting of the supply was by a local gang, as these drugs originated in Chicago.

The *Washington Post* confirmed this by examining a sample of the actual cocaine and the packaging used to transport it from Chicago to New York. All New York samples and packaging were consistent with the Chicago sample.

In describing this transfer, this dealer also noted that the DEA agent who was present at the botched Chicago drug transaction had also visited his apartment and directed him to continue doing what he was doing without arresting him.

The description provided by this source in Chicago matches nearly all the details of the DEA agent who was seen near the Jefferson Memorial before the drop that resulted in the Washington, D.C., "crack house deaths" and another D.C. overdose.

This newspaper knows the exact identity of this DEA agent; however, lacking a direct, indisputable link to the actual tainting of the drugs, we are withholding his name and description.

* * *

Geoffrey Wines omitted several facts from this front-page story: Geoff had learned Clarence's last name was Robinson; that Clarence Robinson was the father of the Eric Robinson who was murdered on Lower Wacker in Chicago; that Eric Robinson's murderer was named Dwight Jones, whose apartment the DEA agent had visited; and that both DEA Agent Charles Harding and Clarence Robinson were guests of President Robert S. Osbourne at Camp David in May, shortly before the first overdose deaths. These omitted facts would need more corroboration before he would write—and the paper would publish—the ultimate story.

Chapter 58

The Oval Office

Because the president was alone, Pat Hayes, his personal secretary, quietly opened the door to the Oval Office. "Mr. President, Attorney General Miller and FBI Director Hunt are here for the eleven o'clock meeting."

"Thanks, Pat. Please show them in…and, oh, this meeting may take longer than planned, so please clear my schedule for the rest of the day."

"Sir? Yes, sir."

Osbourne could tell Pat was surprised and maybe even concerned. But this afternoon would take some time. Osbourne just knew it.

The door closed as Pat left the Oval Office to retrieve the AG and FBI director. Osbourne gathered his thoughts. This could go several different ways.

A minute later, Pat showed Miller and Hunt in. Miller was tighter than usual, with an oh-shit expression. Hunt was his usual poker-faced self. He had no expression, just his typical seriousness and erect posture, as if Joe Friday were a marine.

Osbourne motioned them to take a seat.

AG Miller took the lead. "Mr. President, sir, we better stand for this discussion."

Osbourne briefly looked down and smiled. "Attorney General Miller, please continue."

Miller pulled a letter from his inside breast pocket and handed it to Osbourne.

"Mr. President—President Robert S. Osbourne Jr.—FBI Director Hunt and I are here to formally inform you that you are under investigation for having knowledge of, and therefore being an accessory to, either before or after the fact, the murder of at least one hundred American citizens who were provided with lethal doses of a substance that was laced in illegally obtained street-purchased cocaine. The charge is that your knowledge of this act made it possible for three other individuals to carry out a plan that resulted in these deaths and, in doing so, sabotaged a national security program called Operation Blueprint."

Osbourne let the charges sink in. He looked down at the papers on his desk and then looked up. He noted the sweat beading on Miller's forehead and noted Hunt's cool, collected, unemotional face.

Osbourne had guessed right.

"Gentlemen, let's sit down over there." He pointed to the opposing couches in the center of the office. "I was wondering how long it would take for you to put this all together. But I am afraid your investigation is going down the wrong path. Half of the claims are completely inaccurate, and I do not believe you will want to act on the charge."

"Sir? You were expecting us sooner?" Miller nearly choked on his words.

Osbourne nodded with a slight smile. "Let's take a moment to collect ourselves, and then let's talk. I had Ms. Hayes clear my calendar for the rest of the day, so we have plenty of time." Osbourne walked around his desk and sat on the left-hand couch, with his back to the door. "Oh, and gentlemen, this discussion is privileged, but it will ultimately provide you with important details to use in concluding your investigation."

Hunt spoke up. "Mr. President, I'm not sure we can legally have this conversation."

"Director Hunt, the FBI is investigating this—that is, you. The attorney general, who operates as legal counsel for the executive branch, is also in this room. The subject of the FBI investigation would be against me as the president of the United States, not as a private citizen. And while this discussion is privileged, and therefore my comments are off the record, they can also be used by the FBI in carrying out the investigation. So, I believe we are well within legal bounds."

For the first time, Hunt revealed a hint of emotion by shifting his eyes downward as he considered the president's position.

Osbourne waited, keeping his eyes on the FBI Director's face. Hunt was going to be key in this session and seeing things Osbourne's way.

Hunt looked over to his boss, the attorney general, and nodded.

Miller took the lead again. "OK, Mr. President. Let's talk."

"Coffee?" Osbourne asked. He poured three cups. "So, gentlemen, please tell me the nature of the investigation."

Miller began. "Sir, four months ago, last May, we sat together and reviewed Operation Blueprint. A scheme was set to track the flow of drugs from the cartels to the distributors, to the street, and to the individual users. In doing this, we would be able to build a solid case when we brought major distributors and maybe even the cartels to court. The money was impossible to track, but thoroughly documented tattooed drug samples with distinct markers would provide the evidence needed in court. The Justice Department, the FBI, and the DEA worked together to implement the plan."

Hunt nodded and picked up the narrative. "Almost immediately, we were able to light up the distribution network of the three major cartels. Spring is a particularly high-velocity period, with the cartels filling the pipeline to capitalize on the huge upswing in street usage during the spring and summer.

"But then we started to hear about a rash of overdoses and deaths. First, there was a widespread situation in the Saint Louis area, followed by a major street gang in Washington, D.C., and then a well-respected D.C. attorney. A few weeks later, a bachelor party in New York went wrong with a group of young men overdosing and dying at the Grand Hyatt Hotel. And then a rash of deaths happened in Chicago, with virtually all victims being young professionals. In all cases except the D.C. attorney, we were able to secure samples of the substance. In none of these samples were any of our tattoos."

"None?" Osbourne asked.

"That is right, sir. None. At first, we thought this was due to the immaturity of Operation Blueprint. But as the months progressed, and as we discovered that almost all street product, we intercepted had our markings, it occurred to us something else was transpiring."

Miller stepped in. "As you know, these unexpected deaths caught the attention of the press, and the buried metro stories started moving to page one. We initially thought it was some sort of gang-related and then a cartel-related feud that resulted in the tainting of each other's goods.

"In fact, the *Washington Post*'s Geoffrey Wines, wrote extensively about the deaths and the interviews with cartel associates and even seemed to have an inside track on the cause of it. He reported last week that an analysis of a sample they received from an anonymous source contained an unknown stimulant that caused the heartbeat to accelerate to the point of exhaustion, heart attack, and death."

It was Hunt's turn to speak. "Being a paranoid federal agent, I then asked the FBI in Chicago to start examining how there might be such a concentration of these deaths in the area. We did not bring the DEA into our investigation because, quite frankly, we thought there might be a connection."

Osbourne raised his hand for a moment to let this fact simmer. "You thought the DEA was behind this?" he asked.

Hunt resumed. "This Chicago connection is what clarified the two main suspects in this case: Chuck Harding, a DEA agent I personally handpicked for this assignment; and one Clarence Robinson, who we believe is a longtime friend of yours. The third suspect is a dealer by the name of Dwight Jones."

Hunt continued, maintaining a steady cadence to his accusations. "We know that you had both Mr. Harding and Mr. Robinson as your guests at Camp David on a couple of occasions this past spring. We also know that Mr. Robinson lost his son in what appeared to be a drug-money robbery in March. We now believe Mr. Jones was responsible for the murder because the fingerprints we recently lifted from his mailbox matched the prints found on the top of Eric Robinson's car."

Hunt took a sip of coffee. He was now at the trickiest part.

"We believe we have Harding dead to rights in tainting the drugs. We believe he would tattoo some of the bricks in a shipment and then apply his poison to other bricks. We know this because we have learned that all the cocaine, we have marked, has its own inherently distinct composition, probably due to the specific cartel manufacturer. We now know the signature of each cartel's cocaine from looking at all the samples. It's technical, but we are now able to match sister batches of cocaine. So, if, say, five bricks of cocaine are in a common shipment, we can randomly match those five bricks to each other because they were probably manufactured at the same time. If four have our regular tattoo markers and one has no marker, we still can link their commonality. And as I pointed out earlier, there are no Operation Blueprint tattoos on any of the tainted samples."

"And Clarence's involvement?" Osbourne asked.

"Sir, we believe Mr. Robinson had pressured Mr. Jones, the dealer, to distribute the tainted drugs or be exposed in the murder of Eric Robinson. Somehow, Clarence Robinson learned of Mr. Jones's involvement a few weeks ago, but we're not sure how."

So close, yet so far, Osbourne mused to himself.

Osbourne then excused himself to use the restroom. This would provide a break to the meeting and allow Miller and Hunt to talk.

I guess they figure I'm not a flight risk.

★ ★ ★

Miller and Hunt sat and did not talk.

Osbourne returned and sat on the couch. "So, where does the president fit into this scheme?"

"Mr. President, sir, we believe you were aware of Mr. Harding's and Mr. Robinson's actions and did not alert the proper authorities," Hunt said. "This makes you an accessory."

THE CAMP DAVID CONSPIRACY

"Interesting," Osbourne said. "Yes, indeed, I was fully aware that DEA Agent Harding was tattooing shipments of cocaine as part of Operation Blueprint. And I absolutely knew my friend Clarence Robinson was hell-bent on personally finding who murdered his son because the police had no leads.

"But I am afraid your investigation is completely off base in terms of either DEA Agent Harding or Clarence Robinson having any part in tainting shipments of cocaine that resulted in the deaths of users."

Osbourne leaned forward toward the two men seated across from him. "Do you have any evidence to support the notion that they somehow developed, manufactured, or procured a new substance unknown to the DEA, CDC, or FBI that could kill a person after ingesting such a small amount?"

Hunt looked at Miller. Both shook their heads. "No, sir, we don't," Hunt said. "We don't."

Osbourne sighed. "Gentlemen . . . let's back up a bit and figure this thing out. It is my time to talk about what we know and, quite frankly, what we have accomplished with Operation Blueprint and whatever you want to call the lethal part.

The Attorney General and FBI Director leaned back and let the president speak.

"Director Hunt, in the past three months, you have seen the street usage of illegal drugs, particularly cocaine, drop by half. You have seen the cartels on the ropes as they have tried to figure out what is happening to their shipments. We have seen gang activity, including violence and shootings, come to a standstill as no one is trying to deal or even touch the drugs. This is the type of success that an FBI director only dreams about."

Osbourne then shifted his attention to his hand-picked attorney general. "AG Miller, you now have enough data to prosecute a huge swath of the dealer network. You also have the signature of each cartel's drugs, so you know who is distributing what, even without our tattoos. This is everything you could possibly hope for."

The president paused to let his guests understand his points, both direct and indirect. "Back to you, Director Hunt. If you want to find who is doing this—that is, who is tainting the drugs with a lethal substance—I would submit it is happening right under your nose, inside the FBI."

Hunt flinched, his eyes widening.

Osbourne continued. "Yes, inside the FBI labs and made possible by FBI expertise and the execution of Operation Blueprint." He sensed his points were beginning to sink in. "Did you check each tattoo sample before it went out the door? My guess is you had quality controls in place, but the lethal substance did not need to be in every sample. Even Russian roulette uses a single bullet in a six-shooter. Besides, you did not know what to look for, as this lethal substance is apparently a totally unknown entity. And when you started getting lethal samples back, you said they were not tattooed. Did this cause you to double your internal review to ensure the FBI was not sending the lethal substance out its door in the first place?"

Osbourne was careful not to say that Hunt was directly responsible, but the message certainly was not lost on Hunt—or Miller.

"Now, gentlemen, I do not believe you are in as much trouble as you may think you are. Very early on, when the street deaths started to occur, Mr. Attorney General, you issued a warning to the general public about the presence of some sort of poison being found in cocaine across the country; and the possibility that its presence was part of a drug war between cartels. This probably helped in reducing the demand for street cocaine. The warning also stated that the FBI was investigating. And based on our conversation today, my guess is the investigation is still ongoing and has not turned up anything."

Miller and Hunt were both admirers of and had tremendous respect for President Osbourne. His straightforward assessment was classic for the man. Yet both were thinking, *How does he know so much about this?*

Osbourne gave a brief smile, stood up, and concluded. "I promised you that our discussion today could aid your investigation, because the trail you are on—namely, implicating DEA Agent Harding and Clarence Robinson—will only lead you over a cliff. It is void of critical evidence and would be incredibly embarrassing for the FBI and the Justice Department. I urge you to look internally, and you might solve this case."

Miller and Hunt did not move. Osbourne then continued.

"With the evidence you men just recited and the suspects you have named, I do not believe you will want to move forward, because the evidence does not support your conclusions. In fact, these false charges will be incredibly damning to the FBI."

Osbourne then sat down in his chair behind the Resolute Desk and looked directly at his Attorney General.

"Also, because the president is under investigation, I might add that you will find absolutely no evidence or knowledge pertaining to his involvement. None."

What Osbourne did not say was that he suspected the person behind the last musical message had left the scene, and the FBI would not get their man.

★ ★ ★

The meeting ended. Attorney General Miller and FBI Director Hunt left the Oval Office. It appeared Osbourne would be eating alone at his desk, with the entire afternoon open.

Maybe he would call his friend Clarence to explain how he had just avoided a fight.

Chapter 59

The Washington Post Building

The four toxicology assay reports were spread out on Geoffrey Wines' desk, and each one was nearly identical:

Washington—May 28 (Crack house)
Washington—June 25 Sample (Washer)
Chicago—August 9 Sample (Leo)
New York—August 10 Sample (NYC Bachelor party)

Each sample consisted of pure cocaine and varying amounts of a mysterious compound. There was no known substance in the lab's pharmaceutical database that matched its chemical composition or physiological attributes.

The crack house sample came from the one gram provided by his friend Officer McBee. Geoff was shocked that McBee had fulfilled his request. The sample had arrived via a case of beer at his home's doorstep. McBee was obviously at a loss and figured his journalist buddy could get to the bottom of it. *Boy were they in for a surprise.*

The Washer sample that Emmett's mother had found also contained "compound X." However, it was at a very high level—nearly 2 percent of the substance. *No wonder it killed Mr. Washer before the second line*, Geoff thought. This was the sample Jacob Washington had hand-delivered to downtown D.C. after seeing the man with the scar tampering with it.

The Leo Burnett Building sample's analysis was different. Because it was such a large quantity, ten ounces, the lab had physically portioned the sample into ten subsamples. The report showed the concentration of compound X varied from less than 1 percent to as much as 1.5 percent. A level of 0.1 percent would probably not be harmful, just an added kick. But the report also noted the higher concentrations seemed to be clumped, indicating that the mysterious foreign compound X did not dissolve evenly across the cocaine. It noted that some smaller portions of the cocaine could be as high as 5 percent concentration, which was certainly a fatal amount for the drug.

Wow, this is like Russian roulette, Geoff thought.

Bruce Zimmer's sample from the bachelor party was small, only about one gram. Yet it was perhaps the most telling of all the samples.

The lab, having seen the earlier samples, was on the lookout for varying granular sizes. Dwight had indicated Bruce's sample was the end of a larger sample shipped for the bachelor party. This sample contained only a few granules of the compound X. The lab technician's qualitative notes said it was likely that the larger granules migrated to the top of the total sample as the smaller granules sifted to the bottom. For perspective, the lab pointed out this was a common problem with shipping spice blends. The larger particulate would always work its way to the top of the package.

Geoff thought about the four results. The lab reports indicated the presence of the unknown compound X in all four uncut samples of pure cocaine—and that the compound had to have been added to the bricks after the cocaine had been wrapped and shipped.

If the cartels were blending this compound X into the cocaine, the mixtures would have been more uniform. But these four samples were not uniform. It would appear the compound was somewhere and somehow added across the top of the cocaine and then sent along.

The sample from Mr. Washer's home looked like the usual situation of someone cutting a sample with some bad shit. It too was pure cocaine, but it contained a very high level of the same compound. According to Jacob, it came off the very top of the brick.

The crack house and the Washer samples had an ironclad chain of custody. Jacob had seen someone who matched DEA Agent Charles Harding's description intercept the drop, disappear into a restroom, reappear about ten minutes later, and place the same bag in the same spot.

The sample from Dwight Jones's failed drop in Chicago that Luther Gomez hand-delivered to the *Washington Post* contained the same compound X treatment, as did Bruce Zimmer's sample from New York. They were portioned from the same brick. And DEA Agent Harding had access to Dwight Jones's apartment.

Geoff had been covering the war on drugs for a long time. From interviewing both cops and drug dealers, he knew the expression "prime cut from the brick." It was supposedly the best stuff the dealers would save for only their best customers—or themselves.

Geoff remembered Nicole, the survivor from the mass deaths at the Steuben crack house, had mentioned to Officers Dugan and McBee the men had separated a "prime cut" from the brick to celebrate being back on the Mendez cartel's good side.

Huh. If someone wanted to really fuck with the cartels and the dealers, then altering the "prime cut" would have a disproportionate effect. Just like Dwight Jones said, the government has beaten the cartels. *Man, I'm glad I was able to get my hands on the sample from the crack house.*

And a single DEA agent appeared to have had his hand in each of these incidences. "My God!" Geoff said to himself. "This doesn't even account for the other reported deaths around the country—first near Saint Louis, then Chicago, then Washington, then New York."

"What's that, Geoff?"

Geoff looked up. Emmett Washington peered over the two computer monitors. Geoff hadn't noticed he was there.

"Emmett, you better sit down for this. I believe you had figured this whole thing out—the cocaine deaths, that is. This is your story. I would have missed it."

After a long pause, Geoff cautioned his young intern. "Something else, Emmett. What we have learned could get your brother killed."

Chapter 60

Washington, D.C.

It ended almost as fast as it had started. By September, street deaths associated with bad cocaine had pretty much ended. But from every report, overall usage of cocaine was down, way down. Street prices for cocaine were also extremely low and dropping.

Over the past month, Geoffrey Wines continued to ponder this phenomenon. He could not shake it. Something did not seem right. Things that started and stopped in a definitive manner were operational, reflecting a sequence of planned events—*or interrupted events*.

But on this beautiful autumn day in Washington, D.C., the big news on the drug-wars front was that a large dragnet had arrested over one hundred drug distributors in D.C., New York, Chicago, and Saint Louis.

Today, Luther Gomez, a top lieutenant in the Mendez drug cartel, was being arraigned on charges of massive distribution and sale of cocaine in the United States. The US attorney bringing the charges had publicly bragged the Justice Department had an ironclad case that would convict Mr. Gomez and other top cartel persons, along with numerous distributors.

Geoff thought Nicole's reference to Luther and Mendez at the Steuben crack house was enough to tie Luther to the shipment. Officers McBee and Dugan made specific point of this reference in their police report and on the witness confession Nicole had signed. It was a great piece of police work, but hardly the major score the Justice Department and the US attorney had promised.

But the arrest of Luther and all the others portend something larger.

For this first hearing, Courthouse security was incredibly tight, with attendance allowed only to persons who were well known to the

FBI and Justice Department. A ten-year reporter for the *Washington Post* qualified. Federal officers manned the doors. SWAT teams were also in position around the courthouse.

Geoff sat in the gallery of the Federal D.C. court, where the arraignment was about to begin. Luther Gomez sat his large frame next to his defense attorney, only the two of them. *Interesting show of underwhelming force*, Geoff thought. *Just a small-time cartel guy under the screws of the big, bad US government.*

The prosecution included the US Attorney David Mittman, DEA Agent Chuck Harding, and FBI Agent Charles Bruce. Federal Judge John Paul Grant presided.

US Attorney Mittman stood and cited the case against Luther Gomez: "Mr. Gomez is an important part of the Mendez cartel and responsible for all distribution in the Midwest and East Coast for the cartel. In this capacity, he ensures the distribution network is efficient and works with the dealer networks and individual gangs to make certain their drugs are being sold versus another cartel's."

Geoff clearly knew Luther Gomez, and his role in the Mendez cartel. Luther had personally sought out Geoff, meeting him at the *Post* to convince him that no cartel would ever poison its own nor its competitors' product. "Bad for business," he had said. He must have been right. The charges against him were not for tampering with the drugs but simply for the distribution of them.

US Attorney Mittman began to outline the government's case.

"Last spring, a joint operation between the Justice Department, the Drug Enforcement Agency, and the FBI was implemented to highlight and expose the distribution network of illegal drugs, primarily cocaine. In this operation, DEA agents would intercept various shipments of drugs and inject the shipment with a distinctive marker that we called a 'tattoo.' We would then let the drugs flow into the marketplace. As drugs were intercepted from arrested dealers and users, the paths of the drugs back to the cartels were tracked and recorded. We were not only able to distinguish precisely how the cocaine traveled across the country, cut by various distributors, and sold on the street, we were also able to distinguish one cartel's product from another.

"We will outline the steps that were taken in the field by a skilled team of DEA agents to, one, tattoo bricks of cocaine at various points in the distribution; two, record time, place, and sample of the cocaine; and three, explain the careful double catalog system to ensure accuracy in tracking the samples."

Interdiction. Not confiscation. Distinctive markers. Treating. Post-use analysis. Geoff winced as his head exploded with this revelation. *It was an operation.* It was timed. This was how they did this. The Justice Department, FBI, and DEA were intercepting drugs, marking some, and lacing others with an unknown lethal component. This was how it covered so much territory so quickly and so quietly.

Holy shit. Though Geoff didn't say anything out loud, the assistant attorney sitting in front turned and gave him a stern look.

Geoff brought his physical reaction under control, but his mind still raced as he began to put the pieces together. Bringing someone like Luther Gomez to trial was a huge catch. They must have had a solid case against him and did not want to wait. Surely the government would assess risk and reward of whether someone could tie the tattooing of the cocaine to the strong possibility of the government's role in the lethal tainting of the same cocaine. Geoff had the connection. Did Luther's defense team have it as well?

It was a curious move to have Chuck Harding sit as part of the prosecution team. Did the government know Luther had seen him at the Chicago drug event? Had Harding told them? Had there been any investigation of him after the August "cartel interview" article in which he was all but named?

Surely, he would be well protected. Could that protection, as White House Correspondent Jack Fetterman had found, be a result of his visiting Camp David along with Clarence Robinson, whose son was killed by an unidentified junkie who Geoff knew was Dwight Jones?

Geoff also reflected that the only new news since his summer investigations was that Dwight Jones had been fished out of the Chicago River in early September—a single gunshot through the head. Police determined his fingerprints matched those on the roof of Eric Robinson's car. No mention was made in the press reporting any tie to the sale of illegal drugs. That, too, was curious.

Had Dwight Jones met his demise as a result of cartel caution or at the hands of a loving father, who just happened to be a boyhood friend of President Robert S. Osbourne? Or had it been a DEA agent trying to cover his tracks? Anyway, Dwight wasn't going to be testifying. Too bad he was dead. If the cartel had killed him, they blew an important witness for their case.

Geoff hoped neither the cartel nor anyone else would connect Jacob Washington, Emmett's brother, to Chuck Harding and the Steuben crack house deaths.

It kept getting curiouser and curiouser.

This had to be a very high-level operation, isolated from the rest of the law enforcement sector. There were no leaks. Geoff's usual contacts throughout these departments had not muttered a word about this operation. The Justice Department, DEA, and FBI could all be implicated. Could the president somehow be a part of it, too?

But before this hearing, there had not been a whisper of Operation Blueprint on the street.

Geoff mentally outlined his second Pulitzer Prize–winning story for the *Washington Post*. He understood a lot of it and could prove some of it. But he needed a smoking gun to wrap up the story.

Maybe he would get a break.

Chapter 61

The Washington Post Building

After a few days of consideration, Geoffrey Wines walked into Jack Fetterman's office. The White House correspondent sat busily completing his story for the next morning's paper.

"Jack, how does one make a call directly to the president? And please don't ask me why. You won't want to know."

Jack smiled and looked back at Geoff. He understood. "If I try to set this up for you, there will be too many questions and too many channels. I would suggest you call the White House switchboard, identify yourself, and ask to be put through to Pat Hayes. Tell Pat you want to see or speak to President Osbourne. You may need to tell her what you want. She'll probably find a way to get you through."

"Thanks, Jack. That sounds easy."

Geoff headed back to his desk and made the call.

He was surprised his call was instantly forwarded to Pat Hayes, who answered the phone on the second ring.

Geoff identified himself. She politely told him the president was in back-to-back meetings until 5:00 p.m.

Then she laughed. "But he has been expecting your call for over a month. He asked that if you call, to ask you if you like to fish. And if you do, he would like to have you join him and two buddies for a day of fishing at Camp David."

Geoff agreed.

Chapter 62

Camp David

The black government sedan with a US Navy driver pulled in front of the *Washington Post* building at precisely 9:17 a.m. that Saturday, exactly as planned.

The driver asked Geoffrey Wines to identify himself by name and show his *Post* identification. No problem.

This wasn't exactly a scene from Watergate with a late-night rendezvous in an underground parking facility. This was going to happen in the open, yet in the privacy of the president's own retreat. But Geoff also wasn't going to take any chances.

In the top drawer of his desk, he had placed an envelope with the day's date and two simple sentences: "Going to Camp David today as the invited guest of President Robert Osbourne. This envelope is to be opened only by Leonard Downie—if I disappear." His signature followed.

No one at the *Washington Post* knew he was working on a broader story relating to Operation Blueprint and the mysterious overdoses. All his latest reporting had centered on the prosecutions stemming from the government's action.

Inside the envelope were detailed instructions regarding the location of his notes and the beginnings of his writings concerning the story how the US government, FBI, and DEA had implemented a program to lethally poison supplies of cocaine throughout the country. This program augmented the Operation Blueprint program that was currently being used to convict a significant number of cartel, distributor, and dealer networks across the country. The notes included his discussions with Dwight Jones, Bruce Zimmer, Luther Gomez, Officer McBee, Emmett Washington, and his family; the lab reports analyzing the four samples of cocaine he had acquired; and the Camp David guest list that included visits by Charles Harding and Clarence

Robinson. This evidence would clearly lead a path through the DEA and FBI and strong connections to the presidency. It was clearly the type of investigative reporting that would win a Pulitzer *or get a journalist killed.*

He also stated in the notes he had guaranteed to keep confidential the information from Officer McBee and the entire Gertrude Washington family. Of course, Emmett, working as a reporter, had reporter immunity. Geoff further explained the only reason for leaving this information was to provide truth insurance in case he got "whacked" during his visit to Camp David—or sometime in the near future.

But he fully expected he would return to the office in one piece. If his instincts were correct, he was going to have a bigger story than he could have ever investigated himself.

During the ninety-minute ride up I-270 to Frederick and on US-15 to the Camp David turnoff, he let his mind speculate why he was being invited to the camp to visit with President Osbourne and whom the other two guests would be. He suspected it would be Charles Harding and Clarence Robinson; or maybe FBI Director Troy Hunt.

His articles during the summer had clearly indicated he was on to something: "Cartels Do Not Poison their Own Goods," "DEA Agent Identified by Cartel during Botched Sale," "Chicago Murder Victim Connected to Childhood Friend of President Osbourne."

Did they want to set the record straight? Did they want to convince him to discontinue investigations into the cocaine deaths? Or had they heard that Geoffrey Wines was a great fly fisherman, whatever the hell that entailed.

Regardless, he would see the inside of Camp David.

As the sedan turned left off US-15 and made its way up the drive to Camp David, Geoff took it all in. There were military checkpoints along the way—two, in fact. Security was tight when POTUS was on-site.

★ ★ ★

The car emerged from under the canopy of trees and began its circle up to the main cabin. President Robert S. Osbourne stood at the foot of the cabin stairs, looking entirely relaxed in his white POTUS golf shirt and a pair of South Carolina khaki slacks.

On the porch were two men, also wearing casual golf-type attire. Neither looked as if he were ready to go fishing, at least not to catch the swimming kind of fish.

As the driver opened Geoff's door, Osbourne formally stepped forward. "Mr. Wines, welcome to Camp David."

The two men on the porch joined the president.

"Mr. Wines, I would like you to meet two good friends of mine. I think you might recognize DEA Agent Chuck Harding. And meet Clarence Robinson, perhaps my oldest friend in the world."

After greetings, they retired to the front porch of the lodge. A table had been set for lunch. But they were a bit early, so they pulled the Adirondack chairs around the coffee table on the other end of the expansive veranda. A side table had an ice bucket, two pitchers of iced tea—one marked "sweetened"—an assortment of sodas and brewed navy coffee. No alcohol.

Geoff again noticed no one else was around.

"Mr. President, thank you for inviting me. But I thought we were going fishing, and none of you gentlemen look dressed for fishing—golf, maybe, but not fishing."

Osbourne smiled. "Mr. Wines. I am going to call you Mr. Wines because I want you to know that I and these gentlemen do not take your visit lightly. We know why you asked to see me. And we know it is highly unusual for a president to invite a member of the working press, who is investigating the actions of the government, to his most private retreat."

Am I going to get whacked after all? Geoff thought. The president's words could be taken in a menacing manner or in the straightforward way they had been delivered.

Osbourne appeared to be reading Geoff's face. "I figured you were more interested in catching politicians than fish. So, we are here to talk, if you like. Or we can go fishing. Your choice. Ask us what you want to know, and we will see if we can answer it—off the record, of course."

"Wow. I didn't see that coming." Geoff was surprised as he spoke the words.

He hesitated, contemplating his approach. There would be one set of questions if they were "on the record" and another if they were "off the record."

Could he get anything on the record?

Again, Osbourne seemed to be reading him. "Mr. Wines, we are prepared to discuss your thoughts, theories, questions, and details in depth. But, sir, everything we say here today will be one hundred percent off the record. And because we trust your journalistic integrity, you may take all the written notes you please, but there will be no recordings. And, if need be, I will provide you with full immunity if my Justice Department comes after you."

"You guys are serious, aren't you?" Geoff asked dryly. "The condition of today is that if another on-the-record party comes forward and corroborates anything you have given me, your off-the-record corroboration may be cited anonymously. Is that correct?"

Osbourne and the other two men nodded.

★ ★ ★

Geoff understood the trade-off. He had to be sure he was not falling into the trap of putting the facts of the story into the circular file of off-the-record sources. He visualized his sources and their potential input. He had one ace in the hole whom he was sure the president and the other two men were unaware of.

"OK. We're good. I agree with these terms." Geoff pulled out his notepad and a few extra pens. "So, instead of me asking a lot of questions, why don't you guys just start by telling me your side of the story regarding the war on drugs, Operation Blueprint, and the cocaine overdose deaths, including any government involvement."

The three men looked at each other and shared a mutual nod.

"Gentlemen, if you don't mind, I would like to begin." Osbourne motioned to the others and then turned back to Geoff. "Mr. Wines, have you ever experienced South Carolina in the springtime?"

"No, sir, I have not."

"Mr. Wines, I guess this story needs to start somewhere, and for me it started in 1930s South Carolina . . ."

★ ★ ★

Over the course of the next four hours, with only short breaks for the restroom and to grab the sandwiches the stewards finally brought out at 2:00 p.m., the three men described in detail their experiences, thoughts, sorrow, actions, and frustrations.

Clarence Robinson's anguish over the death of his son was palatable and emotional, as was Chuck Harding's tragedy and the motivation it gave him to move forward. Osbourne shared his deep compassion for his old friend, as well as his budgetary pressures and frustrations of being unable to win the war on drugs. He talked about being in a winnable war and knew what it entailed.

Geoff paid particular attention to Osbourne's telling of the meeting he had with his own attorney general and FBI director when they approached him on being an accessory to a crime and how he denied any knowledge relating to the poisoning of cocaine and their inference that Chuck Harding was some sort of renegade. He outlined his challenge to FBI Director Hunt that he and the FBI look internally for the culprit.

That surprised Geoff. Had the FBI investigated the president of the United States, and Geoff had never heard a word about it?

★ ★ ★

Geoff's notetaking was meticulous. But his mind even sharper in keeping the story lines straight and looking for gaps.

He still needed to get closer to the story.

He conceded the narrative these men told melded completely with his own set of facts. Therefore, it was probably truthful. They appeared to be forthcoming. But one very key piece of evidence was not addressed.

"Sir, if you three men and the FBI and the DEA were not a party to the poisonings as part of Operation Blueprint, then how did it happen?" Geoff asked.

Osbourne looked at him for a moment. "We don't know. Who do you think did it?"

Geoff took the bait. They *were* fishing after all. He was careful not to mention the four samples he had analyzed. "Well, sirs, it had to be an inside job. The source of the poison had to be through the tattooing process. It is reported the poison itself had never been seen before. Yet any evidence of that would have been easily connected to the agent via the markers."

"But there were none," Osbourne said. "The FBI checked, and none of the poison syringes were ever catalogued out or back into the system."

"What about the three-five-zero-zero syringes Mr. Harding here had mentioned?" Geoff thought he had them on something.

"Nonexistent," Osbourne said. "Even Chuck here inquired internally about this. There was simply nothing in the FBI system relating to the three-five-zero-zero markers. No outgoing syringes with that number. No returned syringes. No substantiating data. Nothing."

"What about the person at the FBI, this Dr. Clyde Ostrow? How did he account for those syringes?"

"We don't know."

"You don't know?" Wines retorted skeptically, staring at the president, and then shifting his gaze to the other two men to read their faces.

"He disappeared the day your cartel-interview story broke. Gone. Never to be heard from again. The FBI could not find any trace of him. He had cleared his bank accounts throughout the summer. He has not used one credit card. No passport action, either. Though I would suspect that after thirty years inside the FBI lab, he knew quite a few tricks."

Osbourne continued. "However, Dr. Ostrow kept impeccable records relating to the Blueprinting, the distribution maps, the incoming and outgoing samples, location photos, and everything else the government would need to make the Operation Blueprint prosecutions ironclad. He did not jeopardize the operation; he just added his own touch."

"What about FBI Director Hunt and Attorney General Miller?"

"Baffled, too." Osbourne continued. "Director Hunt had made his thirty-year veteran in charge of all marker production, syringe filling, and cataloging to ensure accuracy while keeping the operation of Blueprint small. It seemed ideal, until it wasn't."

"And none of you had any clue as to what Ostrow was doing?"

Harding jumped in. "Not in real time. Only when it was all over did we understand the clues he might have been sending—the mysterious musical telephone messages we told you about. Today, yes, we can put it together. But not at the time."

"So, Mr. President, without Dr. Ostrow, you guys have complete deniability. Is that right, sir?" Geoff asked.

"I believe so, Mr. Wines. I believe so."

Epilogue

The Washington Post Building

Geoffrey Wines returned to his office in The Washington Post building, eager to publish the fully collaborated story of Operation Blueprint and the resulting tainting of cocaine.

The day at Camp David ended on a non-adversarial note. There hadn't been much socializing after the discussion, only a few pleasantries. He offered his sympathies to both Clarence Robinson and Chuck Harding for their losses. He also offered his gratitude to President Osbourne for bringing him into his war on such a personal basis. It was incredibly disarming to him as a journalist.

He understood the president was not directly involved; he certainly did not order the FBI and DEA to poison shipments of cocaine. But Geoff also understood the president's words and attitudes granted permission for others to act on their own similar instincts.

Osbourne knew Harding wanted revenge for the death of his family and uniquely understood the failure of the war on drugs. He also understood Dr. Clyde Ostrow and, from their discussions during the WWII study group, knew the doctor also believed in the need to fight real wars. Osbourne assumed they would find each other and figure out a way to complete their vision. Dr. Ostrow had even given Harding a way to opt out by using the same 3500 code on all the tainted vials.

He believed Osbourne would not have condoned such an action without deep personal reasons. Clarence's grief hit a raw nerve and allowed the president to risk his personal reputation and look the other way.

Geoff also respected Osbourne's incredibly savvy handling of this situation. He chose not to fight Geoff as an investigative journalist in the public sphere of the *Washington Post*. Instead, he chose to hamstring Geoff by laying out the entire story in an off-the-record confession and appeal to his humanity.

Yes, people died, but they were complicit. Yes, the demand for cocaine was down, and dealer networks were seeking new forms of commerce. Yes, the results were effective. Highly effective.

But Geoff also knew he could place Agent Charles Harding at the headwaters of two of the most horrific episodes. Geoff had Jacob Washington and Dwight Jones as eyewitnesses. And he knew if he exposed Charles Harding by name, it would open-up where and how Harding obtained the poison, which would lead to the FBI, a missing chemist, and a gapping lack of management oversight at the bureau.

Geoff could even make a link between Dr. Ostrow and the president—both WWII vets who were also history buffs.

The articles he could write for the *Washington Post* would create a drip, drip, drip of information that would consume the entire government from the president to the attorney general to the FBI and DEA. It would result in overturned court cases, families with cause seeking restitution, and a distrust in the government that would be hard to reverse.

Lastly, Geoff also understood one immutable fact: President Osbourne had a deep love for both Clarence Robinson and Chuck Harding. He would do everything in his power to protect them.

This loyalty made Geoffrey Wines realize he needed to make the same loyalty assessment regarding Emmett, Gertrude, and Jacob Washington, plus his old buddy Officer McBee, who risked his career in getting the crack house sample to Geoff. The publishing of his complete story would put each of them in danger.

Geoffrey Wines needed to decide if that is a risk he wanted to take?

THE END

Author's Note

This novel takes place in the early 1990's as the drug wars surged; America's annual appetite for cocaine increased substantially; and the War on Drugs budget grew even more.

Now, thirty years later, Marijuana is legal in most parts of the country, yet heroin use is growing and the war on drugs continues.

Instead of Columbia, Mexico and Central America are now the centers for the drug cartels. This closer proximity has fostered the growth of home-grown gangs who fight for distribution rights and ravage the local citizenry, thereby causing a humanitarian crisis to reach our southern border.

In America, the cartels' large city presence has spread to multiple small towns and rural areas. Gang warfare for selling turf results in literally hundreds of deaths each year. Out of control Opioid prescriptions—through legitimate pharmacies—have come and gone. Now Fentanyl tainted drugs permeate the illicit drug landscape as many persons cut off from legal opioid prescriptions seek new remedies for their pain—too often resulting in overdose deaths.

Yet, unlike this novel, the possibility of death from fentanyl laced pain relievers is not alleviating demand for these types of illegal drugs. And America's fruitless war on drugs continues—perhaps necessitating the need for a new *Camp David Conspiracy*.

~Antim Straus

WANT MORE

GEOFFREY WINES?

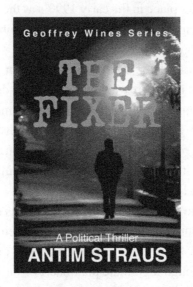

THE FIXER
— A POLITICAL THRILLER—
Book Two in the Geoffrey Wines Series

Washington Post reporter Geoffrey Wines and President Osbourne are back. Now twenty-four years later, Wines is a seasoned journalist, and the president is comfortably in retirement.

But strange events are rocking the presidential election, and an unlikely candidate is emerging. The president has learned this is the work of The Fixer, a mysterious operative he has used in the past, and who is employing a new set of tools and cohorts, to tilt the election.

Available in Paperback, Audible, and E-book on Amazon.

Antim Straus, author of *The Geoffrey Wines Series (The Camp David Conspiracy, The Fixer,* and *The Fixer Returns)* spent a career in new food product development and lives in Missouri with his wife of over 40 years.

Straus holds two U.S. Patents and is also the author of the humorous take on creation entitled *How Mrs. God and I Created the Universe—A Humorous Retelling.* A stage play version is under development.

He also co-edited the trade book *An Integrated Approach to New Food Product Development.*

Please visit Antim at AntimStraus.com to be placed on his mailing list and learn of new projects.

Made in the USA
Monee, IL
06 February 2025

11761822R00177